Stream of Death

An Ed McAvoy Mystery

Bill Stackhouse

Poisoned Pen Press

Poisoned
Pen
Press

Copyright © 2001 by Bill Stackhouse.

First Edition 2001

10 9 8 7 6 5 4 3 2 1

Library of Congress Catalog Card Number: 00-109745

ISBN: 1-890208-56-6

Poisoned Pen Press
6962 E. First Ave. Ste 103
Scottsdale, AZ 85251
www.poisonedpenpress.com
info@poisonedpenpress.com

Printed in the United States of America

Acknowledgments

I can't express enough gratitude to three women, without whom you would not be reading this book.

First, to my mother Eleanor. Some of my earliest memories are of her taking me by streetcar (Yes, I'm that old!) to the public library in Cleveland, Ohio. And when I reached my teens, it was she who introduced me to Rex Stout and Manning Coles, infusing me with her love of mysteries.

Secondly to my editor Barbara Peters. I always thought I had written a good book. She showed me how to make it so much better.

Lastly, and most importantly, to my wife Arlene. When in the throws of mid-life crisis I left a fairly decent job to become a writer, never once did she say, "Why don't you go find yourself a *real* job," although, I'm sure she must have thought it many times.

My heartfelt thanks to all three of you!

CHAPTER 1
(July 1943 - Sicily)

A six-wheeled Mercedes convertible sat parked atop of a hillock near the city of Gela. From a standing position in the driver's side of the vehicle, Oberstleutnant Karl Meitner slowly lowered his field glasses, letting them dangle from the strap around his neck. He removed the leather glove from his left hand and massaged his eyes with the thumb and second finger, then slowly shook his head and sighed equal parts frustration, sorrow, and resignation.

Over a quarter-million soldiers had been deployed to defend the island against an inevitable Allied invasion. However, of the thirteen divisions, only four were German. And although those four included the crack 15th Panzer Grenadiers and the Hermann Goering Panzer Division, they would not be able to repulse the attack alone.

The question had always been, "Would the Italians fight?"

The Abwehr, German Counterintelligence, had sent Lieutenant-Colonel Karl Meitner to Sicily to answer that question.

☙ ☙ ☙

He had had his doubts from the first day of his arrival a month earlier. Oh, the battle plans had been splendidly drawn—on paper. And General Alfredo Guzzoni felt very secure in his Italian Sixth Army Headquarters near Enna, in the center of the island. In fact, the general teemed with braggadocio about the battle-worthiness of his troops, who, he boasted, would fight to the last man if Il Duce so ordered.

Colonel Meitner had snorted contemptuously to himself when he had heard that bold pronouncement. *Fight, indeed,* he had thought. *Fight to the last German, no doubt.*

It had been the little things. The look of defeat had already settled into the Italian soldiers' eyes. But what really bothered the Colonel, above all else, was the fact that the soldiers didn't seem the least bit shamed. If one looked deeper into their eyes, and Karl Meitner was practiced at doing precisely that, behind the look of defeat, he detected relief.

Moreover, the Italians' handling of the partisan problem could only be described as halfhearted at best. Oh, to be sure, perpetrators of blatant acts of sabotage found themselves imprisoned in the garrison, if caught in the act, but nothing of a preventive nature was being effected. The Italians declined to conduct mass reprisals similar to those the Germans levied on the French, Poles, and Slavs. No lessons were being taught to other would-be terrorists except that the price of getting caught was a prison cot and three meals a day. War or no war, Sicilian partisan action was viewed as a dispute between cousins and the Italian Army adamantly refused to participate in genocide against its own.

The dinner party Colonel Meitner had attended three nights prior to the invasion had been a confirmation of all his doubts. "Dinner party"—the Colonel found it a poor choice of words. It had been a lavish grand ball. Held at Il Castello Rimini, a medieval fortress on the northern slope of Busambra Mountain overlooking the town of Villafrati, it had been hosted by la Contessa Sophia Campi, the young widow of Conte Pietro Campi.

Colonel Meitner had watched, horrified, as high-ranking Italian officers, decked out in full-dress uniforms with braid and medals—medals bought rather than won, the Colonel suspected—had fawned over la Contessa. With their tongues loosened by glass upon glass of wine, they had discussed the most sensitive of military preparations with the countess as if she were either a trusted advisor or merely a naive, unworldly *hausfrau.*

From closely observing her at the festivities, the Colonel judged the noblewoman to be neither naive nor unworldly—nor, most certainly, a woman to be trusted.

Dressed in a brocade formal gown, the radiant and beautiful Sophia had flitted about like a white and gold butterfly. Around her neck, she had worn a single twenty-five-carat rose-colored diamond, the famed Isabela Pendant, as her only jewelry. The necklace had been a gift from His Royal Highness, Umberto, Crown Prince of Piedmont, for services rendered in the bedroom, or so the story went.

Although the countess' voice and actions had made her appear to be laughing and joking and flirting with all of the officers in turn, her dark brown eyes, nevertheless, had not laughed nor joked nor flirted. It was those eyes that had most interested Karl Meitner as he silently watched the near-orgy take place. The eyes never lie. And that night, la Contessa Sophia Campi's eyes had told the Abwehr Colonel that here at Il Castello Rimini he would find *a* headquarters, if not *the* headquarters, of the entire Sicilian resistance movement.

Karl had filed his suspicions away. His Italian brothers-in-arms would never have believed him. *But there will come a time,* he had thought, *when acts of treachery will be repaid in full measure.*

❧ ❧ ❧

Colonel Meitner removed the strap of his field glasses from around his neck and rudely tossed the binoculars onto the passenger seat of the staff car. He slid behind the steering wheel, regloved his hand, and resignedly started the engine. He had seen enough.

Patton's Seventh Army had come ashore from the Gulf of Gela on the southern coast of the island. Part of those forces had been engaged east of the city by the German Hermann Goering Division and the Italian Livorno Division. The German tanks were pushing toward the coast road about one mile from the sea. However, the Livorno Division had been repulsed almost immediately and now retreated in tatters toward Vizzini. Some of the troops, officers and enlisted men alike, changed into civilian clothes as they ran and disappeared into the countryside.

The question had been answered. No matter how valiantly the German divisions fought, Sicily could not be held.

Even though the high ground around the Ponto Olivo Airfield near Gela had been taken by the American 82nd Airborne Division, the airfield itself was still in Axis hands. Colonel Meitner could have safely taken off in a small plane, but he had made alternate travel arrangements. The time had come for treachery to be repaid in full. He headed the Mercedes in the direction of another airfield, this one in Palermo where his Focke-Wulf FW190A fighter stood prepped and waiting. The route he chose would take him through the town of Villafrati.

All the lights from Il Castello Rimini were ablaze, like beacons in the night. As Colonel Meitner braked the staff car to a stop in front of the main entrance, he could sense a festive atmosphere inside. Laughter could be heard coming through the open windows on this hot July night.

His pale blue eyes narrowed to mere slits as he thought of the German boys some sixty miles to the south who were dying far from the Fatherland while these Sicilian aristocrats partied. He pounded the folded wire butt of his MP-38 three times on the massive hand-carved front door, then let the machine pistol hang down at his side from its shoulder strap.

The quivering old man who answered the door led the officer into the dining room. The gathering was a small intimate affair attended by only about a dozen or so of the countess' closest friends. La Contessa, bedecked in the white-and-gold brocade gown as she had been the last time Karl had seen her, once again wore the Isabela Pendant about her neck.

Colonel Meitner smiled icily at the merry band of collaborators as he accepted a glass of wine. "*Alla salute!*" he said, raising the glass for a toast and clicking the heels of his highly polished boots together.

The others returned the salutation.

"Have you heard about the invasion?" he asked them, casually sipping the wine while watching their eyes.

"No, no," they replied, feigning surprise. "Terrible, terrible," they said, wringing their hands and clucking their tongues.

The countess rose from her chair at the head of the table and offered a toast of her own, to swift and total victory. The entire company stood and repeated the toast.

Karl Meitner carefully set his glass on the end of the table, took three quick steps backward, raised the MP-38 into firing position, clicked his heels together again, then pulled the trigger back, holding it there until the entire magazine had been expended. Everything had happened so swiftly there were very few cries from the partygoers, just astonishment on their faces as they died. The Colonel bitterly tossed the machine pistol onto the table, unholstered his Walther PPK and walked the length of the room, turning over bodies with his foot and dispensing the occasional *coup de grâce* where warranted.

La Contessa Sophia Campi, severely wounded but still conscious when the Colonel reached her, did not allow her face to register fear, only disdain. She spat at him, the spittle mixed with blood hitting his highly polished boots.

Karl Meitner looked down at the noblewoman with contempt of his own but, as he slowly wiped the boots on her gown, he noticed that her throat was bare. He looked around on the floor in the vicinity of the woman. Nothing. As his gaze came to rest on her closed fist, sheltered under an overturned chair, the countess' dark brown eyes betrayed her sense of alarm.

He righted the chair, put the sole of one boot on the woman's outstretched wrist and shifted more of his weight to that foot. Her hand involuntarily opened and the rose-colored pendant spilled out onto the floor.

The last two things la Contessa Sophia Campi's traitorous eyes saw were Lieutenant-Colonel Karl Meitner pocketing the diamond pendant with one hand and aiming the Walther PPK at her forehead with the other.

Vittorio Gianelli recklessly pushed his motorcycle to the limit as he raced to bring firsthand news of the invasion to his sister and her inner-circle of advisors. Leaving the main road and starting up the mountainside, he almost collided with a German Army staff car hurrying down from the opposite direction. He made an offensive gesture behind him at the disappearing tail lights and laughed. The days of German occupation of his beloved island were numbered.

Vittorio saw the lights of Il Castello Rimini at least a quarter mile before he arrived at the ancient fortress. He hoped that he had not missed too much of the festivities, though if he had, he thought his news would resurrect the merriment.

As soon as he shut off the motorcycle's engine, however, he sensed that something was amiss. Although the windows and the front door were open, no noise issued forth from the building. The oppressive silence caused the hairs on the back of the resistance fighter's neck to prickle. He instinctively drew his Beretta and cautiously approached the entrance, straining to hear any sound, however faint.

Once inside, he stopped and stood immobile in the marble entry hall, listening and watching. Thirty seconds went by during which he neither heard nor saw anything. Flattening himself against the wall, he overturned one of the large bronze braziers that flanked the entrance, kicking it and sending it skidding noisily across the marble floor. Then he heard it, a bare gasp and a stifled whimper from across the entry hall behind the closed cloakroom door.

Vittorio covered the distance in three swift leaps and roughly kicked the door open. He crouched, leveling his pistol and furtively sweeping it from side to side, watching for any movement that would present him with a target. A frail old man huddled in the corner, quivering and crying. The astringent smell of urine permeated the room.

Vittorio Gianelli holstered his weapon as he crossed toward the old man. "Paulo, Paulo," he said softly, gently shaking him by the shoulder. "It's Vittorio. It's all right now. I'm here. Everything will be all right."

The old man broke down, convulsing with sobs, repeating over and over again, "I'm sorry, Master Vittorio. I'm sorry."

Vittorio put his arms around the old man and tried to comfort him. "No, no, Paulo. It's all right. Tell me what happened. Where is Sophia?…Where is the countess?"

But all the old man could do was quiver and sob. "I heard the shots and I hid. I was afraid, Master Vittorio. I was so afraid and I did nothing to help the countess. I'm sorry, Master Vittorio. I know I am a coward, but please do not kill me. I am *so* sorry."

The image of the German Army staff car flashed into Vittorio's mind's eye and even though he guessed at the sorrow that awaited him in the dining room, the young partisan held his fury in check. This gentle old retainer, filled with fear and remorse, could not be faulted for what had happened and should not be subjected to the young man's rage.

He gently helped the old man to his feet. "Go to your room, Paulo. Clean yourself up and then come down and we will talk. I want you to tell me everything that you remember." He affectionately squeezed the old man's shoulder then turned and headed down the hallway in the direction of the dining room.

As a partisan, Vittorio had seen death many times, but the death of valiant warriors fallen in battle, the result of a firefight. The scene in his sister's dining room was carnage—a massacre. As Vittorio slowly walked the length of the room surveying the butchery, the tears welled up in his smoldering obsidian eyes. These were men and women whom he had grown up knowing and loving, an extended family of surrogate aunts and uncles.

When he reached the end of the table, he knelt down, sat back on his heels, and tenderly cradled the body of his older sister in his arms. Only then did the tears finally come. A young Vittorio Gianelli stroked his dead sister's hair and wept uncontrollably and swore a *vendetta*.

Following the evacuation of German and Italian forces from Sicily in August of 1943, after only thirty-eight days of fighting, the Allies did something that would have a profound effect on Sicily, on America, and on Vittorio Gianelli personally. Not wanting to occupy the island, the Armed forces turned over administration of Sicilian affairs to Americans who spoke fluent Italian. Sicilian expatriates living in the States could not believe their good fortune.

Where once Il Duce had all but crushed it in its birthplace, the Allies, in effect, although unwittingly, reimposed Mafia rule in Sicily. And as the new *mafiosi* sought out new recruits, they naturally looked to those young men who had fought so bravely in the Resistance. Vittorio Gianelli was one of the first inducted as a *giovani d'onore*—an honorable youth.

Chapter 2

With his eyes closed it seemed as if he were part of the forest itself. The sounds became so much clearer and sharper. Somewhere to his left, a woodpecker hammered away a territorial warning and crows gossiped among the birches, pines, and poplars that lined the banks of the Esopus Creek. The stream gurgled and splashed over the rocks on its journey down the mountainside toward the Ashokan Reservoir.

He sat there on the cool ground of the stream bank, leaning back on his elbows and resting his back and head against a giant pudding-stone boulder. The scent of pine needles, mingled with the smell of damp loamy soil, filled his nostrils.

Another scent, though, blended with those of nature. This one made his stomach rumble audibly and his mouth water freely. In his mind's eye he could visualize those hunks of bread and meat and cheese that were wrapped in a blue-and-white checkered linen towel, the plowman's lunch his Uncle Roz had fixed for him.

A wicker hamper sat on the ground next to the boulder. Although he couldn't smell them, he could also envision the Ziploc bag of double-fudge chocolate chip cookies that he knew were tucked away in the hamper next to the linen towel. His stomach rumbled again, this time quite loudly.

From beneath the peak of his scarlet, black-and-white Onteora Indians baseball cap, he opened his eyes ever-so-slightly and peered out through his lashes. The shafts of noontime sunlight on this August day, broken up by the over-hanging branches, appeared as sparkling pools of diamonds on the water's surface.

Suddenly, among the other forest noises, one particular sound commanded his attention, a snuffling from somewhere behind him that grew closer and closer. No longer was his the only nose aware of the plowman's lunch in the hamper.

Without opening his eyes or changing the position of his body, he spoke in a soft but firm voice. "Don't even *think* about it!"

The snuffling stopped abruptly with a bit of a snort. The boy opened his eyes and turned his head, looking over his left shoulder. With the end of its pink nose just inches away from the brown wicker hamper, a yellow Labrador retriever had dropped to her belly and lay with her head in her paws, tongue lolling out of the side of her mouth, grinning back at him. Her expressive chestnut-brown eyes said *Who? Me?*

"Yeah, you," the boy answered the unspoken question, taking one of the dog's velvety ears in his hand and affectionately tugging on it.

Requiring no more encouragement than that, the Lab rolled over on its back and panted. The boy could interpret the pants with no difficulty at all. They said, *Pet me, pet me, pet me.* He stroked the pink tummy, causing one of the animal's hind legs to involuntary scratch at the air.

From about fifty feet downstream an elderly gentleman in green waders with Magnum inflatable suspenders and a white Panama hat called out. "You gonna play with that dog or you gonna fish?"

"Play with the dog," the boy called back as he gave the Lab one last pat. He repositioned the baseball cap further back on his head in order to get a better view of the older gentleman in the creek, then shifted his position so that he could reach down into the stream. "Unless you want me to get arrested," he added, proudly raising a string of fish from the water for the old man to see.

A second man, roughly the same age as the one in the waders, groaned from a camp stool on the opposite bank. "You can't have caught your limit already." The man had a brown Donegal tweed hat pulled down over his ears with about every kind of trout fly imaginable stuck to it.

"Hey, you two may be retired but I got a living to make. I can't take all day. Besides, Uncle Roz already has *Baked Stuffed Trout Almondine* scrawled on the blackboard as the catch of the day. Let's see, now,"—the boy made a big show of examining the string of fish—"six browns and four rainbows. Yep, that's the limit all right." He giggled as he let the string slide back into the water.

"The only thing worse than a smart-ass is a young smart-ass," the old man in the waders grumbled to his comrade in the tweed hat.

"Of course that doesn't count the seven brookies I had to release," the boy said. "Uncle Roz doesn't think brookies are big enough to make a decent meal. Umm, how have you more-experienced fishermen done so far?"

The boy's blue eyes twinkled. He knew he was being a smart-ass, but he remembered the first day he had run into Matt and Harvey and he deliberately drew out the words "more-experienced."

Almost every single night for the three months since Christmas, Danny Henderson had practiced casting with the new fly rod and reel that his mom's boyfriend, Ed McAvoy, had given him. He would stand out back of The Plough & Whistle Pub and use the little area his uncle had set aside for an English garden and pretend it was a pond. Come the first of April, he was going to be ready. Fortunately it fell on a Saturday and he and McAvoy had a standing date for opening day of the trout season. Not only mailmen went about their appointed rounds in the snow, the sleet, and the sub-zero temperatures. Danny managed at least a quarter of an hour of practice each night.

The Plough & Whistle, in downtown Peekamoose Heights, deep in New York's Catskills, was home to Danny. He lived in an apartment above the pub with his mother. Although christened Stephanie, everyone called her Stevie, thanks to her small, slight build, short brown hair, and pixyish tomboy looks. In addition to being the barmaid, she was the co-owner of the pub.

Her brother, retired Air Force Master Sergeant Roscoe Jarvis, was her partner as well as the cook and bartender. He also had an apartment above the pub. Because of Roscoe's round body, round head and little ears, everyone called him Porky, except Stevie and Danny. They referred to him as Roz and Uncle Roz, respectively.

As the start of the trout season grew nearer, Danny had honed his skill with a fly rod until he had become deadly accurate. He could hit the frozen water in the cast crushed-stone birdbath, fifty paces away, twenty-three of twenty-five times. The brass sundial, at a mere thirty paces, and the hand-cast, reinforced concrete sculpture of Peter Rabbit, at twenty, no longer offered any challenge at all to the aspiring young angler.

One night each week, McAvoy would come over and give him personalized instructions. In three short months, the boy had learned the forward cast, the roll cast, the side cast, the roll-cast pickup and had also learned to false cast and shoot line. In addition, McAvoy had taught the boy how to tie the various knots he would need, how to read a trout stream so that he could discover where the fish feed and live and, most importantly, how to tie his own flies—even the secret ingredient for the McSuperfly. By opening day of trout season, Danny was ready. Ready with a capital *R*.

❧ ❧ ❧

Bright and early on April first, the fourteen-year-old happily walked directly across Irving Boulevard from The Plough & Whistle to the Peekamoose Heights police station. A yellow dog trotted along at his side. Danny carried his gift rod from McAvoy and a tackle box in one hand and a wicker hamper in the other. The strap of a wicker creel was slung over one shoulder and a landing net was clipped to his belt.

The creel and net he had bought himself, with money his father had sent him for Christmas. Skip Henderson always sent money, never an honest-to-goodness present. It used to bother Danny, but, as he got older, he actually preferred the money. That way he could buy what he wanted. Sometimes, though, he wished that his dad would make the effort to get him something, even if it turned out to be something stupid.

On this first day of April, Danny was ready to fish. What he got was disappointment. He wasn't ready for that.

As soon as he opened the door to the police station Danny sensed it coming. Lucille McAvoy, the police dispatcher as well as Ed McAvoy's sister-in-law, barked orders to someone on the police radio. Her earsplitting, piercing, grating, buzz-saw of a voice filled the entire station.

As Danny entered, he caught the word "roadblock" and his heart began to sink into his shoe tops. Lucille gave him a quick wave and pointed to the row of wooden chairs along the wall. He stood his rod in a corner, set the creel and ham-per down next to it, and sat where he had been directed, shoulders slumped and hands folded in his lap. The yellow Lab lay at his feet with her head in her paws. Even the dog sensed a let-down.

Through the glass into Chief McAvoy's office, the boy watched as McAvoy, Larry Parker, and Jim Culpepper, stood with their backs to him, facing the large detailed map of Ulster County behind the desk. McAvoy did the talking as he pointed to the map and the two young officers nodded and made entries into small spiral notebooks. None of the three was smiling.

Although the door to the chief's office stood open, with Lucille screeching so loudly into the radio microphone in the outer office, Danny couldn't make out what McAvoy was saying. It hardly mattered, though. He knew that whatever was being said would translate into "No fishing today."

The threesome turned from the map, exited the chief's office, came through the gate in the counter that separated the operations area from the waiting area, and hurriedly headed for the main door.

McAvoy noticed the boy and the dog and his gray eyes softened as he paused only long enough to bend down, tousle Danny's straw-colored hair and offer an apology.

"Sorry, Danny. One of those things. I'll catch you later."

The chief grabbed his red parka from the hall tree by the door and followed the two officers outside.

The dog lifted her head inquisitively. Her large chestnut-brown eyes asked, *Aren't we going, too?*

The boy tugged on one of the velvety ears, reading her thoughts. "Not this time, Sandy," he told her. Then, after a brief pause, Danny smiled, not that his loss was less bitter, but because he realized that he could live with it. This hadn't been a personal rejection. It *was* just one of those things. He smiled because he recalled how many times in the three years that his mother had been seeing McAvoy that he had heard the chief break a date with Stevie using almost those exact words: "Sorry, Honey. One of those things. I'll call you later."

"Come on, Sandy," Danny said, rising and crossing to retrieve his fishing gear. "No reason why we can't go by ourselves."

The Lab instantly sprang to her feet, tail wagging with anticipation. Danny waved a good-bye to Lucille, which she acknowledged with a nod and a wink, and he and his four-footed pal returned to The Plough & Whistle to beg a ride from his mom.

Some ten minutes later Stevie dropped the pair off at Maben Hollow Road, just past the town of Slide Mountain on County Road #47 toward Oliverea. It was a sparsely populated spot that Danny had preselected after months of studying the large county map in McAvoy's office.

"Do you have a quarter for the phone?" she asked in that "motherly" tone of voice before Danny could slam the door of the white Trans Sport.

"Yes, Mom." He stood impatiently with his hand on the door handle and shifted his weight from foot to foot.

"And you'll call me by when?"

"No later than two o'clock, Mom." He started to close the door.

"And where will you call from?"

"From the Quick Stop in Slide Mountain, Mom." Then hastily added, "And I'll try not to get my shoes wet, I'll keep my jacket buttoned up and I'll remember to eat my lunch. And, Mom, there's no way I can possibly get lost because if I follow the creek upstream I'll end up in Slide Mountain and if I follow it downstream I'll end up in Oliverea so don't worry, okay? Good-bye." With that, he slammed the door and set off down Maben Hollow Road toward the Esopus Creek, the yellow Lab leading the way, exploring every nook and cranny of the underbrush.

The months of anticipation hadn't even come close to preparing the boy for the real pleasure of fly fishing. In that small stretch of the Esopus Creek, thick with pine, birch, poplar, and undergrowth that completely screened the rill from all telltale signs of civilization, Danny Henderson had found his secret spot. For three hours he had been transported to another world where just he, a yellow dog, forest creatures, and trout lived.

McAvoy's expert tutoring had paid off handsomely. By twelve-thirty Danny had a string of four brownies, three brookies and three of the most beautiful rainbows imaginable—the daily creel limit. Sandy hadn't done too badly either. Danny had seen her hunt up and eat two frogs and a chipmunk. God knew what else might be resting peacefully in the dog's belly. Danny certainly didn't want to know, especially while he sat there eating his lunch. Then, to his dismay, the boy discovered that his secret spot wasn't really all that secret, nor was it all his.

Because of the thick foliage, he couldn't see them coming, but he certainly could hear them. There were at least two, he thought, maybe three, coming down the slope of Big Indian Mountain. One of them had to have been the clumsiest oaf in the forest, stepping on every twig and tripping over every root all the way down to the creek. As they appeared through the underbrush, Danny put a hand on Sandy and stifled a laugh.

There were three men, two somewhat older in their mid to late sixties and a younger man in his mid thirties. One of the older men, a big man with a flushed face and a nose full of broken blood vessels, had on green waders, a white ski parka, and a big white Panama hat. Danny imagined it to have been he who had tripped over everything on the way down. Why he hadn't waited until he reached the creek to put on the waders mystified the youngster.

The other older man had a slight build and a face that carried a perpetually amused expression on it. He wore perfectly pressed tan chinos tucked into the tops of hiking boots, and, underneath an unzipped tan windbreaker, he had on a royal blue fishing vest that sported over two dozen pockets. Trout flies of all sizes and varieties covered every inch of his brown Donegal tweed hat. All in all, he looked as if he had just stepped off the cover of *Field & Stream*. The only item he carried that had no visible purpose for fishing was a gnarled hickory cane.

The youngest of the trio had sandy-colored hair, a friendly sort of face and the build of an athlete—an all-American boy type. But although he looked as if he enjoyed sports, it was obvious from the manner in which he dressed that fishing was not one of them. He wore a blue Harris tweed sport jacket over a cream-colored cable-knit sweater, a pair of blue jeans, and brown Hushpuppy ankle boots. He carried the old man's fly rod and tackle box and two camp chairs, one of which he propped up against a tree at the edge of the woods as he made his way down to the stream. After depositing the rod and tackle box on a large piece of shale that protruded into the water, he proceeded to set up the second chair and assist the man in the tweed hat over to it.

As the old man sat, laid his cane beside the chair, and picked up the fly rod, Danny recognized the effects of arthritis. He had observed Mrs. Winthrop often enough, with her scrimshawed-handled cane, walk and sit in the same manner. The old man did not seem quite as debilitated as Mrs. Winthrop, but the disease was far enough along where he had difficulty standing or walking without the assistance of the younger man's arm or the cane.

The fly rods that both men carried were top-of-the-line Orvis Bighorn Specials with Battenkill reels worth, Danny remembered from three months of reading fishing magazines, over four hundred dollars apiece. He took a quick glance at his own gear, which he knew McAvoy had purchased at the Sears store at the Hudson Valley Mall in Kingston, and was momentarily envious.

But hey, he thought, *I caught the creel limit in a little over two hours. How much better can they do?*

The two elderly fishermen busied themselves with the preparations of tying flies to their leader lines. It surprised

Danny how fast the man with the arthritic condition worked with the aid of a brass knot-tying tool. The younger man retreated the eight yards or so to the edge of the woods, retrieved the other camp chair, and set it up beneath a large clump of birch. Taking a paperback book from the rear pocket of his jeans, he began to survey the area. As his eyes scanned the stream, they suddenly came to a stop on the boy and his dog.

Danny could see that the man was somewhat taken aback so he waved and called out. "Hi. How you guys doing?"

The two older men looked up, somewhat startled to find that they had company. The man in the tweed hat glanced quickly at the young man by the birches then, just as quickly, returned his gaze to Danny and smiled.

"Didn't mean to surprise you," Danny offered by way of an apology.

"Just didn't think anyone else knew about our private spot," the man in the waders said, somewhat tersely.

"No problem, boy," the man in the tweed hat said with a grin. "I'm Matt." Then he pointed to his fishing buddy, "And this curmudgeonly old coot is Harvey. Up there"—he gestured to the young man by the birch trees—"is my nephew Lenny." Lenny smiled warmly and waved, then sat on the camp stool.

"I'm Danny," the boy replied. "And this here is Sandy."

"Hope he don't scare all the fish away," Harvey mumbled as he finished tying a nymph on his leader and stepped out into the stream.

"No, sir," Danny said somewhat defensively. "She's real quiet. She won't bother anyone." The thought that he wisely left unspoken was, *If a clumsy oaf like you doesn't scare them away, stomping around in the creek like a buffalo, my dog certainly won't do any harm.*

"I'm sure she won't, Danny," Matt said, his grin cracking into a genuine smile. "Looks like a fine dog. Harvey here is just one of those no-nonsense fisherman. In fact, Harvey here is one of those no-nonsense anythings." He continued, ignoring the oh-tell-me-about-it glowers from the other man. "Cards, horseshoes, you name it. Old Harvey is out for blood. Pay his grumbles no mind." From his sitting position, Matt fluidly cast his streamer into the creek.

Danny thought that Harvey ought to get together with Ulster County Deputy Sheriff Sergeant Martin Bassett if he really wanted to see someone who went out for blood in a game, but kept the thought to himself and just nodded.

"There's fishing and then there's playing at fishing," Harvey said in an attempt to defend his grumpiness. "We more-experienced fishermen tend to take the sport a bit more seriously. No offense, son." He drew out the phrase "more-experienced" so that it came out very condescendingly and was, in fact, very much intended to offend.

"None taken," the youngster replied as he finished his lunch and closed up the hamper. "It was nice meeting all three of you." He stood and walked over to the water's edge. "But I've got to be getting home now. Good luck with the trout."

"It's skill, son, not luck that separates the fishermen from the would-be fisherman," Harvey pontificated.

"But a little luck would be nice," Matt added. "Harvey and I fished this part of the creek every day last season and I don't think we ever caught the limit between us."

"This is the hardest area there is," Harvey grumbled. "If you wanted to dip 'em out by the dozens, you should be down by The Portal. This part of the creek is for *real* fishermen."

As Danny pulled his string of ten fish from the stream and deposited them into his creel he could tell that the two older men had stopped what they were doing to watch. He didn't look up at them. He didn't have to. The silence said it all as he made a big production out of opening the creel, lowering the string of fish, closing the creel, and picking up the rest of his gear. Only then did he look at the two "more-experienced" fishermen and shoot them a wink and a grin.

Matt Christiansen erupted with laughter. Harvey DuMont grumbled something about beginner's luck and waded away further downstream.

"Where do you live, Danny?" Matt asked, between wheezes.

"Over in Peekamoose Heights," the boy replied, now smiling broadly at the situation.

"That's a long hike." Matt made another expert cast.

"My mom dropped me off. I'm just going to walk over to the Quick Stop in Slide Mountain and give her a call."

"Nonsense," Matt said as he snapped his line back. "You can use the phone up at Harvey's place. Lenny?" he called to his nephew. "Take Danny up to the house and tell Cyn it's all right if he uses the phone."

Lenny motioned for Danny to come in his direction. The boy and the dog did as they were bidden. Danny picked his way across a string of boulders that formed a stepping-stone bridge of sorts. Sandy just jumped into the stream and swam across, vigorously shaking the water from her fur when she reached the opposite bank.

"Is it okay if I come back here to fish?" Danny asked as he walked across the stream bank toward Lenny. "It sure is a nice spot."

"Come back anytime, Danny," Matt replied. "Anybody who can catch the creel limit belongs here." He looked in Harvey's direction and continued in a loud voice. "Isn't that so, Mr. *Real* Fisherman?"

Harvey's grumbled "Yeah, what the hell," was almost drowned out by Matt's laughter.

🐟 🐟 🐟

So it had been since that first Saturday in April. In the four months Danny had been coming to the creek, on those days that he was allowed to go fishing, he had drastically reduced the trout community, catching the creel limit every single day. And Sandy had all but wiped out the frog and chipmunk population in that stretch of the Esopus, as well as putting a sizable dent in the snake clan.

During the school year, the boy could only come to the stream on Saturdays. Since the end of the term, though, he managed to be there three days each and every week. His mother had been a bit difficult to convince, but once he had gotten his Uncle Roz on his side, Stevie soon relented.

Ex-master sergeant Roscoe Jarvis had been the chief cook with the 3rd Air Force Tactical Fighter Wing at the Upper Heyford NATO base near Ardley and Steeple Aston, in Oxfordshire, England. And an excellent cook he was. People would drive from as far away as Kingston and Saugerties for a special dinner at the authentic English Pub in Peekamoose Heights.

One day Porky had innocently wandered into the dispute between Danny and Stevie about all the time the boy was spending at the creek and not helping with the lunch trade at the pub. All Danny had to say was, "catch-of-the-day?" and Porky's little round face had lit up like a Jack-o-lantern.

"I say, Stevie." After thirty years in the Thames and Chilterns region of England, Porky had picked up quite a few British speech mannerisms. "The lad's allowance could just as easily be based on the number of fish caught and cleaned as the number of tables waited, say what?" Then he had turned his gaze on Danny and continued. "Notice the words 'and cleaned,' lad?"

"Yes, sir," the boy had answered.

Porky had rubbed his hand over his bald, round head as he came to a decision. "I'll pay you the same per pound that I now pay Gilland's Fish Market, but that's per pound cleaned.

And no brook trout, mind you. They're not big enough to be bothered with."

The boy had glanced over at his mother who looked at her brother's innocent, smiling, cherub-like face and reluctantly nodded her assent. She did it, though, with a raised finger of caution as she added, "Tuesdays, Thursdays, and Saturdays *only*. You've still got chores to do around here. And," she had continued, "you ride your bike. I'm not chauffeuring you to and from the stream three days a week."

Danny had been about to protest but catching his uncle's wink and slight nod, looked at his mom and simply said, "Done."

❦ ❦ ❦

On this particular Tuesday in August, as Danny Henderson's stomach rumbled again, the long-awaited words rang down from the slope of Big Indian Mountain. "Lunch time, boys."

Sandy was off in a flash, through the stream, across the bank, and into the woods in the direction of the voice, tail wagging. Lunch was one of her favorite words in a very substantial vocabulary.

Harvey waded over to the outcropping of shale, waddled out of the stream and removed his waders. Matt set his fly rod on the rock and turned toward the crackling of the underbrush in the direction of the voice. Danny reached behind him and dragged his wicker hamper over to his side.

A threesome emerged from the woods in the same order as they always did. Sandy first, followed by Cynthia DuMont, and then by Lenny bringing up the rear and carrying an enormous picnic basket that contained the men's lunches.

Early on in their acquaintanceship, Mrs. DuMont had wanted to fix Danny's lunch as well on those days when he was at the stream with the men. While that arrangement would have been all right by him, his Uncle Roz would not hear of it.

"Mrs. DuMont will fix your lunch?" Porky had intoned rhetorically. "DuMont? Sounds French." He let out a derisive snort through his nose. "No nephew of mine will be eating frog food when he can get good substantial English fare. I'll pack your hamper as always, lad."

That had been that.

Cynthia DuMont was almost twenty years younger than her husband and in excellent shape for her forty-some years. Danny Henderson, at fourteen, was just beginning to notice things about women that he hadn't thought much about heretofore. On this hot August day, the tight pink-and-white shorts and matching and equally tight halter top that Cynthia wore didn't require him to tax his imagination too much.

The woman reminded Danny of Lucille McAvoy, but with two big differences. The first, of course, lay in their voices. Where Lucille's sounded like an unmuffled gasoline-powered Weedwacker, Cynthia's was low and sultry. The second had to do with their features. While both women were roughly the same age and both had long, shapely legs, nice hips, and generously endowed tops, Cynthia DuMont had a very beautiful face to complete the package. Lucille McAvoy, on the other hand, had a face like an English bulldog. People in Peekamoose Heights often joked, out of Lucille's earshot of course, that Lucille McAvoy was the best looking woman in New York State from the neck down.

Cynthia held onto a big floppy straw hat with one hand as she directed Lenny where to set the basket and spread the orange-and-brown checkered tablecloth on the outcropping of shale. The men always ate in the same spot every day, where Matt's chair sat. But still, Cynthia always directed Lenny as if he were the village half-wit. As always, though, Lenny wordlessly and genially complied and spread the cloth where he was directed.

Danny had picked up his hamper, crossed the stepping-stone bridge, and joined the foursome on the other side of the creek. He tried to be inconspicuous about sneaking glances at Mrs. DuMont's straining halter as he set out his lunch. When the woman suddenly addressed him, he quickly averted his eyes to look at her face, but he felt his cheeks go flush as Cynthia smiled knowingly.

"I hope you have room for some of my fudge brownies, Danny. I baked them fresh this morning."

"A...a...always, M...M...Mrs. DuMont. Always r...r... room for brownies." He looked away from the woman and nervously routed in his hamper for Sandy's biscuits, gave them to the dog, and shooed the Lab away from the picnic area.

The after-lunch ritual never changed. Cynthia DuMont would stand and say, "Well, I'll just leave you men to your fish stories," then head up the slope toward the house. Lenny would gather up the refuse and follow her. Matt and Harvey would swap lies and Danny would listen to them. Eventually one or the other of the older men would get around to asking the same question of the boy. On that particular day it was Matt.

"Okay, Danny. Badger. What about badger?"

The boy smiled and shook his head. "Nope. Why don't you just pay me the ten bucks and I'll tell you."

"Lemme look at it again," Harvey said. "This is getting ridiculous."

Danny reached into his shirt pocket and handed over a McSuperfly.

"McSuperfly, my ass," Harvey continued as he studied the fly for perhaps the twenty-fifth time, turning it over and over in his hand. "It's a White Wulff!... Sort of."

"Now, now," Matt Christiansen said, gesturing with his head toward Danny.

"Now, now, what? The boy's in junior high school. You don't think he's heard the word 'ass' before?" Harvey tossed the fly back to Danny and dug in his pocket and pulled out a ten-spot. "Now, Matt, here, just guessed badger. We've exhausted all the animals there are—fox, weasel, rabbit...all of 'em."

Danny pocketed the ten-dollar bill and nodded again. "Not quite all."

For the past month the two men had been trying to figure out the one ingredient of Ed McAvoy's McSuperfly that wasn't readily apparent, but with no luck. Finally, Danny had given them a week and bet them ten dollars each that they'd never guess. It was pay-up time.

Matt Christiansen beckoned to Lenny, who had returned from the house. "Pay the boy ten dollars. I can't figure it out and I thought I knew every fly there was."

The young angler safely stowed the second ten-dollar bill in his shirt pocket. "The answer's been so close to you, Mr. Christiansen, I thought for sure you were going to get it. I really did."

"Well?" Harvey grumbled. "Apparently close ain't quite good enough. What the hell is it?"

"It's dog down, Mr. DuMont." Harvey and Matt looked at each other in disbelief. The boy continued. "When I brush Sandy, there's a downy underfur that comes out in the brush with the hair. That's the secret ingredient of the McSuperfly—dog down." He reached into his pocket again, took out a second McSuperfly, and then tossed one to each of the older men. "Here. God knows you two more-experienced fishermen can use all the help you can get."

The boy snickered as he stood up and looked around for his dog.

Matt Christiansen laughed out loud as he placed the McSuperfly in a prominent spot on his tweed hat.

Harvey DuMont grumbled, "Dog down. Shit!" and tossed the fly into his open tackle box.

In response to Danny's whistle, the yellow Lab came out from the underbrush in the direction of the DuMont house, proudly carrying something in her mouth.

"What the hell's it eating now?" Harvey grumbled. "Damn. You're going to have to start feeding that animal more, boy. And don't let it bring the damned thing down here. We just finished lunch, for God's sake."

"Drop it! Sandy, drop it!" Danny commanded. The dog sat on her haunches at the edge of the woods, deposited something small and brown on the stones by her front paws, and wagged her tail with pride as the boy approached.

"Looks like the chipmunk population just went down another notch," Matt said as he leaned over and picked up his fly rod.

The youngster had collected a branch from the stream bank with which to fling the carcass away, but upon arriving at his panting, tail-wagging friend, he discarded the twig, knelt and picked up the dog's prize with his hand.

"It's not a chipmunk, it's a bag," Danny called out as he sat on the bank next to the Lab and attempted to open the small, dirt-covered brown leather pouch.

"What kind of bag?" Matt asked, trading his rod for the hickory cane and hobbling over.

As always, Harvey took a negative tack. "That dog better not be tearing up the trash," he growled as he pulled on his green waders.

"No, no, Mr. DuMont," Danny defended his pal as he brushed the dirt from the pouch. "She didn't get this from the trash. It looks like she dug it up out of the ground or something." Danny was still struggling with the drawstring on the pouch when Matt Christiansen and Lenny reached his side. "The cord's knotted so tight, I can't get it loose."

Lenny reached into a pocket of his jeans and extracted a birchwood-handled Buck folding knife. "Here, just cut the knot and let's see what you've got." He handed the knife to the boy.

Danny severed the knot, loosened the drawstring and poured the contents of the pouch onto a saucer-shaped piece of shale. Rays of noontime sun streaming through the trees broke into a rainbow of color as they refracted through the rose-colored, pear-shaped diamond. The stone was held in a frame of hammered gold and suspended from a gold curb-link chain. Danny could only look up at Matt and Lenny with his mouth wide open in amazement. Sandy, hoping that it was edible, lay down to give the jewel a sniff.

"Well, now," Matt said, as he pulled off his tweed hat and scratched his head.

"Well, now, indeed," Lenny echoed, reclaiming the knife and returning it to his pocket.

Harvey clomped over to the trio, his curiosity having gotten the better of him. "What the hell are you guys staring…" Just then he saw for himself. "Kee-rist!" Harvey made one attempt to kneel, but found that the waders restricted his movement. "Lemme have it! Hold it up here!"

Danny placed the pendant in Harvey's outstretched trembling hand. "Why would someone bury something like this?" the boy asked.

Harvey DuMont was almost salivating. "I'll…uh…take this into a jewelry store and see what they have to say about it. In the meantime, let's just keep this between the four of us, okay?"

"Excuse me?" Matt Christiansen reached over and plucked the bauble from his friend's hand and returned it to the leather pouch.

"It was found on my property," Harvey protested.

"By the boy's dog," Matt said.

"But still—"

"But still nothing." Matt handed the pouch to Danny, who had been just sitting there, with his mouth open. "Go up to the house and call your friend McAvoy, son. Nobody buries a rock like this in the woods unless there's something funny going on. I'm pretty sure the chief will want someone to take a good hard look into this."

"But, Matt," Harvey continued to whine.

"But, nothing. Is it yours?" Matt looked at his friend and there was silence. "Then what kind of example is that to set for the boy?"

Harvey DuMont grumbled something inaudible as he clomped over to the outcropping of shale and sat down to remove his waders.

Matt looked down at Danny again and winked. "Go make the call."

Danny and Sandy both got to their feet and, along with Lenny, headed up the mountainside.

When Lucille put through Danny's call, the chief definitely became intrigued. However, the area where the jewel had been found lay well outside the Peekamoose Heights police jurisdiction. He asked Lucille to notify the Ulster County Sheriff and then hopped into his Jeep and headed out toward County Road #47 to see the necklace for himself.

He always *asked* Lucille for anything, even though he was the boss. Unwritten rule #1: The only member of the Peekamoose Heights Police Force who *told* people what to do was Lucille herself. The sooner new members of the department realized this, the better off they were. Lucille could be a dragon without much effort at all.

As the blue-and-white Jeep Cherokee pulled into Harvey DuMont's driveway, McAvoy smiled when he saw the number 73 stenciled on the rear of the white Chevrolet Caprice already parked there. The chief braked to a stop next to the Ulster County Sheriff's patrol car.

Deputy Sergeant Martin Bassett had just extricated his six-foot-four-inch, one-hundred-ninety-five-pound frame from the vehicle and was adjusting his dark-brown wide-brimmed trooper's hat. Martin cut a fine figure in his uniform. The bluegray trousers with the dark blue stripe down the sides had been pressed to a knife-edge crease and the black shirt had been laundered with just enough starch to preclude casual wrinkling. A gold-plated tie tack in the shape of sergeant's stripes held his bluegray tie in place. Martin's distinguished looks commanded respect. *He* thought so anyway.

"Hey, Deputy Dawg," McAvoy shouted, as he hopped out of the Cherokee. "This must be a mighty important case for them to assign someone of your stature to it."

So much for respect.

The contrast between the two police officers was remarkable. McAvoy, at six-foot-two and two-hundred-twenty pounds, his tummy just beginning to overlap his belt, only dressed in a uniform on ceremonial occasions. Otherwise, he opted for civvies. On this particular day, in his blue chinos, a navy-and-blue tattersall sport shirt, open at the neck, a tan poplin sport coat and tan chukka boots, he looked like a vacationing stockbroker. The chief worked hard to cultivate a relaxed image. People were more at ease with him dressed that way and McAvoy liked people to be at ease with him.

The village of Peekamoose Heights, tucked into the valley where three of the Catskills' mountains—Slide, Wildcat, and Hemlock—all came together, was a community comprised mostly of second homes, some of them quite grand. The wealthy part-time residents seemed to prefer the low-profile look of their police chief to the storm-trooper image. Although all the other eight officers on the Peekamoose Heights police force dressed in standard dark blue uniforms, McAvoy's personal interviewing process screened out any applicants with storm-trooper mentalities.

TO SERVE AND PROTECT was more than just a slogan stenciled on the front fenders of the Peekamoose Heights police vehicles. It was a mission that the entire department took to heart.

"Up yours," Martin growled in response to the chief's verbal jab. "I just happened to be nearby in Winnisook when the call came in."

"Grand opening of a new Dunkin' Donuts?"

"You gonna be a smart-ass or what? What's *your* interest in this, anyway?"

The two men walked toward the front door, the Ulster County Deputy walking a bit slower than usual to allow his friend with the slight limp to keep pace.

"Danny Henderson is the one who made the call."

"Ahh," was all that Deputy Bassett said. It's all he needed to say. No other explanation was necessary. The Deputy, and, in fact, all those who knew McAvoy reasonably well, also knew that the chief and Stevie Henderson were an item.

After the introductions had been made and the story told and retold by each of the two fishermen, Lenny, and the boy in turn, over Cynthia DuMont's recently-baked fudge brownies and freshly brewed coffee, the entire company set out down the path through the woods to the stream and the scene of the find.

While Deputy Sergeant Martin Bassett conducted his official investigation, with Lenny acting as tour guide, Danny took Sandy to their usual spot by the pudding-stone boulder on the opposite stream bank to keep her out of everyone's way.

Cynthia DuMont had Harvey carry Lenny's camp stool down from the shade of the birches to the sunny stream bank. She sat there, leaning back and closing her eyes under the brim of the floppy straw hat, and stretched her exquisite legs out in front of her to work on her tan.

The image of the woman in the tight pink-and-white shorts and halter was not lost on McAvoy but, as he surreptitiously glanced at Cynthia, he spotted something that interested him a bit more. He headed straight for the pair of Orvis Bighorn Specials that were setting on the outcropping of shale. Sighing with envy, McAvoy gazed at the rods with their Battenkill reels.

"Go ahead, Chief, give it a try," Matt Christiansen said as he hobbled up behind McAvoy. He pointed to one of the poles with his cane. "It's a good all-purpose combination rod."

McAvoy picked up the Bighorn Special as if it were the Holy Grail. He looked it over lovingly for a few moments then flicked his wrist and watched as the Kaufmann's Royal Stimulator attached to the leader sailed precisely to where he had aimed it.

He remembered when he had first come to the Catskills after being compelled to take a medical retirement from the Detroit Police Force. The former detective captain, with a left tibia shattered by a drug dealer's bullet, had moved into a little cottage on the bank of Deer Shanty Brook where he wiled away his time tying trout flies and fishing.

The offer of the chief's job in Peekamoose Heights had come in the nick of time. As much as he loved trout fishing, McAvoy had been on the verge of going stir crazy. Aside from fishing, the only thing he had to occupy his time was directing one show each year at Mountain Gap Rep, the local community theater, and although he enjoyed doing it, it wasn't enough.

Now, as he thought back to those days, he missed the fishing. Since becoming chief, he rarely had time and although he had been promising all season long to go with Danny, he still hadn't—not even once.

The Bighorn Special impressed even a longtime fisherman like McAvoy. "Smooth, real smooth," was about all he could say as he repeatedly propelled the fly at various mental targets in the stream. "Great action."

"Why don't you play hooky and join us, Ed?" Matt said, leaning on his hickory cane and beaming with pride. "I'm sure crime won't run rampant over in the Heights if you're away for one day."

"I guess I'm just going to have to make the time. I've been promising Danny for almost four months now and have never gotten around to going with him."

"You and the boy's mom serious?" Matt asked. "Anything imminent? Not that it's any of my business, mind you. It's just that Danny talks about you quite a bit. We've sort of gotten to know you through him."

"It's no big secret," McAvoy said.

He had draped his sportcoat over Matt's camp stool and continued to cast. A .38 caliber Smith and Wesson Model 37, Chief's Special Airweight, was holstered on his left hip with the butt pointing forward in the crossdraw position. For people who still thought that the big man was a vacationing stockbroker, this might have been a tip-off that they were wrong.

"We're"—McAvoy chose his words carefully—"serious about being serious, if that explains anything." He laughed a small self-conscious laugh. Although generally outgoing, McAvoy liked to keep his personal life very private.

Matt sensed the invisible wall go up and backed off slightly. "Well, when or if you decide to take the plunge, you couldn't ask for a better stepson." He nodded toward the opposite side of the stream where Danny sat, back up against the pudding-stone boulder with his furry buddy's head in his lap.

"Yeah, I know." McAvoy's gray eyes moistened slightly as he felt a small pang of guilt for not making the time to take Danny fishing. "Couldn't ask for any better."

"Why don't you come with him this Thursday? Cynthia fixes a great lunch and besides," he looked over his shoulder at the woman sunbathing, then back at McAvoy "you get to watch her serve it." He winked and grinned as the chief snuck another glance at Cynthia's attributes.

Deputy Sergeant Martin Bassett broke the mood. "Hey! Can I tear you away from your games for a few minutes?"

"It's your case, Sarge. I'm just along for the ride." McAvoy nodded a thanks to Matt Christiansen as he handed the Bighorn Special to him, retrieved the sportcoat from the camp stool, and ambled over to the deputy.

"Yeah, but I thought you might have some sort of professional curiosity about this."

What Martin meant was, "Now that I've taken statements from everyone, I haven't the slightest idea what to do next. What would you suggest?" He'd never say that outright, but, nevertheless, that's what he meant and McAvoy knew it.

"You found where the dog dug it up." McAvoy phrased it as a statement; however, it was a polite way of asking a question.

"Mr."—the deputy referred to his notebook—"Leonard Damien and I found a freshly dug hole with paw prints all around it."

"Anything else in the hole?"

"No, and the ground beside it is fairly hard. We poked around a bit with a stick." The second sentence was in response to a McAvoy "Are you sure?" look.

"Then I guess I'd tape off about thirty yards or so around the probable site." McAvoy shrugged his shoulders and stuck one arm into the sportcoat, then stopped. "But before calling in the Wenceslas Brigade, I'd have Dunlavy's Jewelers in Kingston tell you for sure what the piece is and then check the hot-sheet. There's no law against burying jewelry in the woods. We don't really know yet if there's a crime to investigate."

Deputy Sergeant Stanley Jurocik and his rookie sidekick Deputy Tom Lapinski comprised the Ulster County Sheriff's Department's forensic team, hence the moniker "Wenceslas Brigade."

"But why else would someone bury it?" Martin asked.

"Domestic dispute? Who knows?" McAvoy turned his attention to Danny and shouted across the stream to the boy.

"If you're ready to go, toss your bike in the Jeep and I'll give you a ride."

The youngster sprang to his feet, collected his gear, hopped across the boulders in the stream, said his good-byes, and started up the path through the woods to the DuMont house.

Sandy, as usual, took the direct route through the water and raced up the mountainside ahead of him.

McAvoy called after the boy. "Make sure that animal's paws are clean and that she shakes herself off again before she gets into my car."

As Martin Bassett and Lenny went to get the yellow SHERIFF'S LINE—DO NOT CROSS tape from the Caprice, the chief took his leave of Matt Christiansen and the DuMonts. He snuck one last lingering glance at Cynthia's, then headed up the path toward the Cherokee.

Just before he entered the woods Matt called after him, "Hey, Chief, what about Thursday?"

McAvoy stopped and thought for a half second, then grinned and shouted back over his shoulder. "Count me in."

Chapter 3

The *Ashokan Register*, which publishes weekly on Wednesdays, had carried a picture of the necklace with the caption Dog Digs Up Diamond. At press time, no determination had yet been made as to how the jewel had come to be buried on the slope of Big Indian Mountain or if, indeed, it had been stolen. Still the newspaper article had contained all the particulars regarding the find. It also had contained the general location of the DuMonts' home.

Dewey Dunlavy had flown to Amsterdam on a buying trip and would not return until Friday. Consequently, the jewel remained unidentified. As a personal favor to the sheriff, Dewey's wife Kathleen had agreed to keep the pendant in Dunlavy Jewelers' formidable safe rather than have it stored in the Ulster County Sheriff's property locker.

At the DuMonts, Harvey was furious. Waving the newspaper in one hand and pacing back and forth to the extent that the cord would allow, he screamed through the telephone line at Bill Brinkmire, the managing editor of the *Register*. "The public doesn't have the right to know *shit!* What about *my*

right to privacy?! Do you have any idea what this is going to do?! *Do* you? The woods around here will be crawling with bozos!"

Bill found himself at a complete loss for words. The *Register* was strictly a local newspaper, with little coverage of happenings outside Ulster County. Most people in the area not only loved seeing their own names in print but also relished reading all the gossip about their neighbors.

Bill didn't need too many words. An irate Harvey DuMont made a reference to something he assumed Bill did with his mother, then slammed the receiver down before the newspaperman could attempt either an explanation or an apology.

As he hung up his own telephone receiver, Bill Brinkmire was very glad that he had neglected to mention putting the story on the wire and that several other papers in the state had picked it up.

Within an hour after the *Register* hit the streets, the switchboard at the Ulster County Sheriff's office lit up like a theater marquee. Calls ranged from would-be treasure hunters who wanted to know if the necklace had been found on public or private land to those who were sure that it had once belonged to their great-aunt Sadie, Hilde, or Myrtle, and wanted to know how to claim the jewel.

The Sheriff took a bottle of Maalox tablets from his desk drawer and buzzed Deputy Sergeant Bassett. "Martin, better get a couple of people over to the DuMonts to keep the crazies out of the site until we know for sure what we're dealing with."

He hung up the phone and popped four of the lemon-creme tablets into his mouth. *I really needed this. Would all you drug dealers, burglars, murders, and rapists kindly take it easy for today? My deputies've got to baby-sit a hole that some kid's dog dug. Jesus H. Christ!* He swallowed, put a hand to his chest and smiled as a welcome belch relieved some of his heartburn.

❦ ❦ ❦

On the northwestern slope of Balsam Mountain, overlooking Deep Notch in Greene County, the county just to the north of Ulster County, stood a two-hundred-and-seventy-five-room chateau. Built in the nineteenth century by a railroad magnate and christened Winchester House, the four-story European-style building, with its white stone walls, blue slate roof, and four five-story turrets, resembled an Alpine castle.

The one-hundred-and-ninety acres of woods and formal gardens were surrounded by a sixteen-foot high electrified Cyclone security fence, topped with a coil of razor wire. Armed guards, dressed in casual slacks and blazers, manned the entrance gate and also patrolled the perimeter with German Shepherds and Dobermans. These security measures had not been part of the original design of Winchester House, but were added in the 1950s when the ownership of the chateau changed hands and was rechristened Garibaldi House.

It was Thursday evening and a grandfatherly figure sat with his wheelchair pulled up to a white wrought iron umbrella table on the terrace of the chateau. The old man ate his dinner in silence as he surveyed the three acres of manicured lawn beneath him. Although it was a warm summer evening, a charcoal cashmere overcoat with a sable collar hung from his frail shoulders. On his head rested a black fedora. The chateau's maitre d', dressed completely in white, hovered approximately six feet behind the man at the table, trying his best to anticipate what the next request might be.

Groups of other old men played bocce in the half-dozen long, narrow, sand pitches that had been meticulously set into the lawn. The laughter of the players and some of the boisterous shouts in both English and Italian drifted up to the man on the terrace. Occasionally he smiled and acknowledged a particularly good shot with a wave.

Only one of the other fifteen tables had its umbrella raised, and that at the rear of the terrace where a stone staircase from ground level joined it. There, a man young enough to be the old man's grandson, but in reality his eldest son, sat with two friends. Having just completed a round of golf on the estate's executive nine-hole course, Tony sipped a frosted schooner of Genny Light.

On Tony's left, and dressed nearly identically to him in jeans and a sport shirt, Giancarlo Triano, nursing his own schooner of light beer, had recently finished tallying up the two men's scores—for the third time. With the crumpled-up score card in front of him, Giancarlo had begun a discourse on a topic at which he felt a good deal more proficient—the relative sexual proclivities of foreign versus domestic women.

From his clothes, it was obvious that the third member of the trio, a short, swarthy, middle-aged man sitting to Tony's right, had not been out on the course with the other two. Wearing a charcoal silk suit, black shirt, and cream-colored tie, he sat there gazing lovingly at a glass of Donnaz as he swirled the smooth, full-bodied red wine to release its bouquet.

Although he had been listening politely to the story teller, Tony, who considered himself to be a ladies-man without peer, let just a trace of skepticism show on his face. Giancarlo's older brother Giuseppe, however, didn't even attempt to disguise his own cynicism. As the younger Triano extolled the virtues of French women, Giuseppe set his wine glass on the pale-yellow linen placemat and nudged Tony with his elbow.

"Pay attention, Tony. Carlo, here, he knows this subject only too well. You see, he has given his right hand a name. It is Babette."

With that, Giuseppe made a pumping motion with his own right hand toward his crotch. Tony broke out in a raucous laugh. Giancarlo merely raised a middle finger at his brother.

"And tell us, brother Joey, when was the last time *you* had a woman? Heh? Heh?"

"A gentleman like myself, he no kiss and tell."

"He no kiss at all," Giancarlo said to Tony, mimicking his brother's still-lingering Northern Italian accent.

As Giancarlo continued with his dissertation, Tony became distracted by the appearance of another man on the terrace.

A sturdy, bald, middle-aged man had entered at the French doors from the chateau and quickly made his way to the maitre d'. He was impeccably dressed in a gray pinstripe suit. In his hand he carried a copy of the *Greene County Gazette*, a weekly published in the city of Catskill every Thursday afternoon.

Making eye contact with the maitre d', Sal Merlino motioned with his bald head toward Tony's father, a signal which Tony interpreted as an unspoken "How is he this evening?"

The man in white gave a small shrug and a pained expression, a silent "As well as can be expected."

The bald man approached and stood silently at the elderly man's side, fidgeting slightly.

"*Come va*, Salvatore?" Tony heard his father say, as he completely tuned out Giancarlo in order to concentrate on what was happening at the other table.

"Would you like some dinner?" the old man asked, smiling warmly at the bald man and daubing at his lips with a pale-yellow linen napkin.

"*No, grazie, Padrone.* I've just come from the dining room." The *capo subordinato* continued to fidget.

"Sit, sit. Have some Valpolicella and tell me what makes you frown so. It is not like you, *mio amico*. Sit and talk, Salvatore. And remember, I can take any news, good or bad. It is only the lack of information which is dangerous, heh?"

He turned slightly and called to the man in white. "Bruno! *Il bicchiere da vino.*"

Sal gestured at the maitre d' to forget the glass as he sat in the chair opposite the other man and slid the newspaper across the table.

The old man read in silence, looking up only once to fix his obsidian eyes into an icy stare on the messenger across from him. Sal fidgeted even more, unconsciously knotting the linen napkin in front of him.

As Tony watched the scene at the other table, he, too, became uneasy as a memory that he had fought so very hard to suppress engulfed him. In his mind he was transported back four years to his father's Detroit office, shortly before his father's stroke.

It had been a Monday and Sal Merlino had returned late the night before from a weekend "family" meeting in New York City with don of dons Silvio Centofonti. Tony had been lounging in his father's office, long legs draped over the arm of one of the twin button-tufted, cordovan leather chairs, his black Armani suitcoat tossed carelessly over the back of the matching sofa. While leafing through a *Sports Illustrated* and running a comb through his longish, jet-black hair, he only half listened to the conversation at the desk.

Sal was reporting to Tony's father on what had transpired over the weekend. The *capo subordinato* had been fidgety all during the discussion but became extremely so as the talk came to an end and the older man dismissed him. Instead of taking his leave, though, Sal just stood at the side of the desk while Tony's father went back to his paperwork. After a silence of some fifteen seconds, he slid a Sunday *New York Times* across the desk. It was folded open to one of the back sections.

"*Scusi, Padrone,* but there is something here I think you should read."

The old man looked up from his paperwork and barked, "*Mi lasci in pace*! Can't you see I'm busy, *mio amico*?"

The underboss just remained standing there with a pained expression on his face.

Tony's father sighed and resignedly shook his full head of snow white hair, then softened his voice. "So? I don't have time for newspapers, Salvatore. If it is so damned important, tell me what it says!"

Sal simply placed a well-manicured fingernail next to a photograph in the middle of the page and said quietly, "This is something I feel you should read for yourself, *Padrone*."

Vittorio Gianelli looked to where Sal's somewhat trembling finger pointed and the blood drained from his face. "*Il Ciondolo Isabela! Madre Dio*! Can it be? After all these years? Can it truly be?" He picked up the newspaper, grasping it in both hands, leaned back in his chair and read the entire article, suddenly feeling the strain of the nearly three score years since he had last seen the Isabela Pendant around his sister's neck.

The accompanying article told about the semiannual three-day regional jewelry show that would be held at the Plaza the following weekend. All the jewelry manufacturers would be displaying their wares for the thousands of Jewelry Association retail members to view and, one hoped, to order.

The article explained that the highlight of this particular show would be the presence of a small, but trusted, Brazilian cutter-importer-wholesaler. In addition to having a large collection of graded stones for sale, the wholesaler, a Guilherme Meitner who had recently taken the reins of the company after the death of his father Karl—would have on display the famed Isabela Pendant.

The article went on to give a brief history of the pendant; a twenty-five-carat, rose-colored, pear-shaped diamond, held in a frame of eighteen-carat hammered gold and suspended from an eighteen-carat gold curb-link chain.

Originally, the pendant had been a thirteenth-century wedding gift from Frederick II, Holy Roman Emperor and King of Germany, Sicily, and Jerusalem, to his third wife Isabel, daughter of King John of England. It had remained in Sicily for the next six-hundred years, passing from ruling family to ruling family until it was looted by the adventurer Giuseppe Garibaldi when he and his one thousand redshirts captured Palermo in 1860. Subsequently, the pendant had been given as a peace offering by Garibaldi to Victor Emmanuel the First when Victor was proclaimed King of Italy in 1861.

As to how the pendant wound up in Brazil, the newspaper only ventured an educated guess that it had arrived, as had so many other Italian treasures, by way of Germany in the closing days of World War II.

Tony had never witnessed his father in such a distressed state. This was a *capo supremo*. This man had smilingly and unflinchingly opened the car door for Jimmy Hoffa in the parking lot of the Machus Red Fox back in July of 1975 and had climbed in beside the ex-union boss. This man had taken the helm of the Detroit crime family after the death of Joseph Zerilli and had held it together, calling the shots for organized crime in Southeastern Michigan. But now, this same man, after reading a simple newspaper article, had been transformed from a fearsome Godfather into a frail old grandfather.

"Papa?" Tony asked softly as he uncurled himself from the chair and put his feet on the floor.

His father didn't answer and continued to hold the paper in front of him, rereading the article.

Tony tried again, a bit louder this time. "Papa? What is it?"

But Sal Merlino shot him a stern look and gave the boy an admonishing waggle of his finger. Both men remained silent at their stations—Salvatore Merlino, standing motionless by the side of the desk, and Antonio Gianelli, sitting on the edge of his chair.

When Vittorio finally finished reading and brought the newspaper down from his face, he did not even acknowledge the other two men's presence, acting as if he were alone in his office. He simply withdrew a pair of scissors from the center desk drawer, slowly cut the article from the newspaper, then proceeded to smooth it out in front of him on the desk blotter.

Only when he had finished did Vittorio Gianelli look up at his advisor, then over at his son. And as the old man turned his icy gaze from one to the other he tapped the newspaper clipping with his forefinger and hissed out one solitary word. "*Vendetta!*"

❦ ❦ ❦

The plan had been set into motion that very night. There would be no hired help, no wiseguys. Vittorio had insisted. This was to be a family matter. Although Sal Merlino would advise, the operation would be carried out by Tony, with assistance from his younger brothers Johnny and Julie.

They had almost three weeks to plan. After New York, the jewelry show would travel to Atlanta where the Southern Jewelry Association would meet, then on to Detroit for the Great Lakes Jewelry Association convention.

The Detroit site was to be the ballroom of the new St. Aubin Towers, built on the riverfront between the Renaissance Center and the MacArthur bridge, which connected Belle Isle to the mainland. After two weeks of reconnaissance trips to both the New York and Atlanta shows, forged credentials in hand, the trio sat down with their father and Sal Merlino to discuss their plan.

For a small gratuity, underpaid room-service and housekeeping personnel had provided a wealth of information on procedures that could not be directly observed by the brothers Gianelli. In New York and Atlanta, Guilherme Meitner had followed nearly the identical routine. He had spent the night in the hotel where the jewelry show was being held, in a penthouse suite that was accessible only by a private elevator that operated with a special key.

A total of six, four uniformed and two plain clothes, armed guards had been on duty at all times. Two of the uniformed guards had been stationed by the elevator on the exhibit floor. The other two uniformed guards had maintained their watch in the penthouse, always in sight of the elevator. The two plain-clothes guards had never strayed from the Brazilian's side. Moreover, all three pairs had maintained radio contact with each other.

The Gianelli plan was daring but simple. Tony and Johnny would take a room on the fourteenth floor of the St. Aubin Towers, registering under assumed names and paying cash in advance.

The private elevator that serviced the penthouse suite was the end car in a bank of six elevators. After the jewelry show on Saturday evening, the Gianelli brothers would take the fifth elevator and stop it between the fourteenth and fifteenth floors. Fortunately, the emergency stop and the alarm were controlled by separate buttons so no quick rewiring job would have to be performed.

Tony would climb through the access panel on the roof of the fifth car and wait until the private car made its unmanned assent to the penthouse with the dinner trolley. Then he would jump onto the roof of elevator number six as it passed and spend the night on top of the car.

Johnny would return the fifth elevator to active service, get a good night's sleep, and again commandeer that same elevator in the morning.

The boys originally planned on having Tony make his leap during the assent of the private elevator with the breakfast trolley, but Sal convinced them that going the night before would be better. If something went amiss, he explained, they would still have the breakfast run to fall back on.

❦ ❦ ❦

There on the Garibaldi House terrace, Tony remembered that fateful morning as if it had been only yesterday.

He had been sitting on the roof of the private elevator car since about six o'clock the evening before and his legs had begun to cramp. Pulling the glove down just slightly on his left hand, he looked at his Breitling Chronomat once again. Five minutes before eight and just three minutes since he had last checked the stainless steel-and-gold timepiece. He had had no sleep. There had been the constant fear of dozing off and rolling from the top of the car into the shaft below.

Except for the breakfast run an hour-and-a-half earlier, the elevator car had remained on the twenty-fifth floor all night long. Soon, Tony knew, it would begin its second and then, finally, its third descent to the exhibit hall twenty-one floors below. A small measure of revenge would then be exacted—for his family—for his father—especially for his father—but a little bit for himself, too.

As he sat there kneading his leg muscles and waiting, Tony's thoughts were of Rosa and he smiled. *Once this is over, Rosa will respect me.*

It bothered him, though, that it mattered. He knew he could have Rosa Grimaldi's body almost any time he wanted it. Why should he care if he had her respect as well? But Tony did care. It gnawed at him that he cared.

"Wiseguy"—that's what Rosa had called him. Three nights earlier, she had laughed at him when he had told her that he was going to be rich.

"How's a wiseguy like you gonna get rich, huh, Tony?" she had teased him, kneeling there on the couch in her bra and panties. "Your papa gonna raise your allowance, or what?"

He had seen that she was impressed when he told her a little about the plan. The girl's eyes had widened in amazement. And it must have excited her, too, because their lovemaking had been more passionate than ever.

In retrospect, Tony wondered if he had said too much, but, then, shook off his doubts. *A smart girl like Rosa knows what side of the bread's got the butter on it.*

He had impressed Rosa with his talk. He knew that. Once he pulled-off this job, she would respect him, also. This job would make many people respect him. *Thank God for this job. Thank God!*

Tony tensed as he heard the elevator door open and the voices of the guards as they loaded the used breakfast trolley and the dinner trolley from the night before into the car.

This is it—finally.

The car began its descent. Tony fought the almost over-whelming urge to lift the access panel and peek. They had followed the same routine on every day in every hotel, they wouldn't change it now, he told himself.

As the car passed the fifteenth floor, elevator number five had already been immobilized, the access panel lay to one side and Johnny's smiling face poked out through the top of the car. The younger Gianelli sported a wide grin as his brother went by. Tony flashed him a thumbs-up sign and returned the grin.

At the fourth floor, the exhibit hall floor, the trolleys were unloaded. The plain-clothes guard exchanged pleasantries with his uniformed counterparts, radioed the all-clear to the penthouse and the car began its assent back up to the twenty-fifth floor.

For perhaps the dozenth time, Tony checked his Ruger Mark II with its custom-made silencer, this time chambering a round and flicking the safety to the ON position.

Back at the penthouse suite, the second plain-clothes guard and the Brazilian joined the first guard in the elevator. As the car began moving, Tony positioned himself by the access panel, lying on his belly, Ruger in his right hand and panel handle in his left. He took a slow deep breath, then cautiously raised the panel about a quarter of an inch and peeked down into the car while at the same time sliding the Ruger's safety to the OFF position.

The men were in perfect placement. In less than five seconds, all three lay in a crumpled heap on the bottom of the car with .22 caliber bullets in their heads.

The guard carrying the walkie-talkie had been the first target. He took his bullet in the back of the skull. The second guard started to turn in the direction of the *pffft* sound from the silenced Ruger and went down with one to the temple. Guilherme Meitner, who had turned completely around to look up as the second guard fell, had a hole in his forehead.

Ten seconds later, Tony had joined them in the car, tan briefcase on the floor and free hand poised above the emergency stop button. His eyes moved back and forth from the LED floor indicator to his victims as he shot each one twice more in the head for good measure.

The LED indicator changed from eighteen to seventeen to sixteen, each floor about six seconds apart, then to fifteen. Tony counted off two seconds, then hit the emergency stop button. The car lurched to a halt.

He opened the black sample case and looked into it. It was filled with more than fifty small black velvet pouches, each containing ten graded stones, and one slightly larger brown leather pouch. He quickly opened the leather pouch and, just like the picture, only more dazzling, the Isabela Pendant sparkled back at him.

"*Vendetta*," he whispered as he poured the contents from the sample case into the tan briefcase. "*Vendetta* and respect."

As Tony climbed back through the access panel with the briefcase, less than a minute had elapsed since the car had been halted. His timing of the emergency stop had been perfect, also. The top of car number five lay just three feet below him.

Johnny stood in the center of elevator car number five, anxiously looking up through the access panel with his hand on the emergency stop button. As soon as his older brother jumped onto the roof of the car, Johnny pulled out the button and the car resumed its downward passage. Tony tossed the briefcase through the opening to him, swung himself down into the car, pulled the panel shut and removed his gloves.

No sooner had he gotten himself into position when the car stopped at the eighth floor to take on two passengers, each carrying a briefcase, suitcase, and a clothing bag. Tony leaned relaxed in one corner, engrossed in the morning *Free Press*, courtesy of his brother. Johnny stood coolly, business-like, in the other corner, tan briefcase in hand and staring vacantly at the floor indicator above the door.

The two men voiced a greeting. Tony responded with a smile and a nod. The businessmen then joined Johnny in watching the floor indicator as the car made its way down to the main level.

In the lobby, the businessmen headed for the checkout desk. Tony nonchalantly made his way to the main entrance and walked out to the parking lot to reclaim his candy-apple red Fiero.

According to plan, Johnny and the briefcase had remained in the elevator to descend one more floor to the river level. Lobbies of hotels such as the St. Aubin were routinely, although irregularly, staked out by the authorities to discover who was meeting, or sleeping, with whom. If this day turned out to be one of those irregular days, Tony, the older and more notorious of the pair, by leaving through the main lobby, would command the attention of any watchers, allowing Johnny to slip out unnoticed through the riverside exit with the diamonds. From there, Johnny was to casually stroll across the promenade and down to the dock where Julie waited in the *Sophia IV*, a forty-four-foot Tollycraft motor yacht, to take him to the rendezvous point at the Detroit Yacht Club on Belle Isle.

❦ ❦ ❦

Tony cautiously drove the Fiero eastward along Jefferson Avenue, obeying all the traffic laws. He crossed the MacArthur bridge and smiled as he spotted the *Sophia IV* about midway between the St. Aubin and the island. After making a left-hand turn onto River-bank, he drove the length of the island and pulled into the parking lot of the Yacht Club. Easing the car into a space next to a black stretch-limousine with darkened windows, he shut off the engine and got out.

The front passenger door of the limo opened and Tony slid in beside Sal Merlino, pulling the door shut behind him. Vittorio Gianelli sat in the rear seat, an eyebrow raised in an unspoken question. Tony gave his father a big grin, a wink, and a thumbs-up sign. Vittorio smiled in reply and patted him on the shoulder.

From their position in the parking lot, the trio could see the empty slip that belonged to the *Sophia IV.*

"They were about half way to the island when I crossed the bridge," Tony said. "Julie's taking it cool. You know, like a sightseer. He's not gonna take a chance of getting stopped by the river pigs with the cargo he's carrying."

The older men nodded but said nothing. After another twenty minutes, though, Sal Merlino nervously started the engine and drove back the length of the island and onto the MacArthur bridge. As the car slowly crossed the bridge, both Tony and Vittorio Gianelli scanned the river for the Tolly-craft. They could see the St. Aubin Towers on one side and the Yacht Club on the other, but there were no boats the size of the *Sophia IV* in either direction. Turning the car around by Gabriel Richard Park to cross back over the bridge, Sal had to wait as two police cars and an ambulance, sirens blaring, made the turn off Jefferson Avenue and sped onto the island.

Again, the ever-hopeful Tony offered an explanation for his brothers' tardiness. "Maybe they're taking the long way around the other side of the island? You know, so nobody sees them coming directly from the hotel to the club?"

The *capo supremo* and his underboss exchanged skeptical looks. The old man gave a slight shrug of his shoulders, acknowledging that the boy could be correct.

Sal turned the limousine onto the bridge and again made the island-long trip to the parking lot of the Yacht Club. The *Sophia IV's* slip still sat empty. All three men looked at their watches. Over an hour had passed from the time Tony had driven out of the St. Aubin's parking lot. Sal pressed the speaker-phone button on the cellular phone and placed a shore-to-ship call.

A voice that Tony didn't recognize answered the phone on the *Sophia IV.* "Hello?"

"Giovanni? Julio?" Sal asked.

"May I ask who this is, sir?" the voice replied.

"This is Salvatore Merlino. I'd like to speak with either Giovanni or Julio Gianelli. Who is this, please?"

"Are you related to the Gianellis, sir?"

"I am employed by their father," Sal replied. "He is here with me. Who is this?"

"This is Lieutenant-Commander James Enright, sir. U.S. Coast Guard. I'm afraid there's been an…an accident."

The three men maintained their silence as Sal drove the limousine through the gates of the U.S. Coast Guard Station on the southeastern tip of Belle Isle and headed it in the direction of the docks. They glimpsed the command bridge of the *Sophia IV* sticking up above the deck of the cutter moored in front of it. Two police cars and an ambulance sat parked by the side of the pier.

As Sal maneuvered the limo into a space next to one of the patrol cars, Tony became aware of the lack of urgency in everyone's movements and his mouth went dry at that implication. He turned to look at his father and read the sorrow on the old man's face. Vittorio had made the same dreadful inference. The word "accident" had been a deliberate understatement.

At the foot of the gangway leading to the *Sophia IV*, two men stood deep in conversation. The younger man wore a Coast Guard uniform, bearing Lieutenant-Commander's insignia. His companion, a middle-aged black man, had on a wrinkled, brown Sears suit. Sal and the Gianellis knew the black man.

As Sal opened his door to exit the limousine, Tony also opened the passenger door. The underboss shook his head and put a restraining hand on the boy's arm. "Just stay put. I'll handle this," he said in a soft but firm voice.

Tony shook off the other man's hand. "Those are my brothers," he said, fighting back the tears as he put one leg out of the open car door.

A commanding voice from the back seat stopped Tony cold. "Antonio! You will do as you are told."

"But Papa—" the boy said, turning around.

"*Silenzio!*"

Tony pulled his leg back into the car, slammed the door and turned in his seat, again facing the front of the limo.

"That is better, my son. There will be a time for rage. Now is the time for clearer heads. *Capisce?*" Vittorio turned his moist eyes on the *capo subordinato*. "Go, Salvatore. See if there is anything you can learn from Sergeant Gardner."

As Sal Merlino approached the gangway and the Lieutenant-Commander took his leave, Tony lowered his window so that he could at least hear what he had not been permitted to be a part of.

Detective Sergeant Jerome Gardner of the Detroit Police Force cocked his head at the impeccably dressed bald man and clucked his tongue. "Tch, tch, tch, tch. The wages of sin, *Consigliere*. The wages of sin."

"What happened, Sergeant? May I go on board?"

"The answer to the second question is no, not until the lab boys officially tell me what you and I both already know, that there's no physical evidence. As to the first question,"—he pulled a notebook from his pocket and recited in an official monotone—"we have two white males, tentatively identified as Julio and Giovanni Gianelli, the former with his throat slit, the latter blown damn near in half by two shotgun blasts at close range."

Sergeant Gardner replaced the notebook in his pocket. "And I'll also answer your unasked question. No, there's nary a trace of what they were transporting. Just an empty tan briefcase."

The two men stepped aside as four paramedics carefully wheeled two sheet-covered stretchers down the gangway and headed toward the ambulance. Jerome Gardner whistled for them to stop. "You want to save yourself a trip down to the morgue and make the identification here?"

Before Sal could answer, the back door of the limousine opened and Vittorio emerged. Holding up a cautionary finger to Tony in the front seat, he said, "Now you come, Antonio. But not a word do you say."

Sal met them at the stretchers and put his hand on the old man's arm. "This isn't necessary, *Padrone*. I can make the identification."

Patting the younger man's hand, Vittorio said softly, "It *is* necessary, Salvatore. This is family."

Sal simply nodded, then gently pulled the sheets down part way on each of the bodies.

Tony bit his lip to stem the tears that had begun to flow. *How could this have happened?* But then he suddenly went pale and cold as the realization set in. *Rosa!* he thought, fighting the wave of nausea and guilt that swept over him. *Rosa was the only other one. Oh, no! Oh, God, no! This is all my fault!* And as he stood there beside his father looking at the lifeless faces of his two younger brothers, Antonio Gianelli sobbed uncontrollably.

Although the *capo supremo*, too, had tears in his smoldering obsidian eyes, he did not weep. He stood there stroking his dead sons' hair and, through a clenched jaw, uttered only one barely-audible word. "*Vendetta.*"

A nudge from Giuseppe Triano's elbow brought Tony back to the present and a nod directed his attention toward the other table where Vittorio Gianelli's gnarled finger beckoned him.

As he approached, Tony saw that the paper Sal had brought, which now sat in front of his father, had been folded open to a picture of the Isabela Pendant and a reprint of Bill Brinkmire's article from the *Ashokan Register*. The hairs raised on the back of his neck. *My God, can it be?*

"*Dov'è il* Big Indian Mountain?" Vittorio asked Sal.

"Just a few miles south of here, Don Vittorio. In Ulster County."

"Papa, is it —" Tony started, but his father cut him off with a snap of his finger and pointed him into the adjacent chair. Tony sat in silence.

Glancing at the byline of the newspaper article, Vittorio Gianelli's lips curled into a menacing smile. "*Grazie, Signor* Brinkmire. *Tante grazie!*"

Chapter 4

It was shortly before noon and Harvey, in his trademark green waders with the Magnum inflatable suspenders and white Panama hat, was alone with nature. But this Friday, instead of working his usual spot on the Esopus Creek, he fished a stretch of the Woodland Creek on the western slope of Slide Mountain in Peekamoose Heights.

Lenny had driven Matt Christiansen over to the orthopedic surgeon in Kingston for a routine check-up on his arthritic condition. Cynthia, after having packed a hamper for Harvey and getting him on his way, had driven over to Mt. Pleasant for her weekly hair-and-nail appointment. And being a Friday, Danny Henderson attended to his chores at The Plough & Whistle.

It had been early the day before, on Thursday, that Matt Christiansen had telephoned the Peekamoose Heights police station. Since it was the first time that he had had the occasion to dial that particular number, he had not been prepared for Lucille's rasping "Police Department" at the other end of the line. He had to quickly jerk the receiver away from his ear.

With the phone six inches from the side of his face and his hearing still somewhat impaired, he had asked to be put through to McAvoy.

"Matt Christiansen on line one," Lucille shouted and put the call on HOLD.

The chief was just giving last minute instructions to Sergeant Jim Culpepper, the unofficial Assistant Chief of Police. In response to Lucille's holler, McAvoy motioned for Jim to sit and picked up the telephone receiver.

"Hey, Matt. We're just about ready to get under way. What's up?"

"You see the piece about the jewel in yesterday's *Register*?"

"I think it got picked up by every paper in the state," McAvoy replied. "Martin Bassett phoned a while ago. People have been calling the sheriff's office from as far away as Cooks Falls asking about the buried treasure."

"Well, Lenny and I just got to Harvey's and there's at least fifty other people out here, combing the woods with metal detectors and shovels. And you can just guess how well old Harv's taking it. A couple of deputies are keeping them out of the taped-off area, but still, there's no point in you and Danny driving over here. With all the ruckus, no self-respecting trout will come within a mile of this place today."

McAvoy looked up from his desk, through the half-glass into the waiting area. Danny had parked himself on one of the wooden chairs against the wall, Onteora Indians cap on his head and yellow dog at his feet. The boy had finished loading the Jeep and he and his four-footed pal eagerly waited for the chief to conclude the phone call so that they could get going.

"Tell you what, Matt. I've already arranged for the day off and it would be a shame to waste it. After all, the Esopus isn't the only creek with trout in it. I know a spot over here that I think you guys'd like."

Within a half hour, Matt and Harvey had joined McAvoy and Danny at a stretch of the Woodland Creek just down from The Poplars, a small, exclusive forty-eight suite hospital about a half mile west of the village. Of course Harvey had started off the day by grumbling that the fishing couldn't possibly be as good as it was over at his place. However, by the time Lenny, Cynthia, and the picnic basket arrived just shortly after noon, the normally curmudgeonly old man had turned positively cheerful. Both he and Danny had caught the creel limit.

So on Friday, with would-be treasure seekers still covering the slope of Big Indian Mountain like soldier ants, Harvey DuMont had returned to that same stretch of Woodland Creek where Ed McAvoy had taken him the day before. He had parked his car on the roadside next to a mammoth fieldstone arch with the words THE POPLARS carved in Celtic script into the limestone lintel, and had walked through the archway and up the winding private road.

Upon reaching the bridge over the Woodland Creek, he had donned his green waders and stepped out into the stream. As he slowly waddled upstream, he had called out quietly, "Come on little fishies. Come to Uncle Harv."

And they had—eight in a time-frame of less than three hours. On this special Friday, Harvey DuMont was truly a happy man.

The heavy-set black man slowed the metallic jade-green Lincoln's speed to twenty-five miles per hour as he crossed Dutcher Street and entered the downtown section of Peekamoose Heights. He proceeded at that pace westward down Irving Boulevard.

In the back seat of the Town Car, an elderly woman with perfectly coifed silver-white hair, dressed in a pink silk suit, sat and looked out the window at the village she had loved for so many years. One twisted hand rested on the polymer-ivory handle of a walking cane. Scrimshawed on the handle were a pair of full-rigged clipper ships and a wharf scene.

The woman unconsciously traced around the design of the soft green leather on the armrest with her other hand. Although now in her late seventies, and despite the crippling effects of arthritis that were in a far more advanced stage than Matt Christiansen's, Kate Winthrop's mind was as clear as her hazel eyes were bright.

Although she no longer directly ran any of the myriad of corporations that her late husband, George Duffrin Winthrop III, had owned, she still wielded her considerable influence on those whom she had selected as her stewards. This Friday morning's meeting in Kingston, from which she was now returning, had been to exercise some of that influence.

She had strongly "suggested" to the president and other officers of Kingston Tool Works that they rethink their decision to enter into a trade agreement with a Chinese firm, based on the continuing human rights abuses in that country. She would rather they explore what opportunities lay in the now-republics of the former Eastern-block countries instead. When someone with thirty-eight percent of the stock "suggests" something, people tend to give it every consideration.

Kate smiled as she reflected on how liberal she had become, the older she became. The first sign, she thought, although she hadn't realized it at the time, was feeling somewhat ostentatious at calling herself "Mrs. George Duffrin Winthrop III." She now referred to herself simply as Katherine Winthrop—Kate to her small circle of true friends.

Since then, her liberalism had mushroomed into concern for the environment, the underprivileged, the disenfranchised, and the working men and women in her own enterprises. The result had been either corporate policies that supported these ideals, at those firms whose board members were wise enough to adopt her suggestions, or the installation of new members at those who would not or could not be coerced into doing so. Even the domestic Lincoln had been purchased as a bit of social commentary after years of owning Mercedes and BMW touring cars.

Kate almost laughed out loud as she made a mental note to pay a visit to the family crypts in the churchyard of St. Mary's-in-the-Hills Episcopal Church to see if the Duffrin and Winthrop ancestors had, in fact, rolled over in their graves. If voting in the Democratic presidential primary for an ex-senator from Massachusetts some years back hadn't caused it, she thought, then nothing would.

Perhaps, the opening up of the emergency ward of The Poplars, the private hospital she had founded, owned, and where she now lived, to anyone in need *and* the acceptance of what any insurance plan paid as compensation in full, might have had the same effect. Although maybe the relaxation was not all that big a deal since it was only an aboveboard formalization of the unofficial policy that Chief of Staff Benjamin Krider and Head Nurse Millie Larson had been using for years without her knowledge.

As the Town Car approached The Plough & Whistle Pub on the right-hand side of the boulevard, Kate lightly set a gnarled hand on the shoulder of her chauffeur's blue blazer.

"Mr. Douglas?"

"Yes, ma'am?"

"Kindly pull the car over in front of the pub, please."

"Yes, ma'am."

Samuel Douglas and his wife Emily were proprietors of The Then & Now, one of the finest antique stores in the Catskills. Even so, the gentle giant of a man still supplemented his income, although he hardly needed to, by continuing to drive for the woman who had loaned him the money to start his business when no one else would.

Sam eased the Lincoln over to the curb and into one of the two handicapped parking spaces directly in front of the pub.

Danny Henderson stood on a step stool, squeegeeing the outside of the plate glass window. The boy turned as he heard the electric window of the Town Car being lowered. "Hi, Mrs. Winthrop," he said, smiling at the elderly woman and giving her a little salute with the squeegee.

"Good afternoon, Daniel. Would you ask either your uncle or your mother to come out to the car for just a moment, please? I want to make certain that everything is in order for the picnic."

On the Sunday closest to August 15, the feast of St. Mary the Virgin, the Episcopal Church of St. Mary's-in-the-Hills celebrated with a Patron's Day Picnic. Through the years the Winthrops had always picked up the tab for the event. After an almost-disaster two summers ago when two church vestry-men each thought the other was arranging for the catering, Porky and Stevie had come to the rescue at the last-minute. Because of that incident, a resolution had been unanimously passed making The Plough & Whistle the official caterer for the Patron's Day Picnic. Now no one had to worry about who was making the arrangements. Still, Kate Winthrop needed some assurance.

"Mom had to run across the street to the bank and Uncle Roz is working by himself in there, Mrs. Winthrop," Danny replied. "But don't worry about Sunday. All the stuff arrived this morning. I had to inventory it myself.... Honest!" The last word was in response to a look on Kate's face that asked, "Do I trust a fourteen-year-old boy?"

"All right, Daniel." The elderly woman smiled at him. "See you on Sunday." Kate touched the button on the Town Car's arm rest and the window slid up.

Sam Douglas eased the Lincoln back out onto Irving Boulevard and headed westward toward Katherine Winthrop's home, The Poplars.

❦ ❦ ❦

A man dressed in black climbed into a bronze-colored Cougar XR-7, backed out of the parking space labeled CLERGY ONLY, and drove down the winding road away from the private hospital.

This Friday morning he had been Fr. John Desmond, Rector of St. Mary's-in-the-Hills, and had just finished one of his three-times-a-week visitations at The Poplars. He now headed back to his office, next to the police station in downtown Peekamoose Heights. There, he would change out of his collar and black clothes into something a little more businesslike and become John Desmond, small-town-CPA, for the rest of the afternoon.

Instead of running the air conditioner, John had the car windows open so that he could enjoy the aromas and sounds that the Catskills had to offer that day. As he drove, he remembered when he had been John Desmond workaholic-CPA morning *and* afternoon, a rising star at one of the Big-Six firms in Manhattan. That was before a mild stroke had "hinted" that, perhaps, a change in lifestyle might be in order. He deeply inhaled the woodsy air and listened to the forest sounds. A far cry from the smells and noises of Manhattan, he thought and offered a silent prayer of thanksgiving for having had the opportunity for a second life.

As he looked out at nature and pondered his present life, a passage from Gibran's *The Prophet* came to mind: "Who can spread his hours before him, saying, 'This for God and this for myself; This for my soul, and this other for my body?'"

John Desmond smiled and answered the question. *I can.*

❦ ❦ ❦

It was a beautiful day. The sun shone brightly and a soft summer breeze rustled tranquilly through the leaves of the poplars that densely populated that area of Slide Mountain. Harvey DuMont set the butt end of his Bighorn Special down on the rocks and leaned the rod against a branch of a large tree that grew at an angle out over the water. He carefully removed the rainbow trout from his hook and waddled out into the center of the stream with it.

The normally grumpy fisherman had a smile that stretched from ear to ear. *That McAvoy's an all-right guy. One more and I'll have the creel limit for the second day in a row. Damn! I can't remember the last time I did that, except at The Portal. Wait until I tell Matt.*

Holding his catch in the water, facing upstream, he waited for a few seconds until the trout began to wiggle a bit, then released it. The fish gave two swishes of its iridescent tail and quickly darted away.

Even though Harvey DuMont and Matt Christiansen were strictly sport fishermen and rarely kept any of their catch, they still made it a practice to abide by the daily creel limit and would quit for the day when or if they reached that maximum.

As he waddled back over to the stream bank to retrieve his fly rod, Harvey heard a faint rustle of branches. He picked up the Bighorn Special and started to turn to his left to see the source of the sound, but never completed the turn.

The first explosion hit him in the left side, tearing it wide open. The double-aught buckshot lifted the elderly angler off the ground, turned him clockwise almost three-hundred and sixty degrees, and caused his head to whiplash back and his arms and legs to flail wildly like an out-of-control marionette. The fly rod catapulted into the branches of the overhanging tree and the white Panama hat pitched into the water where it quickly sailed away downstream.

As the fisherman's feet hit the water, the second explosion tore open his right side and sent him sprawling backwards into the creek. Now, his nerves caught up with the rest of his senses and an excruciating pain set in. Through his water- and pain-clouded vision, he could only watch helplessly as his life's blood drained out in front of him.

When his beloved Big Horn Special had been involuntarily flung away after the first shot, the fly rod had caught momentarily on the activator cord of Harvey's Magnum wader suspenders, causing the orange flotation collar to inflate. Once again alone with nature, he floated silently with the current, down the Woodland Creek, following his white Panama hat back toward the bridge and the private road to The Poplars.

"What the hell was that?!" Dr. Benjamin Krider asked, looking up from a guest's chart that he had been reading and turning to Lisa Griffin, one of the day-shift Duty Nurses.

"It sounded like gunshots," Lisa replied, somewhat bewildered.

Ben crossed to the window on the south side of the guest wing of The Poplars in an attempt to see what had caused the two explosions. "Get Ed McAvoy on the phone, Lisa. Ask him to send someone up here. If those *were* gunshots, they're too damn close for comfort."

The nurse picked up the phone, punched in the digits from the emergency label on the instrument's cradle and held the receiver a good six inches from her ear. Lisa knew what to expect on the other end of the line.

John Desmond's reverie was shattered by the two gunshots. He slammed on the brakes, skidding the Cougar to a crosswise stop, blocking the road at the north side of the bridge over Woodland Creek. He shut the engine off so that he could hear better.

Some damn fool doesn't know that there are people close by, he thought as he looked around and listened for another sign of the hunter.

John neither heard nor saw anything unusual, just the forest sounds and sights—with two exceptions. As he glanced upstream, he saw a white Panama hat, riding with the current toward the bridge and something bright orange farther away. He climbed out of the XR-7 and walked onto the bridge in order to get a better look.

The hat drifted by him under the bridge but the orange item had become snagged on a tree branch and remained stuck upstream. As the current pulled Harvey DuMont's legs around so that the old man faced the bridge, the priest let out a yell and raced along the edge of the creek bed, vaulting over boulders and calling for help as he ran.

Harvey DuMont felt the tug as John Desmond, knee-deep in water, dragged him toward the stream bank, and he managed to open his eyes as the priest attempted to pull him up onto the embankment. John unfastened the releases on the waders, now full of water, so that the job of lifting the old man would be easier. Through his fading vision, Harvey's eyes half-focused on the priest's black shirt and white collar and he grabbed John's shoulder.

"Don't worry," John panted as he strained to lift the elderly man. "There's a hospital just up the hill. I'll get you some help. Just hang on."

"Bl...bless me, Father, for...for I have sinned," Harvey gasped.

"We'll take care of that later. Right now you need medical attention." John attempted to hoist the wounded man into a fireman's carry but Harvey fought with what little strength he had left.

"Bless me, F...father, for I have sinned!" Harvey insisted.

Only then did John Desmond notice the extent of the man's wounds. *Oh, dear God,* the priest thought, as he gently laid Harvey down on the moss-covered stream bank. *He's not going to make it and he thinks I'm a Roman Catholic priest. I guess now's not the time to tell him differently.*

The honking of an automobile horn made the priest look downstream. A jade-green Lincoln Town Car had stopped on the bridge and Sam Douglas stood at its side.

"Get help!" John shouted. "He's hurt badly." The priest turned his attention back to the wounded man as Harvey began his final confession.

"I...I confess to Almighty God and to...to you, Father. It's been t...ten years since my last confession."

Fr. Desmond made the sign of the cross over the dying man and spoke softly. He hoped that the past decade and the present pain would obscure Harvey's memory enough so that he would not notice that the prayer probably differed slightly from the Roman Catholic version.

"The Lord be in your heart and upon your lips that you may truly and humbly confess your sins: In the Name of the Father, and of the Son, and of the Holy Spirit. Amen." Then, somewhat louder he said, "Go on. I'm listening."

Kate Winthrop, who had lowered her window to better see what was happening, grabbed the cellular phone from its cradle behind the front seat as she spoke to her driver. "I'll call Ben. You go see what you can do to help."

As she began to dial, Sam hurriedly made his way toward the priest and the wounded man, arriving just as John Desmond finished the absolution and Harvey DuMont's spirit was reeled in by the Great Fisherman.

The Poplars was a one-story building in the shape of a giant figure eight with its two circular wings separated by a small square reception building. The Guest Wing contained forty-eight private suites with a nurses' station in the center of the hub. Operating rooms, radiology, and the other medical and service facilities were all situated in the Service Wing. In back of the figure eight, another small rectangular building, connected to the reception building by an enclosed walkway, contained offices. These offices were used by the hospital administrative staff as well as the many visiting specialists who called on The Poplars' wealthy guests. One of those empty offices in the Administration Building had been given over to McAvoy for use as an on-site police station for the investigation into the death of Harvey DuMont.

McAvoy had only just returned from the always-distasteful task of notifying the next of kin.

Since the DuMonts had no other family in the area that the chief knew of, he had checked first with Stevie to find out if Danny knew where Matt Christiansen and Lenny Damien lived. Then, after learning the general location from the boy, he called the Oliverea postmaster to get specific directions.

McAvoy was glad that he had called and had not tried to find the house by himself. The two men lived in a large log A-frame, deep in the woods on the northeast slope of Panther Mountain on the Panther Kill stream.

Matt and Lenny sat there speechless as McAvoy broke the news to them. Fortunately for McAvoy, they considerately volunteered to accompany him to the DuMonts, insisting that Cynthia shouldn't be alone at a time like this.

McAvoy felt relieved. He had hoped for precisely that outcome from his visit.

Cynthia DuMont, all smiles and her usual flirtatious self at their arrival, soon became an emotional basket-case on hearing the report of her husband's death. A call from McAvoy to Dr. Ben Krider back at The Poplars resulted in a prescription for a sedative being phoned in to the pharmacy in Oliverea. Lenny left to fetch the medication and Matt agreed that he and his nephew would stay with Cynthia to help her through her ordeal and make all the necessary arrangements.

After getting Cynthia settled in bed, Matt answered what questions he could about Harvey's background. That information, however, was very sketchy. Even though the two men had both come from Detroit, they had never met until after the DuMonts moved to the Catskills and Matt and Harvey had run into each other down at The Portal.

They had become instant fishing buddies—two fellow ex-Wolverines surrounded by people who didn't seem to be able to pronounce the letter *R* at the end of a word. Matt, a west-sider, had been an investment counselor until his retirement four years earlier. The DuMonts had operated a small chain of dry-cleaning establishments on Detroit's east side up until two years ago.

McAvoy, a west-sider himself, appreciated how the east and west sides of Detroit might just as well have been two different cities, separated by Woodward Avenue running from the riverfront in Downtown Detroit northwest all the way out to Pontiac. A large number of residents on both sides of Woodward managed to live their entire lives without ever crossing that strip of highway.

Matt couldn't think of anyone who disliked Harvey enough to kill him. He freely admitted that old Harv sometimes rubbed people the wrong way. He just couldn't fathom it, though, that someone would blow another person away just because that person irritated people. McAvoy left the DuMont home with Matt's promise that he would call the station as soon as he thought Cynthia could manage to answer some questions herself.

Deputy Sergeant Stanley Jurocik and Deputy Tom Lapinski from the Ulster County Sheriff's Department had finished their preliminary investigation of the murder site and were packing up their forensic gear, getting ready to leave.

Larry Parker, one of the Peekamoose Heights police officers and McAvoy's nephew, had served as guide and liaison to the team. A tall and lanky lad with his late father's rugged good looks and easy demeanor, Larry, at nineteen years old was the rookie on the Peekamoose Heights police force. He had only recently graduated from the Basic Police Training program, conducted jointly by the Kingston Police and the Ulster County Sheriff.

Larry entered the hospital administration office and walked up behind McAvoy, who stood staring at the items resting on a conference table in the corner of the room. The entire body of physical evidence consisted of a Big Horn Special fly rod, retrieved from the branches of a tree that overhung the creek, a white Panama hat recovered from among the rocks and debris in the downstream shallows, and Harvey DuMont's clothing and personal effects, removed from the body at The Poplars. None of the items were of any help in identifying the who or why in Case Number PMH-247-38.

"It looks as if there was just one person, Unc...er...uh... Chief," Larry said, catching himself just before making the blunder of calling McAvoy "Uncle Ed." It was one of the chief's pet peeves when they were on duty. "Some crushed or broken branches by the creek bank and others leading up to the hiking trail, but we haven't had a decent rain in weeks so the ground was too hard to take an imprint of any kind. There was nothing on the hiking trail to tell which way he might have gone. Could have walked down to Winnisook, picked up a car and gone out County Road #47 in either direction, or walked up to the Woodland Valley Campsite and then driven out to Phoenicia. The sheriff is sending a car over to Woodland Valley to check with the ranger and campers but there's not much they can do at the Winnisook end of the trail. Also, whoever it was picked up his empty shells. There's no trace of anything left behind."

During Larry's report, McAvoy pawed through Harvey DuMont's personal effects for perhaps the fifth time with no results. "What could he have done to make someone that angry with him?" he wondered out loud. "If this turns out to be a hunting accident, I'll eat your trooper's hat, Larry.

Someone went to a whole lot of trouble to find him and kill him. This was premeditated."

"Insurance, maybe?" Larry offered.

"We'll check on that angle, but I don't really think so. The DuMonts seem to have plenty of money and, from the looks of the inside of the house, Cynthia hasn't been restrained from spending any of it."

The police officers were interrupted from any further conjecture by Dr. Ben Krider and an Ulster County assistant medical examiner. Usually bodies were sent to the morgue at the Kingston City Hospital. Since Harvey DuMont was already at The Poplars, it was just as easy for the AME to drive up from the city to perform the examination there—or so the story went.

Neither Ben nor AME Miriam Talbot could make eye contact with the chief as they explained the reasoning behind Miriam's visit. McAvoy suspected that he would see them both later that evening at The Plough & Whistle, dining at an intimate table for two.

"It doesn't look like there's any chance that this was a hunting accident," Ben said.

Miriam explained why. "I don't know what you'd be hunting in this area with double-aught buckshot. A rabbit or bird would be blown to bits. Besides, there were powder burns on the clothing. This suggests that the shooting was done at close range. Close enough that the gunman—or woman," she added, "had to have seen what he or she was shooting at."

McAvoy nodded his agreement with the conclusion and the slender attractive brunette continued. "However, the pattern of the shots, and I'm certain that there were two of them, seems to be too large to have been fired from that close of a range."

"Meaning what?" McAvoy asked.

"Meaning, if my guess is right, Chief, when, or *if*, you find the shotgun in question, it'll turn out to be quite a bit shorter than the legal length."

Larry Parker scratched his head, not quite sure he grasped the woman's explanation. "A hit?" He looked from his uncle to the two doctors. "A hit? Here in Peekamoose Heights?"

"Hey, that's your job to find out, guys. I just call 'em as I see 'em," Miriam answered, putting up her hands good-naturedly. "I'll have a formal report ready by Monday afternoon and fax it over to you." She shrugged her shoulders in acknowledgment that her job was finished and she and Ben left the room, barely avoiding a collision with Deputy Sheriff Sergeant Martin Bassett as he hurried down the hallway.

"The Wenceslas Brigade just filled me in," Martin said, not bothering with any preliminary pleasantries. "This necklace thing is getting more and more bizarre, but I sure didn't figure it would lead to murder."

"What makes you think the two are related?" McAvoy asked as he sat on the edge of one of the desks.

Martin smiled with delight. He didn't often get the upper hand in an investigation and relished being able to provide some key information that the chief didn't yet have.

"Well, I'll tell you, Chief," he began, commandeering the desk chair and putting his size elevens on the desk top. "Dewey Dunlavy just got in on a KLM flight from Holland. As soon as he saw that necklace in his safe his eyes fell out of his head and he called the boss. That piece is called the Isabela Pendant and it's part of a multimillion-dollar jewel heist that took place in your old stomping grounds about four years ago. From what he remembers, some people got killed over it."

"Jeez," Larry Parker muttered, scratching his head again.

"Interesting," McAvoy conceded. "What else you got?"

"That's it," Martin replied, somewhat hurt that the chief expected more information out of him. "The boss thought you might want to check it out with some of your Detroit pals and then we'll get together and decide whether we have one investigation or two."

McAvoy picked up the telephone receiver and punched in the number that for the better part of his life had been his. After exchanging good-natured insults with some of his old cronies at Detroit Police Headquarters and catching up on the current gossip, he was finally transferred to Detective Lieutenant Jerome Gardner.

"So you finally passed the lieutenant's exam, huh?" he teased his longtime colleague. "How many tries?"

"Too many, Mac. Too many. And I'm not all that sure it was worth it. The paperwork on this job would choke a good sized goat. I used to be a lot happier out on the streets."

"Yeah, but those streets are a lot meaner these days, Jerry."

After a few more minutes of banter, McAvoy asked about the Isabela Pendant. The lieutenant remembered it all too well and, without the aid of any notes, relayed the basics regarding the theft. He also added his own unsubstantiated educated guess on the perpetrators.

"This had mob written all over it, Mac. Within an hour after the heist, two Gianellis, Julio and Giovanni, were found adrift in their yacht, deader than doornails. The whole thing screamed double-cross, but we were never able to prove anything. The file's still open but nobody's working on it anymore."

An alarm went off in McAvoy's head when Lieutenant Gardner described the way in which Giovanni Gianelli had been almost cut in half by two shotgun blasts at close range.

"Would you check with the mob watchers and see if any of the remaining Gianellis or close associates have left town within the last few days?" He explained the circumstances surrounding Harvey DuMont's death.

"I'll check, but there aren't any Gianellis left here. Don Vittorio suffered a stroke shortly after the death of his sons and went into retirement. I understand that Sal Merlino and number-one son Antonio went with him. But I would have thought you'd know all about that."

"How would I know? I've been pretty much out of the mainstream of things up here in the boonies."

"Where is Greene County in relationship to you, Mac?"

"It's the county just to the north of us. Why?"

"You know of a place called Garibaldi House?"

"The old mobsters' retirement home? Sure, Jerry, but... you're not telling me that—"

"That's where Vittorio Gianelli is. He's been in your own backyard for over three years now."

McAvoy thanked his former colleague for the information, for agreeing to fax the entire file to Lucille, and also for agreeing to run a check on Harvey DuMont.

He looked first at Larry Parker. "Bring the Jeep around. We're going visiting." As the young officer exited the room, the chief again picked up the telephone receiver, but this time he handed it to Deputy Sergeant Bassett. "How about calling your buddies at the Greene County Sheriff's Department. I need a favor."

Chapter 5

McAvoy didn't say a word during most of the drive up to Deep Notch. Finally Larry broke the silence. "Do you know this Vittorio Gianelli guy?"

The chief smiled. "Oh, yeah. We go back a long way. He's got a rap sheet the length of your arm. I even busted him myself on at least a half dozen occasions, but not one of those arrests ever got to trial."

"Pretty bad dude, huh?"

"Ever hear of Jimmy Hoffa?"

"Sure," Larry replied. "He was that Teamsters guy the mob rubbed out about thirty years ago. They say he's buried under one of the goal posts down at the Meadowlands."

McAvoy laughed out loud, partly at the content of Larry's statement and partly because the boy spoke of Hoffa in the same abstract vein as if he were talking about long-dead historical figures like Nathaniel Hawthorne or Washington Irving.

"They're wrong," McAvoy said. "Vittorio Gianelli arranged for the car that drove Hoffa to his last appointment—at the Reynolds Pet Food facility in Wyandotte, Michigan. For months after that meeting an interesting phenomenon occurred." He lowered his voice as if to impart some confidential information to his nephew. Larry sat there nodding, eagerly awaiting the inside scoop. "Dogs from all over the Great Lakes area tried to organize a strike against their masters," McAvoy continued. "They carried little signs in their little paws that said MORE BISCUITS—LESS FETCHING."

Larry rolled his eyes and snorted while McAvoy burst into a hearty laugh as they rounded the final switchback on the northwestern slope of Balsam Mountain.

Just before the road crested and began its twisting descent, they came to an unmarked gravel drive on the left-hand side of the road. The chief had Larry turn the Jeep into the three-hundred-yard long winding private road and follow it back into the woods. After driving about two-hundred-and-fifty of those yards, the main entrance and security building for Garibaldi House came into view.

A mammoth iron gate, set into a sixteen-foot high elec-trified fence, blocked unauthorized entry into the compound. Security cameras, mounted at regular intervals atop the fence scanned the areas on both sides of the enclosure. The dense-ness of the piny woods hid the chateau itself from any prying eyes.

A white Crown Victoria with red stripes, parked on the shoulder some twenty-five yards from the gate, had a large gold star on its door with the words SHERIFF GREENE COUNTY emblazoned over the State of New York seal in its center. Two deputies sat in the front seat.

Larry eased the Jeep up to the side of the Ford and McAvoy lowered his window and introduced himself.

"You all clear on what's going down?" he asked.

The driver's mouth broadened into an expansive grin. "I wouldn't miss this for all the pasta in Italy," Sergeant Pete Myrick said. "Go ahead, Chief, it's your show. We'll back you up all the way."

As Larry drove the Jeep the remaining distance and pulled up next to the security booth, the two Greene County Sheriff's deputies climbed out of the Crown Vic, leaving the engine idling and the doors open. They moved to the front of the vehicle, faced away from Garibaldi House and chatted between themselves.

At the Jeep's approach, one of the two security guards exited the gate house. Although middle-aged, he appeared to be in excellent physical condition. He was dressed in red slacks, a white knit shirt open at the neck, and a green blazer. From the bulge under his left arm, McAvoy suspected that a Beretta Model 92F accessorized this colorful ensemble.

Both McAvoy and Larry got out of the Cherokee but Larry remained beside the car as the chief approached the security guard.

"I'm Ed McAvoy, the Chief of Police over in Peekamoose Heights. I'd like to speak with Vittorio Gianelli, please?"

The guard quickly glanced through some papers on a clipboard then looked at McAvoy. "I'm sorry, sir," he said politely, "but I don't find your name on the appointment calendar for today. Perhaps if you were to telephone and make the necessary arrangements?"

Out of the corner of his eye, McAvoy noticed the guard's partner inside the gate house pick up a telephone receiver. "I don't have an appointment," the chief said. "Is Don Vittorio here?"

Again, the guard exuded politeness. "I'm sorry, sir, but I am not allowed to divulge that sort of information. Our guests here at Garibaldi House are very privacy conscious and I —"

"This is official police business," McAvoy interrupted.

"With all due respect, Chief McAvoy, Garibaldi House is hardly within your jurisdiction."

"But it *is* within the boundaries of Greene County." McAvoy nodded toward the two deputies with their backs turned to the gate. He was impressed, though, by the security guard. This was no run-of-the-mill wiseguy.

"But, sir, unless the local officials have reasonable cause to believe that some statute has been violated, they, too, must phone for an appointment. That *is* the law."

The guard tried his best to remain polite and not to smirk, even when he raised his upturned palms and slightly shrugged his shoulders as if to say, "What's a poor country boy to do?"

"I'm sure if they heard gunshots that they thought came from within the compound, that would be reasonable cause enough," McAvoy said, not even attempting to disguise *his* smirk.

The guard was momentarily taken aback as he tried to decipher the chief's meaning. During the conversation, both he and his partner on the telephone in the gate house had been concentrating on McAvoy. They had not seen Larry Parker remove his Smith & Wesson Model 5906 from its holster and hold it down at his side. At a slight nod from the chief, Larry rapidly fired three rounds into the ground, then immediately reholstered the stainless steel semiautomatic and stood there, innocently, looking as if nothing out of the ordinary had happened.

The guard who had been talking to McAvoy instinctively reached for his Beretta but was restrained by the chief. The second guard exited the security booth at a run, weapon drawn.

The two Greene County Deputies jumped into their car. Sergeant Myrick jammed the shift lever into DRIVE and floored the accelerator pedal, causing the Ford to fishtail up the drive to the gate in less than five seconds, spraying gravel all the way.

"Open that gate!" Myrick shouted to the guard with the gun. "*Now* or I'll ram it!" The sergeant revved the car's engine to give emphasis to his command.

The two guards looked at each other in bewilderment, then the disembodied voice of Sal Merlino crackled through a loudspeaker on the side of the gate house. "*Ignorante!* Let the gentlemen from Peekamoose Heights through....Mr. Gianelli will see you on the terrace, Captain McAvoy."

Grinning like a Cheshire Cat, Deputy Sergeant Pete Myrick backed his vehicle away from the gate, again taking up a position about twenty-five yards away. The guard who had been inside the security booth reentered the building and activated the gate mechanism. McAvoy and Larry climbed back into the Jeep.

As Larry slowly drove through the now-open gate, the first guard gave a slight smile and nod to McAvoy. It was clearly a token of admiration from one professional to another. It said, "You're good. You are *really* good."

The blacktopped driveway from the gate to the chateau wound its way circuitously through the woods. On two occasions along the route the policemen encountered guards with dogs, but as the Jeep approached them, the men waved politely. McAvoy noticed, however, that as soon as they had passed, each one raised a walkie-talkie to his mouth.

On the other side of the woods, the driveway continued on up to Garibaldi House, straddled by a nine-hole executive golf course. The course was deserted, with the exception of another security guard in an electric golf cart, who met them nearly halfway to the chateau. The guard politely suggested that if they were to take the road around the right-hand side of the building by the tennis courts and the pro shop they could drive directly to the rear terrace.

McAvoy thanked him and Larry did as the security man had suggested, not doubting for a minute that the suggestion had really been an instruction.

As the Jeep rounded the corner of the chateau, McAvoy noticed that the tennis courts and bocce pitches were as equally devoid of players as had been the golf course. He smiled to himself, wondering how many faces of mobsters who had supposedly been deported long ago peered out at them from behind curtained leaded-glass windows.

Two men stood at the foot of a stone staircase that ascended in a sweeping curve up to the terrace. A bald, middle-aged man wore a three-piece dark blue pinstripe suit. Another, much younger man had on the prescribed green blazer, white shirt, and red slacks. Larry drove toward the pair and parked the Cherokee at the curb in front of them.

"Ahh, Captain McAvoy." Sal Merlino smiled expansively as he came around the car to open the passenger door for the chief while his partner did the same for Larry. "It's so good to see you again," he said, proffering his hand.

"And you, *Consigliere*," McAvoy replied with equal insincerity, taking the hand in a firm grasp.

"I'm terribly sorry about the little mix-up out there at the front gate," Sal continued. "Some of our guests are quite paranoid about their security. If you had but called ahead, I would have happily added your name to the visitors' list and we could have avoided any...unpleasantness."

"No problem," McAvoy said and, as the foursome moved toward the steps, he made the introductions. "Sal this is Officer Parker. Larry, Salvatore Merlino, Mr. Gianelli's... advisor."

Sal smiled in recognition. "Ahh, Colleen's boy." He shook Larry's hand. "Following in your uncle's footsteps I see."

The hair on the back of Larry's neck prickled as he shook hands with the *mafioso* lawyer. *How does he know about me? And about Mom.*

Sal's remark was not lost on McAvoy, either. It was a carryover from the old Detroit days when he had been trying to bust the Gianellis' hold on just about every unsavory enterprise in the city. The *consigliere's* innocent-sounding comment conveyed a much darker message. "We know who you are. We know who your relatives are. And we know *where* they are." That kind of verbal intimidation never did work on McAvoy—not then and, certainly, not now.

"So, Sal, do you and the old man get out and about much these days?" he asked as they climbed the stone staircase, which Sal Merlino deliberately took at a slower-than-usual pace to accommodate the chief's old injury.

"My duties require me to be away from the chateau quite often, but as for Mr. Gianelli, since his stroke—you heard about that, I imagine?" McAvoy nodded in the affirmative. "Since his stroke, he hasn't ventured forth more than a half dozen times in the three-plus years we've been here."

"One of those times wasn't this morning, by any chance, was it, Sal?"

"Oh my goodness, no," Sal replied with a chuckle.

Just then the four men reached the top of the stairs and McAvoy realized that he could abandon any thoughts he might have had about Vittorio Gianelli himself being the trigger-man in the Harvey DuMont execution.

Of the sixteen white wrought-iron umbrella-tables set around the slate floor of the terrace, only one, next to the stone railing overlooking the bocce pitches, was in use. A frail figure sat there in a wheelchair, dressed in a charcoal cashmere overcoat and a black felt hat. He could hardly have crossed the distance from the table to the French doors leading into the chateau by himself, much less have trekked through the woods on Slide Mountain to the banks of Woodland Creek.

Bruno Seracino, the chateau's maitre d', hurriedly set the three remaining places at the table. The slight bulge beneath his white jacket attested to the fact that his job description included other responsibilities as well.

Vittorio Gianelli raised a hand and weakly waved McAvoy over to his table. "*Buona sera, mio amico! Come sta?*"

Sal and the two police officers approached the table while the green-jacketed security guard took up a position to one side of the French doors.

"I'm fine, Don Vittorio. Just fine," McAvoy replied, trying his best not to let the shock register on his face at seeing the former gangland boss in this debilitated state. "I'm sorry to interrupt your dinner, but there's a matter I'm looking into and I need to ask you some questions."

Vittorio shook his finger at McAvoy in mock reproach. "You say 'matter' but what you are really talking about is a crime, heh?"

McAvoy smiled and gave a slight inclination of his head.

Vittorio laughed heartily. "It is just like the old days, heh, Sal? Whenever a crime is committed, Captain McAvoy comes to question poor Vittorio Gianelli. Sit, sit, all three of you. You will have some *vino*, some *osso buco,* and we will talk. I know it is probably early for your dinner, but these days I eat early, go to bed early, and pray to the Virgin that I die peacefully in my sleep."

As the three men sat, Sal and McAvoy flanking and Larry across from the *capo supremo*, Bruno appeared with three more plates of braised veal shanks on beds of saffron rice.

Sal Merlino reached for the carafe of Umbrian Torgiano, topped off Vittorio's glass, and poured wine for the two policemen and himself as he introduced Larry. "*Padrone*, this young officer with Captain McAvoy—or I should say *Chief* McAvoy, now—is his sister Colleen's boy, Larry Parker."

Vittorio's tired eyes brightened as he sized Larry up. "*Il nipote.*" He nodded his head approvingly then switched his gaze to McAvoy. "It is nice to have somebody to follow in the family business, heh, Captain?" He raised his glass with a shaky hand. "*La Famiglia!*"

The other three men joined him in the toast.

"And speaking of family," Vittorio continued, "if this old brain does not fail me, is not Colleen the Mayor of your Peekamoosey village?"

"Peekamoose Heights," McAvoy corrected him.

Again, the hair stood up on the back of Larry's neck at hearing his mother's name on the old mobster's lips.

"A family-run operation, heh? I can, how do you say... relate to that." Vittorio laughed again.

After another ten minutes or so of small talk, during which he savored the veal shanks and rice, McAvoy decided that the time for business had come. He described the murder of Harvey DuMont, carefully watching the faces of both Sal and Vittorio. The eyes of the two *mafiosi* quickly met but their voices remained silent. Even the mention of the Isabela Pendant barely got a rise out of either of them.

"I remember that name," Vittorio began in a forcedly detached manner, but the tears that welled up in his eyes gave away his true feelings. "On the very day my Giovanni and Julio were killed, I remember reading that a piece of jewelry by that name was stolen from an exhibit of some sort. It is my understanding that the police never caught the thieves." He hesitated and a quietness came over him as he continued. "Just like they never caught the *bastardi* who murdered my sons."

McAvoy passed on the opportunity to suggest the connection between the Gianelli boys and the robbery. No point would be served by rubbing salt into the man's wounds. He also passed on offering any condolences. No point would be served by hypocrisy, either. But, before he could move the conversation in the direction he intended it to go, Vittorio obliged him by doing so himself.

"*Scusi*, Captain McAvoy?" he asked, with a mixture of feigned shock and innocence. "You think that *I* had something to do with this murder over in Peekamoosey?" Then shaking his head, as if dumfounded at the notion, he looked across the table at Larry and pointed his finger at the young officer. "You hear how cynical a lifetime of police work makes you? Your uncle, here, he thinks that a sick old man in a wheelchair can do murder?"

McAvoy couldn't help but smile, but instead of replying, he fixed his gaze on Sal Merlino. "May I ask where *you* were at about noon today?"

"Why here, of course," Sal answered and quickly followed up with, "If it becomes necessary, I can produce a variety of witnesses."

"Ones who wouldn't be afraid to be seen by a government agency?" McAvoy joked and waved off Sal's protest as he continued. "Do you mind telling me where your son Tony is, Don Vittorio?"

Again there was the briefest of glances between the two mobsters before Sal answered. "Antonio is away from the chateau at the moment. He left about an hour and a half ago."

"You remember how it is to be young," Vittorio added with a shrug of his shoulders. "*Amore.*"

"Only vaguely," McAvoy replied, then handed Sal a business card. "I would appreciate it if you would have him call me when he gets back. I have a few questions." He pushed his chair back and stood. Larry did likewise. "Thanks for the dinner, Don Vittorio. My compliments to the chef."

Vittorio put a restraining hand on McAvoy's arm. "You cannot leave yet, *mio amico.*" He gestured toward the maitre d', who had just come through the French doors, carrying a tray with four long-stemmed desert glasses. "*Zabaione!*" Then he nodded his head in Larry's direction. "You would make the boy miss dessert?"

McAvoy looked at Larry as he retook his seat. "The man who controlled loansharking, bookmaking, prostitution, protection, and drugs in Greater Detroit is worried that you won't get your dessert."

Larry Parker remained standing and the hair on the back of his neck tingled once more. He avoided Vittorio's obsidian eyes and looked straight at McAvoy. "I'm not all that sure I want dessert from a man who would sell drugs to school kids." The blood drained from Vittorio Gianelli's already-sallow face. He crashed his hand down on the table top, causing wine to slosh out of all four glasses. Bruno froze in his tracks, halfway between the French doors and the table, and Sal Merlino sat speechless with his mouth wide open. McAvoy let just a trace of a smile cross his lips.

"*Non per i bambini!*" Vittorio screamed hoarsely. "Never did the Gianellis sell drugs to the children! Never! The niggers sell to *bambini*, not the Gianellis!" He began to cough uncontrollably and wheeze.

Sal Merlino jumped up and removed a vial of pills from Vittorio's coat pocket. Forcing one of the capsules between the old man's lips, he picked up the wine glass and got him to drink. The wheezing subsided somewhat as Sal held Vittorio Gianelli in his arms.

McAvoy rose from his chair. "I think we'll skip dessert, Don Vittorio." As he ushered a bewildered Larry toward the stone staircase, he shouted over his shoulder. "We'll show ourselves out, Sal, but don't forget to have Tony call me. *Capisce?*"

Sal Merlino nodded and waved them away as the guard in the green blazer moved to the head of the staircase and escorted them down to their vehicle. Once inside the Jeep, all McAvoy said was, "Drive! And don't dilly-dally!"

"I'm sorry, Uncle Ed," a still-shook-up Larry said, forgetting about McAvoy's pet peeve. "I didn't know it was the blacks who sold drugs. I always thought it was the mafia."

McAvoy chuckled as he turned in his seat for a last look at the chateau before they entered the woods. "Don't worry about it. You did just fine. It's a false point of honor with people like Vittorio Gianelli. You see, he and his kind don't sell drugs to kids directly. They merely sell drugs to the people who in turn sell them to kids." He patted Larry on the shoulder. "It's nice to know that you have some principles. You did good, *Officer* Parker." The accent on the "Officer" let Larry know that his use of the familiar "Uncle" had not gotten by the chief unnoticed.

As the Jeep cleared the main security gate, Larry heaved a sigh of relief and both he and McAvoy waved as they passed the Greene County sheriff's car, still parked on the shoulder. The deputies returned the acknowledgment, cranked the Crown Vic into a U-turn and followed them out the gravel driveway and back down Balsam Mountain.

McAvoy plucked the mike from its holder on the police radio and depressed the TALK button. "PMH-One to base. PMH-One to base. Over."

Lucille's croak came back over the speaker. "This is PMH-Base. Go ahead. Over."

"We're on our way home, Lucille. Anything important?"

"Matt Christiansen called about a half hour ago. Apparently the sedatives have worn off and Mrs. DuMont is awake. He says that she's managing to keep herself together and he thought she might be up to answering some questions if you wanted to stop by."

The chief looked over at Larry but didn't have to say anything. Larry nodded at him and stepped a little more firmly on the accelerator pedal.

"Thanks, Lucille. PMH-One clear," McAvoy said and hung the mike back on the holder.

❧ ❧ ❧

The dinner trade had settled their tabs hours ago and now only the usual Friday night bar crowd remained at The Plough & Whistle, except for McAvoy and one middle-aged couple at a cozy, dimly lit table for two in the corner. Ben Krider and Miriam Talbot lingered over coffee, dessert, brandy, and each other.

From his customary table by the dart board, the chief had an excellent vantage point from which to observe both the big screen TV and the intimate table for two. He switched his gaze back and forth from two sheaves of papers on the blue-and-white checkered tablecloth in front of him, neatly stacked in manila folders; to the Yankees-A's game, which had just gotten underway out on the west coast—and over to the middle-aged mating ritual.

How the hell is he going to sneak her in and out past the nurses? McAvoy wondered, sipping from his mug of Hudson Lager, one of the three specialty brews that Porky kept on tap year-round from the Woodstock Brewery in Kingston. The chief let himself fantasize for just a moment and conjured up a mental picture of Ben Krider tiptoeing along the darkened hallways of The Poplars, pushing a hospital gurney containing the sheet-covered form of the very attractive Dr. Miriam Talbot. Snickering out loud as his imagination exaggerated the contours of the sheet, he turned his attention back to the two manila folders on the table top.

Lieutenant Jerry Gardner had faxed both the Gianelli brothers murder and the Great Lakes Jewelry Association robbery files to Lucille. Two handwritten notes from the lieutenant had accompanied the material. The shorter note contained just two sentences. One read, "See page four of the Jewelry file—Cleveland businessman." The other said, "See page seven of the Gianelli file—Rosa Grimaldi."

The longer, three-page note had been Jerry's analysis of what he thought had really happened but couldn't prove. McAvoy deliberately avoided reading it until he had poured through the other documents himself. He didn't want his own opinion colored by the lieutenant's summary.

The Cleveland businessman note referred to a machine tool salesman who had stayed at the St. Aubin the week of the theft. News of Giovanni and Julio Gianelli's murders had been picked up by one of the wire services and reported nationwide, accompanied by with pictures of the unfortunate brothers. The salesman had contacted the Cleveland Police to say that he thought one of the victims, Giovanni, whose photo he had seen in the *Plain Dealer,* had ridden down to the lobby in the same elevator with him and two other men on the morning he checked out of the hotel. He hadn't recognized the picture of the second murdered man. After a series of faxes from Detroit to Cleveland, the businessman picked out the photo of Antonio Gianelli as one of the other two men.

Interesting, McAvoy thought. *Johnny and Julie get whacked and Tony is nearby. Very interesting.*

The Rosa Grimaldi note referenced a report from the Ontario Provincial Police. Rosa's body had washed ashore near Great Western Park on the Canadian side of the Detroit River, downstream from Belle Isle where the Coast Guard had found the drifting *Sophia IV.* Miss Grimaldi had had her throat slit.

Three other related documents were the autopsy reports for both Rosa Grimaldi and Julio Gianelli and the detective's notes compiled from questioning Rosa's friends and co-workers. The medical examiner reported that the throats of both Julio and Rosa were slashed in nearly an identical manner and both wounds could have been made with the same weapon.

The detective's notes revealed that Rosa had been Antonio Gianelli's longtime, on-again-off-again girlfriend, although close friends thought that she had recently started seeing someone else. No one knew anything about Rosa's new love interest except that the girl had talked about calling it quits with Antonio, this time for good.

Well, she certainly did that. McAvoy thought.

Jerry Gardner's analysis matched the chief's own conclusions. In short: the Gianellis had planned the jewel heist and a not-too-awfully-bright Antonio had bragged about it to his lover Rosa. Rosa told her new boyfriend and the boyfriend not only double-crossed the Gianellis but killed Rosa to cover his tracks when the girl arrived at the yacht with the pickup boat.

McAvoy couldn't imagine how Harvey DuMont fit into this web of theft, murder, and love. *If there is no connection, that would mean that the Gianellis had Harvey whacked simply because the Isabela Pendant had been found on his property.*

The chief didn't believe in coincidence, but found it even more difficult to accept that the mob could be that sloppy, unless raw emotion had overruled sound judgment.

Deputy Sergeant Martin Bassett had called earlier in the evening with a piece of not-so-good news. The sheriff's patrol that had been sent to check out the Woodland Valley Campsite had come up with nothing. Neither the campers nor Donald Janeczek, the Park Ranger on duty, had noticed anything or anyone suspicious.

Some three hours later, Tony Gianelli had called from Garibaldi House, with Sal Merlino on an extension to assure that the boy did not say anything stupid. Tony provided McAvoy with the names of the other three members of his golfing foursome who would vouch for his whereabouts at the exact time of the DuMont murder.

Tony switched tone as the conversation came to an end. "Your nephew upset my father—"

"But Mr. Gianelli is doing just fine now, Chief McAvoy," Sal interrupted, before Tony could shoot off his mouth. "He wishes you well on your hunt for this killer. If there is any other information we can provide, please, don't hesitate to give us a call."

After the telephone connection had been broken, McAvoy could imagine Sal Merlino chastising Tony Gianelli with colorful words such as "*Stupido*" and "*Ignorante*". The younger Gianelli had no finesse, no class. He'd always be just a wiseguy. Threats were never to be made openly. They were always veiled in civility, like Sal's earlier remark about Colleen's boy in reference to Larry Parker. The chief had no doubt that someday Tony would wind up on a morgue slab as had his brothers.

❧ ❧ ❧

McAvoy's visit to the DuMont home on the way back from Garibaldi House had been equally fruitless. Cynthia held up quite well during the questioning and she looked fantastic, dressed in a revealing black lace peignoir and sitting teary-eyed on the love seat with her legs tucked up under her.

With about ten inches of shapely, tanned thigh peeking out through the slit in the widow DuMont's robe, McAvoy found it difficult to concentrate on the investigation. As it turned out, though, he didn't really need that much concentration. Cynthia couldn't provide him with anything remotely resembling a motive for her husband's murder. Harvey didn't owe anyone money. No one owed Harvey money. He hadn't made any enemies in the two years they had lived in the Catskills nor had he any lifelong enemies back home in Detroit.

Matt Christiansen had seen to the funeral arrangements. Harvey's body had already been transported from The Poplars to the Wagner Brothers Mortuary in Boiceville and Lenny had driven over and dropped off the clothes Cynthia had picked out. The body would lie in state on Sunday evening from seven until nine o'clock. A requiem mass would be offered for the repose of Harvey's soul on Monday morning at Boiceville's Our Lady of Sorrows Catholic Church, with interment at the Mt. Hope Cemetery immediately following the service.

Although Matt had volunteered that he and Lenny would stay the night, Cynthia insisted that she had recovered enough to be by herself and shooed the two men home when the chief took his leave.

McAvoy finished his beer, straightened the piles of papers in front of him, removed the half-frame reading glasses, and rubbed his eyes. A fresh mug of Hudson Lager appeared on the table and a pair of soft but strong fingers massaged his shoulders and the back of his neck.

The lingering image of Cynthia DuMont, waving good-bye, framed in the doorway to her home on Big Indian Mountain and back-lighted so that the flimsy black lace peignoir became almost transparent, suddenly disappeared. McAvoy reached up and took one of Stevie Henderson's hands and nibbled at her knuckles.

Stevie kissed the top of his slightly balding head. "Things are starting to slow down around here," she whispered. "Roz can handle the place by himself, if you'd like to come upstairs for a little while."

McAvoy feigned a protest. "But I've got this full mug of beer."

"See what you can do about emptying it in the time it takes me to make one more pass around the room," she said as she gave him a bump with her hip. She set his empty mug on her tray, then bounced away to make the rounds of the other tables.

McAvoy put the reading glasses back in their blue corduroy case, returned the case to its customary place in his shirt pocket, and picked up the beer mug. As he sipped the ice-cold lager, Porky Jarvis approached the table.

"I say, Ed," he began, in his assimilated British speech pattern. "Any idea who might have offed that poor bloke this morning?"

"A pretty good idea, Porky."

"Ahh, then, just a matter of time, what?"

"Afraid it's not that simple. There's a little matter of evidence." In answer to Porky's quizzical look, McAvoy elaborated just a bit. "We have none."

"You mean you haven't found it yet," Porky said. It was now McAvoy's turn to look baffled so Porky explained his remark. "I'd rather imagine your investigation is somewhat akin to me developing a new recipe. All the ingredients are there in front of me. It's just a matter of finding the right ones for the dish I'm preparing."

He then changed the subject to the one that McAvoy suspected had brought him over to the table in the first place. "Have you talked to the lad this afternoon?" Porky asked, gesturing with his thumb toward the ceiling and the apartment beyond.

"Not since lunch. Why?"

"He took the news of Mr. DuMont's death rather badly. You might want to have a word with him before Stevie finishes up here. The lad's very confused. A man-to-man without his mum around may be what the doctor ordered, hmm? Feel free to take the suds with you." Porky winked and retreated behind the bar to resume his duties.

McAvoy picked up the mug and made his way toward the door marked PRIVATE and to the stairway that led to the second floor living quarters, stopping just long enough to exchange pleasantries with Ben Krider and Miriam Talbot.

Chapter 6

As the Monday graveside service for Harvey DuMont came to an end, Fr. Jerry Tomlinson, Pastor of Our Lady of Sorrows Catholic Church, reverently closed his prayer book, handed it to one of the acolytes, and took the aspergillum from the boy. He sprinkled holy water onto the lid of the bronze-tone casket in the sign of the cross and intoned the final words. "May his soul and the souls of all the faithful departed, through the mercy of God, rest in peace."

The small crowd standing at the grave site, neighbors of the DuMonts mostly, mixed in with a few parishioners who attended all the funerals for lack of anything else to do, responded with a devout "Amen."

Four of the attendants from Wagner Brothers Mortuary lowered the casket into the ground, then the mourners, individually or in pairs and trios, stepped forward. Spending a moment or two, each looked into the grave and offered either a silent prayer or farewell, depending upon their religious persuasions.

Cynthia DuMont, flanked by Matt Christiansen and Lenny Damien, went first. Even in widow's weeds Cynthia looked ravishing. The black crepe dress, hemmed slightly above the knee, had an inset of sheer silk chiffon above the yoke that made a modest, if not very effective, attempt at concealing her ample cleavage. Silk chiffon also formed the sleeves of the dress. A black lace mantilla covered her long chestnut-brown hair, which had been done up into a French braid for the occasion.

Cynthia stooped down, picked up a handful of freshly dug earth, and scattered it over the casket. After blowing a final kiss to her late husband, Matt and Lenny led her away to the small tent-like gazebo that Wagner Brothers had erected near the cemetery entrance. Each person leaving the grave site stopped at the gazebo and offered Cynthia renewed condolences.

Danny Henderson had attended the service with McAvoy. He didn't have to be coerced. He had asked to come. After three-and-a-half months of fishing with Harvey, Danny would miss the old curmudgeon. For all his gruffness, Harvey was okay in Danny's book. He had shared his piece of the creek with the boy.

As an acolyte at St. Mary's-in-the-Hills, Danny had participated in many funerals and noticed that after the service, the majority of mourners would pluck flowers from the various sprays and toss them down onto the casket. The boy stood there, waiting his turn to approach the grave site, fingering an item in the jacket pocket of his confirmation suit.

When he and McAvoy finally stepped up to the open grave, Danny removed a McSuperfly from the pocket, smiled, and tossed it onto the coffin lid among the flowers. *Maybe this'll help. And remember, there's no creel limit up there.* Then the boy looked over at McAvoy and gave a slight nod. He was ready to go.

The twosome made their way over to Cynthia DuMont and expressed their sympathies. Danny's blue eyes moistened as Cynthia kissed him on the cheek and thanked him and McAvoy for coming. He turned from the woman and fought back the tears as he and the chief walked toward the blue-and-white Jeep Cherokee.

The weekend had brought no new developments in the investigation. Lieutenant Jerome Gardner had telephoned with the preliminary results of the Detroit Police Department's inquiries into Harvey's past. So far as they could tell, during his years in Detroit he had had no arrests or citations other than the occasional traffic violation.

Harvey's dry-cleaning business, on the whole, had also come up clean. Jerry had been proud of his pun. There were only a few complaints on record with the Better Business Bureau regarding items damaged during the cleaning process— quite low, they reported, for a dry-cleaning establishment. Apparently the DuMonts had been extremely quality-oriented and had promptly settled most of the few damage claims they received directly with their customers.

No visible connection to organized crime had been found but Jerry had stated that the police would keep that avenue of their investigation open. As a former insider, McAvoy knew that keeping the avenue of investigation open was a euphemism for "We won't close the case but we won't be devoting any manpower to it, either."

Late Saturday afternoon, the chief had driven into Kingston for a meeting at the Ulster County Sheriff's office. Deputy Sergeants Martin Bassett and Stanley Jurocik, from the Forensics Department, had attended as well.

After a rehash of the facts, the non-facts, and guesses surrounding the Isabela Pendant and Harvey DuMont's murder, the sheriff had decided to lump both investigations into one. The consensus of opinion held that the finding of the jewel was tied to the murder. Since the murder had occurred within the Peekamoose Heights police jurisdiction, the sheriff had asked McAvoy to head up the total investigation, with the sheriff's office providing whatever support he required.

Had the Peekamoose Heights Police Chief been anyone other than Ed McAvoy, the sheriff probably would have assigned one of his own investigators to the case. With McAvoy's background, though, plus the fact that the sheriff had the county jail to run, forty-one miles of Hudson River waterways to patrol, and all of rural Ulster County to police, he welcomed one less case with which to occupy his time, budget, and manpower.

McAvoy had attempted to help Danny Henderson through his grief over Harvey's passing. The boy was stunned over the sudden and tragic death, and although he had tried, he couldn't make any sense out of someone deliberately hunting down and killing a harmless old man.

McAvoy had reassured him that those feelings were normal and okay to have. "If something like this ever *does* make sense," he had told the boy, "then you'd better start questioning your outlook on life." Murder had never made sense to McAvoy—well, almost never.

Fortunately Danny didn't have too much free time to think about Harvey's death. He couldn't have gone fishing that particular Saturday even if he had wanted to. The better part of the day had been spent helping his mom and uncle prepare the food for Sunday's Patron's Day Picnic at St. Mary's. Although Porky made the desserts on Saturday, all the other main and side dishes would be cooked on-site during the picnic itself. The portly pubkeeper adamantly refused to acknowledge the invention of the microwave oven.

"If we're going to use that contraption," Porky had been quoted as saying two years ago, "we might as well serve them TV dinners, what?"

Consequently all the preliminary food preparation had to take place at The Plough & Whistle the day before so that on Sunday, the dishes could go directly from the refrigerator to the parish hall stove and ovens.

The picnic itself had been a huge success as usual—much to Kate Winthrop's delight.

Sam and Emily Douglas had driven over to The Poplars on Sunday morning, left their Dodge Caravan in the parking lot, and had taken Kate to St. Mary's ten-thirty service in her Lincoln Town Car.

At the picnic, the elderly woman held court in a lawn chair under a large old oak tree, holding her scrimshawed-handled cane like a scepter. A combination surrogate Godmother and unofficial goodwill ambassador, she managed to catch up on all the news of the parish as everyone stopped by to pay their respects.

Luckily, Danny was so involved with the food preparation that he didn't have time to think about Harvey on Sunday morning either and, in the afternoon, the softball game occupied his thoughts. He managed to go two for four, with a single and a double, driving in three runs. At his second base position, he caught Fr. Desmond's blistering line drive for the final out as his team won by a score of seventeen to fourteen.

With each hit or catch he made, Danny glanced over to where Brigid O'Seamus sat on the grass with some other girls from the Onteora Junior and Senior High School. Although he tried to play it cool, it secretly delighted him that she clapped and cheered for him.

Brigid was there with her grandfather, Patrick Blackstone, and her Auntie Fee, Patrick's daughter, with whom the young girl lived. Patrick, a retired magician, owned a magician's supply house called Gandalf's Cave, and Fee, an herbalist, was a librarian at the Olive Free Library. Both were avid members of The Society for Creative Anachronism and had arrived at the picnic in full medieval costumes.

Patrick, dressed as Merlin the Magician and carrying an enormous cypress-wood staff carved with the face of an old man, went about the grounds pulling coins and eggs from people's ears and making smoke appear from the ground.

Fee wore a black satin gown trimmed in silver brocade and a roundlet of flowers about her head. A tall, beautiful, but enigmatic, girl, she moved from area to area playing a variety of hauntingly beautiful airs and walking songs on her Celtic harp.

Since The Plough & Whistle had begun catering the event, not only parishioners but people from miles around would come to the festival, most of them for the food. And because Winthrop money footed the bills, Porky used the event as a showcase for what the pub had to offer.

This year, in addition to the traditional roast leg of lamb with mint sauce, roast rib of beef with Yorkshire pudding, and fish and chips, Porky had bowed to pressure from Danny and included a main course more attractive to the younger attendees. Although outwardly this dish had the appearance of corn dogs, in reality, its batter-dipped pork sausages were an adaptation of an English dish called Toad-in-the-Hole. To further the illusion, Porky served them on individual sticks rather than in the traditional method, in a baking dish covered with batter.

Kate Winthrop beckoned McAvoy over to her from his onlooker's position along the first-base sidelines. Although he had been a decent outfielder in his younger days, the stiffness in his left leg now relegated him to permanent spectator status.

"Are we all to be murdered in our beds, Chief McAvoy?" the elderly woman asked pointedly as he approached her.

McAvoy saw the twinkle in her hazel eyes and realized that the question contained more sarcasm than accusation. He played along with her. "Jeez, I don't know Kate. Do you often sleep out in the woods these days?"

She poked him in his slightly protruding tummy with her cane and motioned him over to a second lawn chair under her oak tree throne canopy. "Smart-ass! In all seriousness, though, Edward," she asked as he sat down, "is this something about which we ought to concern ourselves?"

"I don't think so. This wasn't a random act. It was deliberate. No one else needs to worry."

"How's the boy taking it? I understand he used to fish with Mr. DuMont."

Just then, Danny Henderson cracked a double down the left-field line. McAvoy gestured to the boy as Danny rounded first. "He'll be all right. Kids bounce back quicker than we do."

They were half way out of Mount Hope Cemetery to where the Jeep stood parked with the other cars that had made up the cortege when McAvoy stopped and put his hand on Danny Henderson's shoulder. "Go on ahead," he said. "I'll be along in a minute."

The youngster did as he had been instructed while McAvoy waited until he could catch Matt Christiansen's eye. Matt's main concern seemed to be Cynthia's welfare. He never looked away from her. However, Lenny glanced over and McAvoy signaled to him.

The young man ambled over. "What's up, Chief? Anything we can do?" He had abandoned his usual blue jeans and sport shirt for the occasion and was dressed in a more conservative camel blazer and brown slacks that made him look almost ivy-league.

"I've got Harvey's personal effects in my Jeep," McAvoy said. "I was wondering when your uncle thought it might be a good time to bring them over. In addition to the clothes he was wearing, I've got his wallet, rings, and pocket stuff, as well as his fishing gear."

"Let me check." Lenny walked back and whispered into his uncle's ear.

Matt looked over at McAvoy, raised his finger in a just-a-minute gesture and spoke with Cynthia. The widow said something back to him and then raised her handkerchief to her eyes. Matt nodded, patted her hand, and started hobbling over toward McAvoy. His dress, too, had changed radically from when the chief last saw him. Instead of the *Field & Stream* look, Matt could have stepped off the cover of *GQ*. He almost rivaled Ben Krider, in McAvoy's opinion, for the title of best dressed man in Ulster County.

The chief met the man half way to save him the pain of crossing the entire distance himself.

"Hi, Mac," Matt greeted him, leaning on the cane. "Cyn wonders if you could dispose of the clothing for her. She really doesn't want to see it."

"No problem, Matt, but I had to ask."

"Just give me the personal stuff. I'll take it with me. Also, Cyn would like Danny to have the fishing gear. She knows he'd appreciate it and care for it the way Harv did."

"That's very generous of her," McAvoy said with a smile. "The boy'll like that. I'll have him call in a few days to thank her."

"Call, hell, Mac. Have him come over tomorrow, just like before. He and I'll catch the creel limit and dedicate it to old Harv's memory."

"I'm not sure he'll be up to it."

"It'd be the best thing for him. Hell, it'd be the best thing for both of us. Talk to him, Mac." Matt winked, gave the chief a slap on the leg with the cane, then hobbled back to the side of the widow DuMont.

McAvoy removed a Ziploc bag from the back seat of the Jeep, tousled Danny's straw-colored hair and said, "Be back in a minute." He then took the bag of personal effects over to Dwight Deavers, the driver of the Wagner Brothers limousine. "Give this to Matt Christiansen, would you, Dwight?"

Dwight nodded and set the bag on the front passenger's seat. "Sure thing, Chief. And tell Lucille I'll be back to work this afternoon."

Dwight worked for the Village of Peekamoose Heights, taking care of the municipal vehicles and doing handyman chores. He never took a vacation to go anywhere for the fun of it but saved up his time and took it a day or a half-day at a time to work for other people and make more money. Dwight was at the top of Jerry Wagner's list of on-call pallbearers and drivers.

When McAvoy returned to the Jeep, he found Danny sitting there in silence. The boy had removed his tie and absently knotted it around his hand as he glumly stared out the window in the opposite direction from the cemetery.

The chief started the engine and slowly drove in the direction of Peekamoose Heights. Neither he nor the boy spoke during the trip home.

Over lunch at The Plough & Whistle, McAvoy broke the news to Danny that Cynthia DuMont wanted him to have Harvey's Big Horn Special with the Battenkill reel as well as the rest of her husband's fishing gear. With mixed emotions, the boy gathered up the bequest from the back of McAvoy's Jeep and took the fly rod directly out to the garden for a few practice casts at the crushed stone birdbath. As he stored Harvey's gear in the shed out back with his own fishing paraphernalia, he silently thanked the old man, promising to take special care of everything.

When the chief saw him about a quarter of an hour later, Danny had changed out of his suit into jeans and a T-shirt and set about his chores at the pub. The boy's despondent look of the morning had been replaced by his usual sunny smile.

McAvoy's assessment of the resiliency of kids, as expressed to Kate Winthrop the day before, had proven to be accurate. Danny *had* bounced back quickly. The chief was happy for the boy. After signing his tab, he collected his Smith & Wesson from behind the bar, clipped the holster to his belt, and walked across the street to the police station.

McAvoy had had to check his revolver at the bar when he arrived because Porky Jarvis had a hard and fast rule at the pub. No one wore a gun in his establishment unless that person was there on official police business. There were no exceptions. The rule applied to McAvoy and Martin Bassett as well as to everyone else. Years ago in England, Porky had seen an off-duty MP shoot up a pub something awful before being subdued by one of the patrons. That patron had been Master Sergeant Porky Jarvis himself, armed with a heavy pint beer mug.

For most of the afternoon, McAvoy waded through the stacks of paperwork that Lucille had placed on his desk. He reviewed duty rosters, field reports from the eight Peekamoose Heights police officers, copies of traffic citations, and parking tickets—an altogether boring afternoon.

At about four o'clock, a croak from Lucille, at her desk outside McAvoy's office, interrupted the tedium. "Ed! Phone call from Lenny Damien on two. He says it's important."

Although there was an intercom, Lucille never bothered using it, and the chief had long ago given up trying to get her to do so. With a voice like Lucille's, an intercom was superfluous anyway.

McAvoy picked up the telephone receiver and punched the button for the second of five outside lines. "Yeah, Lenny, what's up?"

"You'd better get over here, Chief," Lenny said without any preliminary pleasantries. "After all the neighbors and church people left, Matt fixed Cynthia a couple of drinks... you know, trying to relax her enough so that she wouldn't have to take the sedatives? Well, she got sort of loaded and she's talking…she's talking about diamonds and ranting and raving about always knowing something bad would come from it and…anyway, Matt thinks you'd better come over."

"Be there in fifteen minutes." McAvoy hung up the phone and jumped up from the desk, leaving his office at a half run. "Where's the tape recorder?" he asked Lucille.

She had been talking with Larry Parker as the young officer sat at one of the twin duty desks across from her, getting ready to start his watch. Larry and Jim Culpepper had drawn the afternoon watch for this particular two-week period.

"It was just gathering dust in the cabinet so I lent it to Heather for class."

In the evenings, Officer Heather Larrabee attended the State University of New York in New Paltz, working toward an Associate Degree in Police Science.

"Then you'd better come with me," McAvoy said. "And bring your pad. Larry, you've got the phones."

Lucille picked up her steno pad and followed McAvoy out to the Cherokee. Larry gave the twosome a little two-fingered Cub Scout salute as they left and turned his attention back to the duty roster.

The first order of business at the DuMonts had been for McAvoy to caution Cynthia that she didn't have to say anything to him or answer any of his questions. He also advised her that she could phone for an attorney if she wanted to.

"I've lived with this lie for too long, I just want to be rid of it once and for all," she said with tears streaming down her cheeks. "My Harvey's dead. There's no point to it anymore. I just knew it would end up like this."

Cynthia DuMont sat on the love seat as she had the last time McAvoy had questioned her, with her legs tucked up under her. Only this time, instead of the back lace peignoir, she had on the black dress she had worn to the funeral.

In between sobs, Cynthia described the horror of her last two years in Detroit, constantly being afraid of strangers and nervously looking over her shoulder every time she ventured out in public. Finally she convinced Harvey to sell their business and move somewhere that offered a greater measure of safety and security. A secluded home in the Catskills on the slope of Big Indian Mountain seemed to fit the bill, or so they thought.

Cynthia professed not to have known about Harvey's part in the much-publicized jewel robbery and murders until months afterwards. Even then she maintained that she only found out about it accidentally.

An avid gardener as well as a fisherman, Harvey split his leisure time between puttering in the yard and wading the many streams in southeastern Michigan. Cynthia had been after him to repot a small palm tree that they had brought back from a Florida vacation, and after several weeks, when he still had not gotten around to it, she decided to do it herself. As she troweled a combination of compost and dirt from a bin in the potting shed, the small shovel uncovered a brown leather pouch.

When confronted by his wife, Harvey had confessed to the robbery. As for feeling guilty about how the stones were acquired, Harvey rationalized that since he had taken the jewels from mobsters, no harm had been done to "decent citizens." Harvey had never confided in her how he knew about the Gianellis' plan. He claimed that the less she knew, the better off she would be. He had hid the pendant in the potting shed at their east-side Detroit home for the same reason that he had buried it in the woods on Big Indian Mountain. It was the only piece from the heist that could be positively identified. The loose stones, Harvey told her, couldn't be traced.

Cynthia claimed not to know how many of the diamonds remained or where they were kept. She agreed, though, that the next morning she would voluntarily accompany McAvoy to the Phoenicia branch of Mountain Valley Bank and Trust and open her safe-deposit box. Since she had not yet notified the bank of her husband's death, the lock-box would not be sealed.

A series of procedural calls from McAvoy to the Ulster County Sheriff and the District Attorney's office resulted in an arrest warrant being issued for Cynthia DuMont for aiding-and-abetting in the Gianelli brothers' and the Rosa Grimaldi murders.

Both the sheriff and the assistant district attorney agreed with McAvoy that Cynthia was no danger to society, wouldn't run out, and, at her trial, would probably get probation anyhow. Consequently, they allowed as how she might just as well spend the night in her own home. In the morning, Martin Bassett would meet McAvoy and Mrs. DuMont at the bank and take her and any evidence into custody at that time. The ADA would schedule an arraignment for the afternoon and would not insist on bail. Cynthia DuMont would be released on her own recognizance and be back home in time for dinner. It would take the DA a few days to work out the extradition details with his counterpart in Wayne County, Michigan, and until then, Cynthia could remain at her own home.

Assistant District Attorney Frank Ledbetter finished the conversation with a plea. "Mac, make sure she understands that she's not to leave Ulster County before checking with our office?"

McAvoy explained all of this to Cynthia and she accepted the arrangements without any protest, seeming relieved just to finally have the matter out in the open. However, Harvey had apparently neglected to tell her about killing Rosa Grimaldi. She seemed truly shocked, in fact, horrified, when told about that aspect of the case.

McAvoy tactfully asked her about a possible relationship between her husband and Rosa and hinted that maybe that's how Harvey had found out about the Gianellis' plan.

Cynthia laughed off his suggestion. "I can't believe it, Ed. Not my Harvey. He would never cheat on me. I don't mean to brag on myself, but do you really think Harv needed anything else?" She uncurled her long legs from under her and stretched out, panther-like, on the love seat to emphasize her point. "There must be some other explanation for the Grimaldi girl's death."

However, the woman was at a loss to come up with one and McAvoy could tell that her mind was uneasy. Doubt was beginning to seep in.

Understandably, he thought. *She's just discovered that someone she loved lied to her. Not only that, but while she could justify in her own mind the killing of mobsters, she's having a difficult time applying that same rationale to Rosa Grimaldi.*

Since Cynthia obviously had no more useful information regarding the case, McAvoy and Lucille took their leave. On the way to the Jeep, Matt Christiansen told McAvoy that he would contact the Lawyer Referral Service of the New York State Bar Association and have an attorney lined-up and waiting for them at Cynthia's arraignment.

During the drive back to the office, Lucille, always pragmatic about her plus and minus features, cackled as she hiked her skirt up to mid-thigh. Stretching out her own exquisite legs and pushing forward her substantial bosom, she duplicated, as best she could in the passenger seat of the Jeep Cherokee, Cynthia DuMont's panther-pose. "You know, Ed," she croaked, "if that woman and I had shopping bags over our heads, you'd be hard-pressed to tell us apart."

McAvoy looked over at his sister-in-law and, while he gave her a wink and nod of approval, he couldn't resist a good-natured jab. "As long as you kept your mouth shut under that bag."

Lucille swatted him in the shoulder as she returned her body to a more ladylike position and rasped, "Asshole!"

After a moment or two of silence, they glanced at each other and both burst into laughter.

Chapter 7

The Tuesday afternoon arraignment had gone quickly, and with a minimum of distress, as McAvoy had predicted to Cynthia that it would. Deputy Sergeant Martin Bassett had testified that Mrs. DuMont was cooperating fully and voluntarily with the authorities. Consequently, Judge Keith Elliott had released Cynthia on her own recognizance and Matt had driven her home.

The inventory of the DuMont's bank safe-deposit box that morning had revealed a cache of sixteen diamonds, worth approximately one-hundred-thousand dollars. The diamonds were transported to Dunlavy's Jewelers to be kept as evidence along with the Isabela Pendant.

An investigator from the DA's office had followed Matt and Cynthia home from the courthouse, with Cynthia's knowledge and agreement. He wanted to see if anything in Harvey's personal papers or files would point the way toward other safe-deposit boxes containing any more of the stolen diamonds. The DuMont lifestyle, although quite comfortable, did not explain why only sixteen of the more than five-hundred diamonds taken in the heist remained. The search had proved futile and the investigator had returned to his office to contemplate his next move.

As he left Cynthia's arraignment, Bill Brinkmire churned with mixed emotions about the entire Harvey DuMont story. While happy to have so big a tale set in his own backyard on which to report, he lamented the fact that the arraignment had been held early in the afternoon. The weekly issue of his *Ashokan Register* would not be published until the following afternoon, but, the *Kingston Chronicle*, which published daily, would now be able to run the story in its Tuesday evening edition.

Bill decided to grab a copy of the *Chronicle* and see how thorough a job it did, then determine what tack he would take for his own article. He secretly hoped that, in the *Chronicle's* haste to meet the press deadline, it would leave some important angle unreported. Such were the trials and tribulations of a small-town weekly newspaper man.

Agnes Berman, the police-beat reporter for the *Kingston Chronicle,* had been quite thorough in portraying the facts of the case, considering the short time in which she had to compile her account. On the previous Friday, the *Chronicle* had only included the bare facts surrounding Harvey DuMont's murder. Now that the story had grown larger, with Cynthia's revelation of the diamond robbery and Detroit murders, Tuesday's paper not only included the specifics of the Detroit cases but recycled the facts of the Harvey DuMont murder in much greater detail. It noted both the previously-unreported particulars of Fr. John Desmond finding the body and the assistance of antique dealer Samuel Douglas in extricating Harvey from the creek.

As he sat in his office reading the competition, Bill Brinkmire soon realized that there were no interviews with any of the principals involved in the case. He chuckled as he reached across his desk for the telephone. For the price of

Plough & Whistle dinners for himself and for Ed McAvoy, which he would write off as a business expense, he just might be able to go the *Chronicle* one better in Wednesday's *Register*.

⚜ ⚜ ⚜

In an adjoining county, another hand also reached for a telephone. This hand was wizened with age and it reached across a white wrought-iron umbrella-table and punched a single button on the telephone which the waiter had just brought and plugged into a wall outlet.

"I want Salvatore and Antonio! *Immediato!*"

Vittorio Gianelli set the receiver back in its cradle and returned his attention to the article in the *Kingston Chronicle*. He merely picked at the bowl of *zuppa di pesce* in front of him. Although the look in his obsidian eyes revealed a deep hunger, he no longer had an appetite for food.

⚜ ⚜ ⚜

Dr. Benjamin Krider signed the credit card receipt, thanked Ralph Donovan, and eased his Toyota 4-Runner out of Donovan's Shell Station onto Van Winkle Street. When the traffic light changed, he made a left-hand turn onto Irving Boulevard for the half-block trip to The Plough & Whistle. The anticipated flavor of roast squab with rosemary jelly already teased his palate. As he turned the corner, he noticed that a black Mercedes touring sedan had taken his place in front of the full-service gas pumps. The darkly tinted windows prevented him from seeing whom he should be envious of but he did note that the car bore Greene County license plates.

Probably lost and looking for directions, Ben thought, then sighed and continued down the boulevard.

He really would have enjoyed owning a car like the sedan and could well-afford it since he received a six-figure salary from The Poplars *and* free room and meals, those meals that he didn't choose to take at The Plough & Whistle. But Ben Krider was a frugal man—frugal with a capital *C*, as in cheap.

His only expensive habits seemed to be clothes and food. The doctor always looked like he had just stepped out of a Brooks Brothers ad, and he dined at The Plough & Whistle at least four times weekly.

As he made the U-turn across the boulevard in front the police station and into the last street-side non-handicapped parking space by the pub, the rumbling of his stomach made Ben push the Mercedes into the recesses of his mind.

"Fill 'er up?" Ralph Donovan asked cheerfully as the electric window slid down on the driver's side of the black sedan.

"No thank you," Sal Merlino replied. "We just need some directions, if you don't mind."

"No problem. Where you headed?"

"We're trying to locate an antique dealer in this area by the name of Samuel Douglas. Do you know where his shop is located by any chance?"

Ralph pointed south on Van Winkle Street. "Sure. Corner of Van Brummel, the next block up, on the left. The shop's called The Then & Now. But you may be too late. I think he closes up at six-thirty."

Sal glanced at the dashboard. The digital clock read six-fifty-three. "We'll go by there just in case. Thank you very much." He pushed the button that raised the window, then made a left turn out of the Shell station onto Van Winkle.

"What do we do if he ain't there?" Tony Gianelli asked.

"Look at the business hours he has posted and come back when he *is* there."

"Papa wanted some answers tonight." Tony's tone contained a hint of a threat.

"Your father wants a discreet inquiry made. *You* are along for the ride. Just listen and learn. And, if you feel the urge to say anything at all...don't. *And*, if you can't control that urge, do not, under any circumstances, come on like a hoodlum."

Sal had been against having Tony accompany him on this errand. Vittorio, however, had insisted.

"I know the boy is stubborn and has to learn...how do you say...subtlety, *mio amico*. But who better to teach him then you, heh?" Patting Sal on the cheek, ha had continued. "But just because he is my son does not mean you have to take any *crapola* from him." Then Vittorio had winked. "Teach him well, Salvatore. Teach him well. I cannot bear the thought of losing another one."

Sal had smiled softly and nodded. He was dedicated to the old man.

Tony sat there sulkily without replying. His day would come and then he'd show the too-cautious Sal Merlino and the too-old Vittorio Gianelli. *What the hell good is having power if you don't use it? One of these days I'll show them all.*

Sal parked the Mercedes across the street from The Then & Now. The lights inside the restored Victorian home showed a man and a woman, moving furniture around.

"Must be the cleaning crew," Tony said as the two men crossed the street.

Sal tried the doorknob. The door opened, hitting a little bell hanging down below the top of the door frame.

Sam Douglas, struggling, with pitifully little help from Emily, to lift a Regency green marble-topped rosewood table, turned toward the sound.

"We're closed," he said automatically, but then noticing the quality of the suit worn by the impeccably-dressed Sal Merlino, he quickly followed up with, "But feel free to look around if you'd like. We're just doing a little rearranging."

Emily used the interruption to sit on a nearby comb-back side chair and rest.

In two-months' time the Douglasses would be exhibiting, along with one-hundred and ten other dealers from twenty-two states, at the Fall Antiques Show at The Pier in New York City. In anticipation of the event, they had been on a series of recent buying trips. Their normally tidy and tastefully laid-out shop resembled a Salvation Army warehouse rather than one of the premier antique shops in the East. Sam and Emily were trying to rearrange some of the pieces to best utilize their rapidly shrinking floor-space.

"There're some lovely things here," Sal said as he looked around the well-appointed shop. "But we're not really in the market for anything just now. We were hoping to catch Mr. Douglas before he left for home."

Emily and Sam glanced at each other, suppressing all but the smallest traces of smiles. Had they a dollar for everyone in this ninety-nine percent WASP enclave of Peekamoose Heights who assumed that because they were black they were the janitorial service, they could sell The Then & Now and retire on a quite comfortable monthly allowance.

Sam offered his hand to Sal Merlino. "I'm Sam Douglas," he said and then gestured with his head toward Emily. "And this is my wife Emily."

Although Tony stood with his mouth agape, Sal exhibited only the briefest of hesitations before taking the outstretched hand. "How do you do, Mr. Douglas? I'm Roger Manetti from Empire State Casualty. And this is Jim D'Angelo."

Sal had learned years before that in making up an alias, it had better suit your looks. He and Tony hardly looked like a Patrick O'Shea or an Angus McDuff.

"We've got all the coverage we need, Mr. Manetti," Emily spoke up from her perch on the side chair. "And besides, Andy MacPherson, here in the village, handles our insurance."

"I'm sure you're well-taken care of, Mrs. Douglas," Sal said with a laugh. "Jim and I aren't salesmen. We're claims' adjusters. We need to ask you some questions about the Harvey DuMont shooting, if you don't mind." He turned to Tony. "Did you bring the file in with you, Jim?"

Since Sal had not briefed him, Tony Gianelli stood there doing his deer-in-the-headlights impression. "Um…no…um… Mr. Manetti. I…um…left it out in the car."

"No matter," Sal replied, taking a small notebook from his inside jacket pocket. Then to Sam he said, "The questions are pretty routine. We've reviewed the police report, of course, but there are just a few clarifications we need."

Sam Douglas looked around at the mess in the shop and ran his hand over his closely cropped graying hair, thinking that now he and Emily would be there all evening, straightening up.

Sal read his thoughts. "We won't take up too much of your time. We can see that you're busy. In fact, you can work while we talk. If Mrs. Douglas will direct traffic, young Jim, here, will help you move the heavy items while I ask the questions."

Before Sam or Tony could raise an objection, Emily hopped up off the chair and gratefully accepted the offer. "You've convinced *me*, Mr. Manetti."

She directed Tony over to the marble-topped table with which she and her husband had been grappling. "If you'll grab one side of this table, young man, it needs to be taken over there by the window. And please do be careful," she quickly added as she quite accurately sized-up Tony as someone who had no appreciation for the splendid antiques in her shop. "That table is well over a hundred-and-seventy years old."

Tony looked over at Sal but Sal merely gestured with his head toward the table. An unspoken command was issued by the *capo subordinato* and Tony reluctantly obeyed.

During the next fifteen minutes of small-talk about the antique business mixed with skillfully framed questions about the murder, both jobs got completed. The Douglasses had their shop rearranged to their liking and Sal Merlino had learned all that Sam Douglas knew about the DuMont shooting, which hadn't been much since Harvey had died just as Sam had gotten to him.

Unknowingly, though, Sam *had* imparted a single, very important piece of information that had not been contained in any of the newspaper accounts. Nor had it been documented in the police reports, copies of which had been delivered to Garibaldi House, unbeknownst to the Ulster County Sheriff's Department. Sal now knew that Harvey DuMont had made a deathbed confession to Fr. John Desmond, Rector of St. Mary's-in-the-Hills Episcopal Church.

As Sal finished stroking the Douglasses, an exhausted Tony, not used to manual labor, sat on a maple Chippendale parson's bench, mopping his brow with his handkerchief. Because of the Beretta in his shoulder holster, he had had to work with his suitcoat on. As he sat and rested and looked around the shop, he thanked the saints that he had not been forced to move the walnut Queen Anne kneehole desk and the Portsmouth tall-case clock as well.

"Take Van Brummel two blocks west and you run right into St. Mary's," Sam directed Sal. "The rectory is on the left side of the church as you face it."

Emily thanked Sal and Tony for their assistance. Sal thanked Sam for his information and the two *mafiosi* departed.

Emily and Sam watched through the leaded glass window of the front door until the black sedan had made a right-hand turn onto Van Brummel Avenue and disappeared from view. As Emily locked the door and switched on the alarm system, she remarked, "Insurance claims' adjusters must make a pretty good salary. That's a Mercedes touring car they're driving."

"Maybe they get a percentage of anything they save the company," Sam said as he set the telephone answering machine to pick up after the fourth ring.

"Could be," Emily agreed, then noticing what her husband was doing, she added, "Why don't you set it on automatic pickup? I know it's only seven-fifteen but I'm beat. All I want to do is eat dinner, take a quick shower, and hit the sack. If anyone calls, they can wait until tomorrow to talk to us."

Sam did as she requested and flipped off the lights to the antique shop as he wearily followed his wife through the blue velvet drapes and up the stairs to their living quarters. He felt the effects of the furniture rearrangement in every one of his middle-aged muscles.

❦ ❦ ❦

St. Mary's-in-the-Hills Episcopal Church was patterned after an old English village kirk. Light-gray stone blocks formed the walls for the church itself as well as for the adjoining rectory, with black slate tiles used for the roofs. A crenellated wall topped the three-story bell tower, sporting parapets on all four corners. The imported light-gray marble of the floor, the dark wood of the pews, and the thickly-padded deep-violet velour material covering the seating surfaces and kneelers gave the interior of the church a regal appearance.

On this Tuesday evening, the nave was in darkness and only a solitary light had been switched on in the sanctuary to illuminate the massive wooden altar with its white marble top. A single figure knelt on one of the red kneeling pads at the edge of the second of three dark-gray marble tiers comprising the sanctuary floor. John Desmond's face registered the distress that twisted his insides as he knelt at the foot of the altar.

"Dear Lord, let your light shine upon me," he prayed, "so that I might clearly see the path that you would have me follow. And give me the courage, the strength, and the grace to follow that path to the honor and glory of Your name."

❦ ❦ ❦

Mondays were John's days off. Rarely would he hang around the rectory on those days because if he did, someone would find him for something. He also would set the answering machine on automatic. Its prerecorded message gave the telephone number of St. Gregory's Episcopal Church in Woodstock as the number to call for emergency clerical services.

John didn't go into his CPA office in town on Mondays, either, except during tax season. He used the day to run personal errands or even take in a movie, or just bum around, window shop, and loaf. He needed the time to himself, to put the business of both the parish and the accounting firm out of his mind and recharge his energies.

On the Monday of Harvey DuMont's funeral, John had driven up to Albany to meet three of his CPA buddies for a round of golf, followed by an evening of dinner, drinks, and good conversation. Having arrived back at the rectory late that night, some sixty dollars richer for his golfing efforts, he had had no opportunity to hear the news from anyone in town regarding Cynthia DuMont's revelations about her husband's past criminal activities.

On Tuesday, John didn't go into his CPA office in town at all, but spent the entire day visiting clients in the New Paltz area. Consequently, no gossip reached him on that day, either. He returned to the rectory with barely enough time to change for evening vespers, which were read on Tuesday and Thursday evenings at six o'clock. He hadn't even bothered to put his car in the garage. He just left the Cougar in one of the parking spots out in front of the rectory.

As he intoned the opening greeting, John noted that only the regular quintet was in attendance, and, as Episcopalians are wont to do, each person had his or her own separate pew. In the Lenten or Advent season, sometimes the turnout would soar into double digits—on one occasion topping out at a record high of twenty-seven. At most other times of the year, though, just the "regulars" attended—Sara Lawson, Doreen Schumann, Phillip McMannus and Sally Burnside, all retired, and Al Epworth, the Senior Warden.

At the end of the service, Fr. Desmond shook hands with each of them in the nave by the steps up to the chancel and thanked them for coming.

Doreen said to him, "Terrible thing about that poor man, Mr. DuMont, isn't it? Such a nasty business. It only goes to show that you reap what you sow." She clucked her tongue and left the church by the north transept exit to the parking lot, feeling most self-righteous.

John just smiled and nodded, puzzled at the reaping-and-sowing remark but, since he hadn't yet had his dinner, he didn't want to prolong the conversation by asking Doreen to elaborate. She would have been only too happy to oblige and dinner would be put off for at least another forty-five minutes.

Knowing that Al Epworth would lock up and turn out the lights, John quickly doffed his alb and stole in the sacristy, then made his way down the south transept, through his office, and into the rectory, stopping only briefly in the office to check the answering machine for messages. There were a few that could be dealt with in the morning.

The day's mail and paper sat in their customary place in a wicker basket by the door from the office to the rectory, placed there by Marsha Daniels. Marsha came in and spent the day on Mondays and Fridays, giving the rectory and office a thorough cleaning. She stopped in Tuesday, Wednesday and Thursday afternoons for an hour or so after leaving her other clients just to tidy up. Saturdays and Sundays John was on his own.

He picked up the basket's contents and carried it into the kitchen with him. As he set the envelopes and Tuesday's edition of the *Kingston Chronicle* onto the kitchen table and reached for the handle of the refrigerator door, the newspaper flopped open. A subheadline below the fold caught his eye. It read "Catskill Slaying Linked to Detroit Robbery and Multiple Murder." Seized with curiosity, John sat at the table and read Agnes Berman's article about the Cynthia DuMont arraignment.

So that's what Doreen meant, he thought as he read about the murders of the Gianelli brothers and Rosa Grimaldi. *I guess that would constitute sowing and reaping, all right.*

A growl from his stomach interrupted his contemplation. Part of the remains of Sunday's picnic had found its way into John's refrigerator and another, larger part, had managed to wrap and label itself and climb into the freezer.

After selecting some sliced lamb and mint sauce and some leftover wild-rice pilaf from the refrigerator, John crossed toward the microwave, built into the cabinets on the adjacent wall, but stopped halfway there. He returned to the table to reread the piece in the *Chronicle,* an eerie feeling having crept over him.

While his body sat there at the kitchen table in the rectory of St. Mary's-in-the-Hills, John Desmond's mind returned to the banks of Woodland Creek where he knelt, cradling the dying Harvey DuMont in his arms.

Bless me, Father, for I have sinned, Harvey had gasped. *I confess to Almighty God and to you, Father. It's been ten years since my last confession.*

Ten years? John asked himself. *Is that what he said? Ten years?*

The priest replayed the scene again and again in his mind and Harvey's words came out the same each time. *Yes. There's no mistake about it. He said ten years.*

And then John looked down at the *Kingston Chronicle* on the table in front of him. His eyes focused in on the words "Four years ago" in the text where Agnes Berman began her recap of the Detroit jewel robbery and the murders of Julio and Giovanni Gianelli and Rosa Grimaldi.

John closed his eyes and tried to recall the substance of Harvey's confession. During the years since his ordination he had developed a knack for forgetting confessions once he had pronounced the words of absolution. The reasoning behind this deliberate forgetfulness was simple. In most cases he came into contact with these same people at least on a weekly basis. If he were to be able to minister effectively and compassionately to them, he had to see them as individuals, not as lists of sins. Besides, by virtue of the Sacrament of Reconciliation, those sins had been "loosed in heaven." They had to be loosed from his mind as well.

Slowly John pulled Harvey DuMont's last confession from the recesses of his memory, his recollection now quite vivid. But he was also confused and read the newspaper article again.

The case was virtually closed. In her report, Agnes Berman repeated police speculation that the accidental finding of the Isabela Pendant on Harvey DuMont's property had been a tip-off to the mob of Harvey's whereabouts and Harvey had been murdered by a professional hit-man to fulfill a *vendetta*. Agnes also surmised that the widow DuMont would get nothing more than probation since her only crimes were silence and loyalty to her husband over the years.

Oh, good Lord, John thought, and was halfway to the telephone to call Ed McAvoy when the reality of the situation hit him. *I can't tell Ed anything. The only reason I know what I know is because of Harvey DuMont's confession.*

A sickening feeling settled in the pit of his stomach. It didn't take a scholar in Canon Law to understand his obligation under the Seal of Confession. It was absolute. Nothing a penitent said could be revealed—ever—for any reason whatsoever.

Although he knew what it would say; nevertheless, John needed to read it again. He crossed into his office, took down his volume of *The Oxford Dictionary of the Christian Church* from the bookcase wall, sat at his desk and opened the book to the appropriate location. The words he knew he would find were still there. The rules of Canon Law had not been miraculously repealed in order to spare him this ethical dilemma.

"...and admits of no exception, no matter what urgent reasons of life and death, Church or state, may be advanced."

John Desmond had an urgent reason of the state on his hands but that reason was not good enough. No reason was good enough to break the Seal.

He unconsciously reached for one of his four Turkish meerschaum pipes in the ebony rack on the desk, each one elaborately carved with the personage and symbols of one of the four evangelists. The set had been a Christmas gift some years ago from Kate Winthrop. John selected St. Mark, depicted accoutered in bishop's garb and seated with a pen in his right hand, the gospel in his left, a winged lion at his feet, and a scroll winding around the bowl and up the barrel with the inscription, "Peace be to thee, O Mark, my evangelist." Stuffing the pipe with a special apple-scented mail-order blend from the humidor and striking a flame to it with his lighter, he thought back to his seminary days at the University of the South in Sewanee, Tennessee.

He remembered the "what if" scenarios the seminarians used to concoct for their instructors. Seminarians were very good at concocting "what if" scenarios.

David Blanchard spoke up, half smirking because he thought he had just been able to ethically rationalize his way around the Seal.

"But, Father, what if someone confessed that he were *going* to kill someone. Besides trying to talk him out of it, couldn't I take steps to prevent the killing without revealing that I received the information in confession?"

Fr. Daniel McWherter sat on the edge of his desk, sighed and looked around the room with his tired eyes. Then very deliberately and very quietly, he answered the question for David Blanchard, using the same words that he had used to answer it for every class since he began teaching some thirty-five years earlier.

"Not even if that someone confessed that he were going to kill *you* could you take any steps to prevent it."

The silence in the room was oppressive as the seminarians shifted their eyes from one to the other to see if their comrades had heard the same words and understood them in the same way.

Fr. McWherter continued. "We are talking about an absolute, ladies and gentlemen. There are no situational ethics that can make it otherwise. It is an absolute obligation, even unto death."

"What about simply calling the police and saying, 'You guys might just want to have a policeman standing by at the corner of such-and-such and whatever at ten o'clock tomorrow morning.'?" another seminarian asked. "You're not really revealing anything that you know."

"Do you not understand the meaning of the word 'absolute,' Mr. Desmond?" Fr. McWherter asked in return. "In all your years as a CPA, have you never once come into contact with that word?"

❧ ❧ ❧

John thought about placing a call to New York City. He even had the telephone receiver in his hand. The Suffragan Bishop was known for her liberal views. Perhaps if he explained the situation to her, she might…

But Fr. McWherter's voice echoed through time and space. "Do you not understand the meaning of the word absolute?"

John resignedly replaced the telephone receiver in its cradle. He knew that although the bishop might be liberal on social issues, no way would she even entertain the thought of giving him a dispensation from the Seal. This was strictly a matter for him and his conscience.

He replaced the meerschaum in its proper spot on the ebony rack, next to St. Matthew on the left-hand side of the humidor, rose and, crossing through the south transept, entered the church. Switching on only a solitary light in the sanctuary, he knelt and prayed for guidance.

Sal Merlino braked the black Mercedes to a stop where Van Brummel Avenue teed into Church Street. St. Mary's-in-the-Hills loomed directly in front of him.

A solitary light in the sanctuary illuminated the stained glass Resurrection scene in the east-facing rose window. Lights also showed through a few windows in the adjoining rectory. The large parking lot to the right of the church was empty and only one car, a bronze-colored Cougar XR-7, sat in the small parking lot in front of the rectory.

From his vantage point across the street, Sal could see only a small section of a third parking lot behind the church by the main entrance through the bell tower. He eased the sedan across the street and up the driveway on the north side of the church, slowly circling the complex. The Cougar turned out to be the only car in any of the parking lots.

"Suppose he's got company?" Tony Gianelli asked.

"Only one way to find out." Sal steered the Mercedes into the rectory parking lot and pulled into the space next to the Cougar.

The two men got out of the car and walked up to the front door. Sal pushed the illuminated button, activating Avon-calling chimes. They waited a few moments, but when no one came to the door, Sal gave the doorbell another poke. Still no answer. He tried the door handle but the door was locked.

"Now what?" Tony asked.

"Maybe he's in the church. I noticed a light shining through the stained glass window as we drove up."

"How do we get in?"

"You go around to the right and check out the doors on that side of the building. I'll take the left side and we'll meet at the bell tower in back."

"What if I find an open door?"

"Then tell me about it when we meet at the bell tower," Sal snapped.

The two men parted, Sal heading out to circle clockwise around the complex. The rectory had a double-width attached garage and Sal checked out both the overhead doors as well as the back doors to both the garage and rectory.

A parish hall—of a much more recent construction date than the original church and the rectory, Sal judged, by the type of brick used and style of roof—had been built behind the rectory. It was connected to the earlier structures by a corridor off the south transept. He found all four of those outside doors locked as well. Finally arriving at the bell tower and the main entrance to the narthex of the church, he tried the double-doors in front of the tower and both side doors. Al Epworth could take pride in being thorough. Nothing had been left unlocked.

Sal glanced at his watch then looked around the side of the church in the direction from which he expected Tony to momentarily appear. He saw no one. Another thirty seconds went by and still Tony Gianelli didn't show.

Beginning to feel uneasy about the situation, Sal started walking along the north side of the building toward Church Street, his steps becoming quicker with each passing second. When he came to the door at the north transept, bile rose up in his throat and he emitted a slight groan. Light, freshly cut gouges near the lock stood out from the dark varnished surface of the door.

Dear Lord, don't let me be too late, he silently prayed as he pulled open the jimmied door.

There was no one in sight. Sal stepped inside the transept and, holding onto the door, slowly let it close behind him. He crossed silently toward the double doors to the nave at the opposite side of the transept and nervously looked though the windows in the upper half of the door frame. Although a light was lit in the sanctuary, the entire church was vacant. He waited for a few moments, letting his eyes become accustomed to the relative darkness and allowing his anger to rise.

Father or no father, when I get a hold of that little son-of-a-bitch I'll... Then, realizing that he had to *find* Tony in order to kick his ass, he calmed himself slightly, grasped the handle and started to open the left-hand door to the nave.

Tony Gianelli had hurried around the front of St. Mary's so that he wouldn't be exposed for too long a time to any traffic on Church Street. Except for the side door in the bell tower, the north transept contained the only door on this side of the church. He wiggled the handle. Although secured, the lock-set in the door was not a dead bolt type. A credit card could open it, but Tony had something much better. He reached into the pocket of his gray silk suitcoat and withdrew a pearl-handled knife hilt. With just a push of a button on the hilt, a five-inch blade sprang forth. Ten seconds later Tony was inside.

At the other end of the transept, a light shone through the windows in the double doors to the nave. Tony hugged the wall as he tiptoed across the marble floor and peered through the windows. Up beyond the choir stalls in the chancel, a priest knelt at the foot of the altar. Tony looked around the darkened nave and, not seeing anyone else, slowly pulled one of the doors open. It squeaked. He froze.

John Desmond thought he heard the transept door open and turned in that direction, but, because of the lighting in the sanctuary and the darkness of the nave, he couldn't see anyone there. Shading his eyes from the sanctuary light with his hands, he called out, "May I help you?"

Tony Gianelli hesitated for a moment, then walked up the main aisle between the two sets of choir stalls and approached the communion rail. "Excuse me, Father. I... um...tried the bell at the rectory but...um...nobody answered."

John rose. "No problem. I'm John Desmond, the rector here. Would you like to come into the office and talk?" He motioned toward the south transept as he stepped through the opened gates in the communion rail and down into the chancel.

"Yeah. If that'd be okay, Father. My name's...um...Jim D'Angelo, I got some questions that I need answered."

John could see that the young man was uneasy about something. *Oh, well,* he thought. *Dinner will have to wait a little longer.*

No matter what the hour, he never told someone who needed to talk to come back at another, more convenient, time. His experience told him that people who sought out a member of the clergy had usually mustered all their courage for that one moment. Any delay and that bravery would dissipate and the opportunity to counsel someone might be lost.

"I hope I have the answers," John said smiling, then looked back in the direction from which Tony had entered the church. "How did you get in here?"

"The outside door was unlocked," Tony lied. "I saw the light shining through the stained glass window when I drove up so I went around the building and tried all the doors. That one was open."

John decided against locking the outside door at that moment but also made a mental note to check the doors himself in the future rather than relying on Al Epworth. Instead, he led his visitor through the south transept and into the office, leaving the office door open.

Crossing to one of the guest chairs in front of the desk, he gestured toward the other. "Have a seat, Jim, and tell me what I can do for you."

"I'm a...um...claims' adjuster for...um...Empire State Casualty," Tony said, thankful that he had paid attention when Sal Merlino had introduced himself to the Douglasses. "I need to ask you some questions about the DuMont murder."

John hoped his face did not betray his thoughts. *An insurance man? I'm going to put off my dinner for an insurance man?*

But since he *had* asked the young man in, he could hardly now say, "Why don't you call me tomorrow?" It did strike him as odd, though, that someone would come to question him about a matter on which he had been praying so intently. Nevertheless, he reasoned that the quicker he complied with the request, the sooner Jim D'Angelo would leave.

For perhaps the half-dozenth time, John retold the story, starting from the point at which he first heard the gunshots to where he and Sam Douglas carried the body to the bridge and placed it on the gurney brought by The Poplars' ambulance. He omitted, of course, any reference to Harvey DuMont's confession.

"And he never said who shot him?" Tony asked.

"He died within minutes after I found him."

"The colored guy who helped you—"

"Sam Douglas," John supplied the name.

"Yeah, him. He said that this DuMont made a confession before he died."

John began to get an unsettled feeling. "Yes he did, but surely you know that I can't reveal anything regarding what was said."

"How's about I ask you some questions. If what I ask was part of the confession than you take a pass on the answer. If it wasn't, then you answer it, okay?"

"I'm sorry, Jim," John said, reaching across the desk for the pipe he had smoked earlier. "It doesn't work that way. Not only can't I reveal what Mr. DuMont *did* say, I can't reveal anything about what he *didn't* say, either." He proceeded to clean and scrape St. Mark's bowl, readying it for a fresh plug of tobacco. "By process of elimination, that would be the same thing as telling you what he said. Do you understand?"

"The guy's dead, Father. What's the big deal?"

"The sanctity of the confessional, *that's* the big deal."

"Well, I've got a deal here that you might just find even bigger," Tony Gianelli said as he reached his right hand underneath the lapel of his suitcoat in the direction of his left armpit.

Chapter 8

Ben Krider hurriedly entered The Plough & Whistle and went directly over to the blackboard that listed the daily specials. He heaved a sigh of relief. *Squab* was still scrawled on the board.

The Plough didn't have menus. Twice weekly, on Monday and Thursday mornings, Porky would go to market in Kingston and buy the best ingredients he could find at sensible prices. Each day's menu depended on what Porky had been able to procure. This arrangement suited everyone. The pub could offer a variety of dishes at reasonable prices and the customers never tired of having to choose from the same selections day after day.

People like Ben Krider and Ed McAvoy, who took most of their meals at the pub, especially liked this arrangement. The only downside was that if Porky had only been able to purchase a dozen of an item, such as squab, then when that dozen was gone, the item was erased from the blackboard.

Early on, Porky had allowed people to call in and reserve dinners that were in short supply but that policy had lasted less than two weeks. Telling someone that there was no more of an item and then having them see the reserved item served to another patron who had come in later resulted in too many hard feelings. Now the pub ran on a strictly first-come-first-serve basis—no exceptions, not even for regulars like Ben and McAvoy.

As Ben turned from the blackboard, Stevie Henderson passed by on her way to the bar with an empty pitcher. He pointed to the item on the board. "Squab, Stevie. Get my order in quick for a squab, okay?"

"I'll see to it, Doc," she said with a laugh and kept right on going.

Ben followed her for a few steps. "I've really got my heart set on that squab. You didn't write it down."

Stevie stopped and turned to him. "Ben, how many people do you see here taking dinner orders?"

He quickly glanced around the pub. Danny, wearing a white bib-apron and plastic gloves, brushed crumbs from the blue-and-white checkered cloth on an empty table. A plastic dishpan, full of used plates, glasses, and silverware, sat on one of the chairs. Porky could be seen through the doorway to the grill, ladling Cockaleekie into three bowls.

Ben looked back at the barmaid. "Just...just you, Stevie."

"Then when I tell you I'll see to it, I will see to it. Maybe not right this very instant, but I *will* see to it. Now, go sit down and relax or you'll screw up your digestive system." She turned from him and resumed her trek to the bar

With his mind more or less at ease, knowing that a squab figured in his dinner plans, Ben looked around the room again, this time for a place to sit. McAvoy, at his customary table by the dart board, caught the doctor's eye and waved him over. The chief and Bill Brinkmire had just ordered but had not yet received their meals.

"We got us a live one here, Doc," McAvoy said, gesturing with his thumb to Bill Brinkmire. "Our ace reporter is buying dinner for anyone connected with the Harvey DuMont murder who will give him an interview."

The frugal Ben Krider looked at Bill with an "Is that so?" look.

Bill chuckled and motioned Ben into the chair next to him. "You better have something worthwhile or you buy your own dessert."

Sitting where he had been directed, Ben rubbed his hands together in anticipation of the free meal. "Well, there's a certain matter regarding the shot pattern and the powder burns, discovered in the medical examination, that should get me dessert *and* an after-dinner drink."

"You don't say?" Bill turned a page of his notebook and picked up a pen.

McAvoy reached across the table and covered the paper with his hand. "Sorry, Bill. Not for publication."

"Why not?"

"Yeah, why not?" Ben echoed, afraid of having to buy his own dessert.

"Off the record?" McAvoy asked Bill.

"Do I get an exclusive when it can be told *on* the record?"

McAvoy nodded and began to reveal his thoughts and assumptions about the case. Since he had read the files that Jerry Gardner had faxed from Detroit, he was able to fill in quite a few of the gaps in Agnes Berman's article from the *Kingston Chronicle*. He also told Bill about Vittorio and Antonio Gianelli residing at Garibaldi House. The reporter furiously took notes in his own special shorthand.

McAvoy finished up his dissertation with an answer to Bill's original question regarding the powder burns and shot pattern. "Chances are that whoever killed Harvey DuMont has already disposed of the weapon. But maybe, just maybe, he hasn't. I might still be able to find someone wandering around here with a sawed-off shotgun in his possession. Even though it can't be positively tied to the shooting, at least I'll have a piece of circumstantial evidence and right now we don't have any evidence of any kind against anyone. That's why I can't let you print anything about the murder weapon. If the killer knows that we suspect that the shotgun used is a sawed-off, he'll dispose of it for sure. Other than that, and actually accusing the Gianellis outright, you can use anything else I've given you."

Bill readily agreed. "So you really think the killer is sitting up there in Greene County, fat, dumb, and happy, watching you spin your wheels?"

"And the happier he is," McAvoy said, "the more complacent he may become."

"You know, speaking of Greene County," Ben interjected, "I just saw the most beautiful black Mercedes up at Donovan's on the way over here tonight."

The other two men looked at him in puzzlement. "How the hell does talking about Greene County tie into a Mercedes?" McAvoy asked.

"The Mercedes had Greene County plates."

An alarm went off in McAvoy's head. "In Donovan's?"

"Yeah. Just a little while ago. Why?"

The question went unanswered. McAvoy leapt to his feet and headed for the telephone at the end of the bar. He grabbed the receiver, opened the slim local phone directory and punched in the number for Donovan's Shell Station.

After the ninth ring McAvoy looked at his stainless steel Seiko and silently cursed. *Shit! They close at seven and it's seven-twenty.*

He looked up two other numbers from the D-column, a Donovan, Ralph and a Donovan, William. *If it was just before Ben got here, Ralph would have been on duty by himself. Bill leaves at five.*

He punched in Ralph's number. Linda, Ralph's wife, answered on the second ring. McAvoy was in luck. Ralph had just gotten home and yes, he remembered the black Mercedes.

"Can you describe the driver?" McAvoy asked.

"Sure, Chief. Big bald guy in an expensive suit. Also, there was a younger greaser-type in the car with him."

"Did you notice which direction they went?"

"Better than that, Chief. They wanted to find Sam Douglas. I pointed the way for them. That was okay, wasn't it? I mean, I didn't do anything wrong, did I?"

McAvoy assured him that he had not and quickly broke the connection. A half-dozen more names down the D-column was Douglas, Samuel. McAvoy punched in that number and waited.

The Douglas' answering machine picked up on the first ring, informing him that business hours were from ten in the morning until six-thirty in the evening. McAvoy didn't bother listening to the remainder of the message. He slammed the receiver down and let go with a medium-loud "Shit!"

Stevie looked over at him from behind the bar and arched an eyebrow. "Problem?"

"Give me my gun! Hurry! I gotta go!"

She fished out his Smith & Wesson from under the bar and handed it to him as he hurried toward the front door. He was still clipping the holster to his belt as he ran, with his hop-skipitty gait, across Irving Boulevard toward the police station. Stevie watched him from the doorway, saying a silent prayer as she always did when he rushed away on police business.

As she started to let the door swing closed, Bill Brinkmire came up to her. "Where's he going?"

"I really don't know, Bill." Her voice had a worried tone to it.

"Put everything on my tab," he shouted, taking off across the street after McAvoy. "And give Doc Krider an after-dinner drink."

Stevie let the door swing closed and resumed her duties, going first to a bewildered Ben Krider to deliver his squab, which he would now have to eat by himself.

Bill Brinkmire caught up to McAvoy at the front door to the police station. The chief was standing in the doorway.

"Where's Jim?" McAvoy shouted to Larry Parker.

"Out on patrol, Chief."

"Switch the phone over and let's go." McAvoy turned from the door and almost collided with Bill. "You want an exclusive? Get in the Jeep!"

He ran down to one of the two blue-and-white Jeep Cherokees parked in the circular drive, climbed into the driver's seat and started the engine. Bill Brinkmire hopped into the back seat just as Larry Parker joined them and scrambled in beside McAvoy. The chief made a U-turn on Irving Boulevard and headed west toward Van Winkle Street.

Larry grabbed the mike from its holder on the radio and pressed the TALK button. "This is PMH-One to PMH-Two. PMH-One to PMH-Two. Come in PMH-Two. Over."

Jim Culpepper's voice answered back through the radio. "This is PMH-Two. Is that you, Larry? Over."

"Yeah, Jim. I'm with the chief. We're on our way to…" he looked over at McAvoy, realizing that he didn't know where they were going.

"Sam Douglas' shop," McAvoy said as he made the left turn onto Van Winkle.

"The Douglas' antique shop," Larry relayed. "I've got the phone switched. Over."

There were only two officers on duty during the afternoon and night watches. Normally they took turns patrolling and riding the desk. In the event that the second officer needed to leave the station, he put the telephone on call-forwarding to Lucille's home phone.

"I'm on my way in. Give me a shout if you need backup. PMH-Two clear."

"PMH-One clear," Larry replied and hung up the microphone.

McAvoy braked the Jeep to a stop in the exact spot where the black Mercedes had been parked just minutes before. "Wait here," he told Bill Brinkmire.

Bill nodded and McAvoy and Larry got out of the vehicle.

Directing Larry to a point on Van Brummel Avenue where the young officer could observe that side as well as the back of the shop, McAvoy mounted the three steps to the porch and poked the button for the doorbell. An obnoxious buzz sounded from inside. He waited a few moments and pushed it again, this time leaving his finger on the button so that the buzzer sounded continuously.

A few moments passed, then lights came on inside the store and an angry Sam Douglas bulled his way through the blue drapes that hid the staircase from view. He was dressed in a yellow, red-and-brown dashiki and matching kofi, the garb he wore in the privacy of his home. He also carried a knobkerrie in his hand.

When he saw that his supposed jackass-leaning-on-the-buzzer was, in fact, the chief of police, he set the African war club down, changed his expression from anger to one of curiosity, then deactivated the burglar alarm and opened the door. He never got the opportunity to voice his curiosity.

"Two men in a black Mercedes," McAvoy said. "Were they here?"

"The insurance investigators? Yeah. They left about twenty minutes ago. Why?"

"Insurance investigators?"

"Yeah. They were investigating the death of that DuMont fellow. They had a few questions."

"Damn! Twenty minutes, you said?"

"At the most, Chief. But you should be able to catch up with them. They were on their way to St. Mary's to talk to Fr. Desmond."

Larry had joined the chief during the conversation. At Sam's last remark, both he and McAvoy automatically turned and ran for the Jeep. McAvoy shouted a, "Thanks, Sam," over his shoulder.

A perplexed Sam Douglas stood in the doorway and watched as the Cherokee sped away, then shook his head, relocked the door, and reset the alarm. Picking up his antique war club, he switched off the lights and went back upstairs.

After making the right-hand turn onto Van Brummel and speeding to Church Street, McAvoy pulled over to the curb at the corner and turned off the headlights. Two cars were parked in the lot in front of the rectory, John Desmond's Cougar and the black Mercedes.

Bill Brinkmire tapped McAvoy on the shoulder and pointed toward the north side of the church. A solitary figure had come around from the back of the building. In the fading twilight the three men watched as the figure made its way along the wall from the bell tower to the transept.

"Where's the other one?" McAvoy wondered out loud.

"Maybe around back," Larry replied.

"Or still in the car?" Bill offered.

Just then the figure opened the door in the north transept and entered the church. McAvoy eased the Jeep across Church Street, without turning on the headlights, and up into the driveway about twenty feet from the transept door.

"Let's go," he said, shutting off the engine and opening his door. Then realizing at the last moment that he hadn't clarified the command, he turned and grabbed Bill Brinkmire by the jacket collar as the newspaper man, too, had opened his door. "Not you," he said with a note of exasperation in his voice as he hauled the reporter back into the Jeep.

"Oh, right," Bill replied, carefully and quietly pulling the door closed and sitting back down in the seat with his hands in his lap.

McAvoy and Larry took off at a run in the direction where the figure had entered. Upon reaching the north transept, they each took up positions on either side of the door, sidearms drawn and cocked. At a nod from McAvoy, Larry yanked the door open.

The chief, crouching low, his Smith & Wesson extended in front of him and held in a two-handed grip, quickly moved into the open doorway. "Freeze!" he commanded in a hoarse whisper.

Sal Merlino, who had started to open the left-hand door to the nave, turned himself into a statue, but emitted an audible sigh.

"Where's the greaseball?" McAvoy asked as he approached Sal.

"I'm not altogether sure, Captain," Sal replied, still frozen in position.

McAvoy grabbed him by the collar, swung him around face-first into the stone-block wall and set the barrel of his revolver at the base of Sal's skull. "Don't fuck with me, Sal! Where's Tony?" He kicked the bald man's legs away from the wall.

"I think he's inside," Sal answered with another sigh, as Larry Parker, who had holstered his sidearm, began to pat the *mafioso* lawyer down. "And this really is unnecessary," Sal added. "You know I don't carry."

"He's clean, Chief," Larry said as he removed a set of handcuffs from the pouch on his belt and snapped one side onto Sal's right wrist.

"Captain McAvoy—" Sal began.

"Shut the fuck up!" McAvoy ordered. Then to Larry he said, "Bring him along with us, but if he starts to open his mouth or resist in anyway whatsoever, smack him over the head with your piece." He took Sal by the collar again and turned the bald man's head so that they were face to face. Tapping his revolver on Sal's nose, he said, "*Capisce?*"

Sal closed his eyes and gave one small nod as he visualized his hands around Tony Gianelli's neck, squeezing tighter and tighter.

When McAvoy released his grip, Larry twisted both of Sal's arms behind the man's back and cuffed the other wrist. Then the young officer grabbed Sal by the collar with his left hand, took out his semiautomatic with his right hand and placed the end of the barrel between the lawyer's shoulder blades. He looked over at the chief and nodded.

McAvoy slowly opened the door to the nave. The hinges squeaked. All three men froze. After a few moments, McAvoy opened the door wider and they entered the church, silently making their way across the nave to the double doors leading to the south transept.

Stopping there, McAvoy cautiously looked through the glass in the upper half of the door frame. The lights from John Desmond's office at the far end of the transept illuminated Tony Gianelli, sitting with his back to the open office door. McAvoy motioned for Larry to stay put and slowly opened the transept door. Larry nodded as he tightened his grip on Sal Merlino's collar.

Fortunately, the hinges on this door didn't squeak. As McAvoy silently inched his way down the hallway, his back to the wall and his service revolver in his hand, the conversation from the office became clearer.

"Do you understand?" John Desmond asked.

"The guy's dead, Father," Tony answered. "What's the big deal?"

"The sanctity of the confessional, *that's* the big deal."

"Well, I've got a deal here that you might just find even bigger," Tony Gianelli said as he reached his right hand underneath the lapel of his suitcoat in the direction of his left armpit.

The chair in which Tony sat was about three feet from the office door to the transept. No sooner had he placed his hand inside his jacket then the chief leapt into the room.

McAvoy grabbed Tony by the hair with one hand, pulling his head over the chair back, and stuck the barrel of his service revolver into the young man's ear. "Don't even *think* about it," McAvoy said.

Tony Gianelli, dark brown eyes wide open in surprise, gazed up into the chief's face. His hand rested on the butt of a Beretta but he had the good sense not to draw the weapon.

John Desmond dropped the St. Mark pipe on the floor and almost fell off his chair in fright at McAvoy's sudden appearance. "Ed, what do you think you're doing?" he asked as he stood up and started to cross to Tony's aid.

"Don't come any closer," McAvoy said.

The tone of the chief's voice made John stop as he had been directed. "But, Ed, this young man—"

"This young man," McAvoy interrupted, "unless he wants me to clean the wax out of his ears, is going to extract his pistol, using only his fingertips." The chief looked down into Tony Gianelli's eyes. "*Capisce, Paesan?*"

Tony slowly brought his right hand from underneath his jacket. He held a Beretta model 92F semiautomatic between his thumb and forefinger. At the sight of the weapon, a dumfounded John Desmond, who had stooped to retrieve his pipe, cautiously stood and backed up to the rectory doorway.

"Toss it on the carpet over by the bookcase," McAvoy instructed. Tony complied. The chief motioned with his head toward the desk. "If you'll move out of the way, Father."

John edged along the wall to get behind his desk, replacing the pipe in the rack when he got there. Once the priest had moved, McAvoy lifted Tony Gianelli out of the chair by the hair.

"God damn it, you son—" Tony started but McAvoy propelled him across the room toward the doorway to the rectory and slammed his head into the doorjamb before he could finish the sentence.

"You're in a church, Greaseball. Don't use that kind of language in here."

A futile attempt at resistance and the beginning of another epithet, regarding McAvoy's relationship with his mother, earned Tony a second close encounter with the doorjamb. He abandoned any further thoughts of smart-mouthing or fighting back.

"Assume the position," McAvoy hissed.

Tony braced his hands on the doorjamb, took two paces backward and spread his legs.

"You've done this before," McAvoy remarked, sarcastically, then to the priest he said, "Father, would you tell Larry to bring the other one in?"

John Desmond scurried down the transept hallway and reemerged a few moments later preceded by Larry Parker and a handcuffed Sal Merlino. A buoyant Bill Brinkmire, who had not been able to contain his curiosity, had joined Larry and Sal in the church and followed them into the office. Larry still had hold of Sal's collar and had his weapon drawn. Bill had a notebook and a pen.

"Offer Sal a seat, Larry, then come over here and give me a hand," McAvoy said.

Larry pushed Sal into the chair in which Tony had been sitting, holstered his semiautomatic, then patted Tony down.

"I want these cops charged with police brutality," Tony shouted. "Look at my head." He turned his head as far as possible with McAvoy still holding onto his hair to show Sal the cut on his forehead. Blood trickled down the side of his face.

Sal Merlino, struggling to a standing position, managed to control both the rage he felt toward the arrogant young man and the delight brought on by seeing Tony's battered skull. "Would you kindly remove these handcuffs, Chief McAvoy? I assure you I will not cause you any trouble."

McAvoy nodded at Larry, who had extracted a pearl-handled stiletto from Tony's pocket and had tossed it on the floor next to the Beretta. The young officer removed the cuffs and Sal crossed to Tony and McAvoy.

Grabbing a handful of Tony's hair next to where the chief still held on, the lawyer said, "May I please have a word with my client?"

McAvoy released his own grip, stepped back a pace or two and holstered his revolver.

"I'm not sure whether or not Chief McAvoy has told you that you have the right to remain silent," Sal said quietly to Tony. "But as your *father's* attorney, I'm advising you to *shut your mouth!*"

Sal's rage had overcome his delight and he needed to get that feeling of delight back again. He concluded his advise by ramming Tony's head into the doorjamb for a third time and twice as hard as McAvoy had done on the two previous occasions.

Tony's knees buckled and he sprawled to the floor, blood spurting from the now-enlarged gash.

Sal turned to John Desmond. "My apologies, Father. None of this was supposed to happen."

"Will someone please tell me what *this* is all about?" a confused John pleaded from behind his desk. He looked from McAvoy to Sal to Bill.

Bill Brinkmire didn't see the look. He stood in the corner of the room, furiously scribbling in his notebook. Sal turned away from the priest and retook his seat in the guest chair closest to the transept, shaking his head in frustration at the predicament that Tony had gotten them into.

"Later, Father," McAvoy replied, picking Tony up by the hair and a shoulder. "I'll tell you all about it later."

Larry, who had pocketed the Beretta and the stiletto, now handcuffed Tony's hands behind him and jammed the young *mafioso* into the guest chair by the rectory doorway. Tony just sat there, silently glaring at Sal through the rivulet of blood running down his face.

McAvoy turned his attention to Sal Merlino. "Under the circumstances, I don't imagine you'd have any objections to me searching your car, would you, *Consigliere?*"

"Are you planning on charging me or my client with any crime?"

"No," McAvoy answered, again with sarcasm. "I'm just going to ignore the fact that he broke in here and threatened a priest with a gun."

Sal held up a cautioning finger and smiled slightly. As angry as he was with Tony for what he had done, the *consigliere* for Vittorio Gianelli had a job to do. "What threat?... And what gun, might I ask?"

McAvoy gave him one of those "pull-the-other-leg" looks.

Sal elaborated. "You acted too quickly, my friend. You and I may surmise what Antonio *intended* to do, but no threat was actually uttered and no gun was ever drawn."

McAvoy started to protest but Sal waved him off. "I could make the case that my client was merely reaching for a pocket handkerchief when you accosted him. And when I put Fr. Desmond on the stand and ask him if my client threatened him or pulled a gun on him, what will he say?" Sal looked over at the priest.

John nodded and shrugged his shoulders at McAvoy.

Sal continued. "And as for breaking and entering, did *you* see who forced the lock on that door? It could have been anyone. Maybe it wasn't forced at all. Maybe someone left the door unlocked. I assure you, this will not even make it to an arraignment. Mr. Ledbetter, your supremely-cautious ADA, will want more than supposition."

Sal may have been a mobster but he was also a topnotch attorney. He also knew when to stop backing someone into a corner and he had reached that point with McAvoy.

"Certainly, as a punitive measure, you can hold Antonio in your jail overnight until I can get a writ. But, if it is chastisement that you want, I assure you that a more severe punishment awaits him at Garibaldi House." He gazed over at Tony Gianelli, smiled a cold thin smile, and winked.

The tough-guy facade began to crumble and a look of panic crept into Tony's eyes as Sal's words registered on him. McAvoy switched his focus from Sal to Tony and then back again to Sal and repeated his prior question. "Do I get to look in the car?"

Let's make it a win-win outcome, Sal thought. *Toss him a bone.* "Be my guest, Chief McAvoy. We have nothing to hide."

"Larry, you take the greaseball out to the Jeep. I'll be along in a few minutes," McAvoy said.

Larry did as he had been instructed, guiding a sullen Tony Gianelli out through the front door of the rectory and around the side of the church to the police car.

McAvoy gestured toward the front door. "Lead on, Counselor."

To John Desmond, Sal said, "Again, my sincerest apologies, Father. And, believe me, Antonio will be severely reprimanded for his actions." He turned and also headed toward the front door.

Before leaving with Sal, McAvoy spoke to both John Desmond and Bill Brinkmire. "John, I'll talk to you later. But in the meantime would you drive Bill over to the pub?"

Before the priest could answer, Bill asked a question of his own. "You had dinner yet, Father?"

John, remembering the cold lamb in the microwave, shook his head.

"Then it's my treat. The squab over at The Plough & Whistle looked delicious." He clapped John on the shoulder. "Besides, you and I have a lot to talk about." And before McAvoy could say anything, he added, "I'll be there when you get back and you can review my notes."

McAvoy nodded his approval and joined Sal at the front door.

The search of the Mercedes turned out to be a waste of time—no sawed-off shotgun in the trunk or under the seats. McAvoy hadn't really expected to find anything, certainly not in Sal Merlino's car. The search had only been a form of harassment anyway. McAvoy even admitted it to himself—a venting of the frustration he felt at knowing who had killed Harvey DuMont but not being able to prove it.

During the inspection, John Desmond and Bill Brinkmire left the rectory and got into the Cougar, John having first relocked the north transept door and returned his lamb, mint sauce, and rice to the refrigerator.

From the passenger seat of the priest's car, Bill caught McAvoy's eye. The chief, standing next to Sal Merlino's Mercedes, gave a slight negative shake of his head. Bill gave a "too bad" shrug of his shoulders and the Cougar pulled out of the parking lot and headed toward town.

Sal Merlino recognized the search as harassment, also, but thought it better to allow McAvoy to direct his obvious frustration at the car rather than at his client. When the chief had finished, Sal looked over at McAvoy and raised an upturned palm, an unstated "Have you decided what you're going to do?"

"You lead the way," McAvoy said. Then, pointing to the cellular phone in the Mercedes, he said, "Tell the old man I'm bringing his son home and also tell him what that little asshole did. When I get there I want that gate open and I expect Don Vittorio to meet me on the terrace. He opened the door to the Jeep, which Larry had pulled alongside during the search of the Mercedes, but stopped and turned back to Sal. "And, Sal, I'm in no mood to be fucked around."

Sal let out a submissive sigh and gave a single nod of his head.

McAvoy climbed into the passenger seat of the Jeep and signaled Larry to wait until the Mercedes pulled out of the lot first.

Although the nod and sigh were submissive, the delight had returned to Sal's heart. He would thoroughly enjoy telling Vittorio Gianelli that his asshole of son had broken into a church to threaten a priest at gunpoint. As he made a left turn onto Church Street, he picked up the cellular phone and punched in the number for Vittorio's private phone line at Garibaldi House.

The drive up to Deep Notch proved to be uneventful. A handcuffed Tony Gianelli slouched sullenly in the back seat of the Jeep and didn't utter a word during the entire trip. As Larry steered the Cherokee down the gravel drive, the flood lights, mounted on either side of the entrance to the Garibaldi House complex, showed them that the massive iron gate had already been rolled back.

Sal Merlino's Mercedes sat idling in the opening. When the Jeep neared the gate, the Mercedes eased forward and picked up speed, leading the way down the curving driveway through the woods.

A green-jacketed guard, the same one who had been on-duty during their previous visit, stood next to the security booth. As the Jeep passed him, the guard smiled at McAvoy. The look on his face said, "You sure got balls, McAvoy. I'll give you that."

As had been the case the last time they made the drive from the gate to the chateau, the only people McAvoy and Larry saw wore red slacks, white knit shirts, and green jackets. When they reached the terrace, a waiting attendant took Sal's Mercedes and drove it out of sight around the back of the building. Sal stood at the foot of the staircase and waited for McAvoy. Mercury vapor floods illuminated both the staircase and the terrace. Larry parked the Jeep and, as McAvoy joined Sal, the young officer opened the rear door for Tony Gianelli.

The would-be mobster had reassembled his facade and again played the tough-guy. He shook off Larry's hand as the officer attempted to help him from the car. As he sauntered over to Sal and McAvoy, the expression on his face threatened, "Just wait until my papa sees what you've done to me." On the inside, however, his mind cringed as he anxiously wondered, *What will my papa do to me?*

Sal and McAvoy started up the stairs in silence with Larry and Tony a few steps behind them. As the foursome reached the terrace, they could see that two of the white wrought iron umbrella tables had been set with yellow placemats, matching napkins and silver and crystal service. Bruno Saracino, the white-clothed maitre d', stood at attention near the French doors to the chateau, a covered, wheeled serving cart at his side.

One of the tables, the one where Vittorio Gianelli customarily held court, contained place-settings for three. Vittorio sat in his wheelchair sipping a glass of Verdicchio, black cashmere overcoat draped about his shoulders and black fedora on his head.

The second table at the near end of the terrace, down front by the railing but out of earshot from the first, had been set for only one person.

Vittorio put down his wine glass, dabbed at his lips with the napkin, then pointed a bony index finger at Tony and beckoned him over to the table. McAvoy nodded to Larry, who removed the cuffs from Tony's hands.

The young man quickly approached his father, mustering all his cockiness for a frontal assault, hoping to deflect Vittorio's anger away from himself and onto McAvoy.

"Papa, look what that bastard—"

"*Silenzio!*" the old man commanded.

"But, Papa—"

"*Si accòmodi!*" Vittorio pointed a finger at the chair on his right—the only one at that table with no place-setting in front of it.

Tony shut his mouth and sat.

Vittorio shook the finger in his son's face. "You break into a church, Antonio?!"

Tony opened his mouth to answer but the look on his father's face told him that the question had been rhetorical. He wisely closed his mouth and let Vittorio finish.

"*La chiesa di Santa Maria?!*" Despite being a mobster, Vittorio had a devotion to the Virgin that approached something mystical. His voice rose in volume as his anger increased. "And you pull a gun on God's priest?!"

"I never pulled a gun, Papa," Tony replied, testily. "And besides that, he ain't even a real priest. He's a Protestant."

"A man of God!" Vittorio screamed. "In a church dedicated to the Holy Mother!"

"So? God is going to strike me dead, or what?"

Vittorio Gianelli took in a gasp of breath, his eyes widened and he crossed himself, muttering a prayer that the Lord would forgive his stupid and irreverent offspring. Then he crooked his finger and motioned Tony closer to him as he picked up the wine bottle with his other hand and refilled his glass.

Tony leaned forward in the chair, thinking that his cockiness had paid off. He expected Vittorio to impart some sage but otherwise foolish fatherly advice to him and offer him a drink. This audience was going far better than he had hoped—or so he thought.

When his face was but a foot away from his father's, Vittorio, with an agility and speed that defied his infirmity, swung the half-empty wine bottle at his son, catching him squarely in the forehead with it. Tony tumbled from the chair, blood gushing anew from the seemingly ever-enlarging gash on his head and mixing with the wine from the broken bottle.

"Do not mock the Lord, Antonio!" Vittorio hissed, looking down at the semiconscious Tony sprawled out on the slate floor. "Never, ever, mock the Lord or his Holy Mother!" He then crossed himself again.

An instant after Tony Gianelli hit the floor, Bruno opened one of the French doors. Four men entered the terrace and approached Vittorio's table. Two of the men, young and muscular and dressed in the red, white, and green, each grabbed Tony under an armpit and hoisted him to his feet. The other two men, older and dressed in white, one with a broom and dustpan and the other with a wet mop, quickly cleared the broken glass, wine and blood from the terrace floor.

Vittorio smiled and nodded a "thank you" to them as they retreated inside the chateau. He then turned his attention to the two security men with his son. "Take him to his room and see that his cut is fixed. But he is not to leave. I will deal with him later." He gave a dismissive gesture with the back of his hand.

"Yes, *Padrone*," both men said in unison and half-walked and half-dragged Tony into the chateau.

The maitre d' closed the French doors behind them, then pushed his serving cart over to the three men standing by the staircase who had silently, but delightedly, watched the domestic dispute unfold. "The *Padrone* would like you and Captain McAvoy to join him at his table," he said to Sal. "But, after what transpired on his last visit, I think the Captain's nephew will be more comfortable over there." He turned his attention to Larry and gestured toward the table with the lone place-setting. "If you would be so kind, Officer Parker?"

Larry glanced at McAvoy, received a barely noticeable nod, and proceeded to the table to which the maitre d' had directed him. Sal and McAvoy crossed halfway across the terrace to Vittorio Gianelli. The old man motioned them to the seats with place-settings—McAvoy at his left and Sal across from him.

"He is young. He is eager to please his papa. But he does not have the brains of a jackrabbit," Vittorio said, tapping his temple with the fingers of his right hand.

"And his funeral will occur before your own, Don Vittorio," McAvoy replied.

"Julio had the brains, Captain McAvoy. Of the three, Julio had the brains. A lawyer, that one. Maybe even a *dottore* or, if God had been willing, a priest. Maybe even a priest." Tears welled up in Vittorio's eyes as he reminisced about his youngest son and he brushed them away with his hand.

As the chief looked at his grieving host, he almost forgot whom he sat next to. He had to remind himself that this frail old man would rip the heart out of anyone who stood in his way. "More than likely a lawyer," McAvoy replied. "Very few priests I know these days are so greedy that they would commit murder or steal diamonds."

As the three men sat in silence, Vittorio Gianelli's obsidian eyes bore into McAvoy. Finally the old man spoke. "There is a difference between greed and *vendetta*, Captain McAvoy."

"In your book, maybe, Don Vittorio, but not in mine."

"I do not expect you to agree with me, *mio amico*. But Julio was a good boy. We were going to keep him a good boy. That is why we only let him drive the boat."

"*Padrone*, please!" Sal interjected. "Before you say anything more." He looked from Vittorio to McAvoy. "Would you please stand up Cap...excuse me, Chief McAvoy?"

"I'm not giving up my piece, Sal. Forget about it."

"No, no, no, Chief. I don't want your gun. But before Don Vittorio continues, I must check you for wires or recording devices."

"Are you serious?"

"Most serious. If you would please stand up and open your jacket."

McAvoy complied with the request. Vittorio had whetted his curiosity and he wasn't taking a chance on getting thrown out now. He spread open the lapels to his navy poplin sportcoat. Sal Merlino expertly checked the lining of the jacket and patted him down, front and back. When he was finished, Sal thanked him and they both sat back down.

❦ ❦ ❦

If Larry Parker had felt the least bit sorry for himself at being segregated from the others, that feeling sprouted wings the moment the maitre d' lifted the cover from the serving cart and began setting a variety of desserts in front of the young officer.

"*Zabaione*," the man in white said, pointing to the long-stemmed glass he had just set down. "A custard, with strawberries and a touch of Marsala," he explained with a wink as he shook out the yellow napkin and placed it on Larry's lap. "Try this first while it is still hot. *Molto bene!*"

He then identified the other desserts that he had placed on the table. "*Crostata di Ricotta*—a cheese pie. *Cenci alla Fiorentina*—deep-fried sweet pastries. You've probably had them before and called them angel wings, heh? *Cassata alla Siciliana*—a Sicilian fruitcake with chocolate frosting. And finally, *Pesche Ripiene*—baked peaches, stuffed with macaroons. *Squisito!*" He kissed the thumb and second finger of his right hand for emphasis. "Since you are on-duty, I bring you this to drink." He set a large glass of milk on the table.

Larry picked up a spoon to eagerly dig into the *Zabaione*, but then remembered something else. "Maybe you'd better take care of these," he said, extracting the Beretta from his belt and the stiletto from his pocket and plunking the gun and knife down on the table top. "They're Tony's."

With a pragmatic shrug of his arms and shoulders, the maitre d' transferred the weapons to his serving cart and covered them with a yellow napkin.

"My name is Bruno," he said. "Now, you need anything else, you just signal me and I come, okay?"

Larry nodded in the affirmative as he scooped a spoonful of custard into his mouth.

Bruno started toward the table with the threesome, stopped and turned back to Larry, waggling a cautioning finger. "But not while I am at the *Padrone's* table, though, heh?"

Larry gave him a thumbs-up sign and the maitre d' winked and pushed his cart over to Vittorio Gianelli's table.

"You were saying something about Julie not killing anyone or stealing anything and only driving the getaway boat?" McAvoy prompted Vittorio.

Vittorio nodded. During the time it had taken Sal to frisk McAvoy, Bruno the maitre d' had brought brandy, steaming cups of cappuccino, and a tray of desserts. As they ate and drank, Vittorio proceeded to tell McAvoy the story of the Isabela Pendant, starting with that night so many years ago in Sicily and ending with the trip to the Belle Isle Coast Guard Station.

At the end of the story, McAvoy asked, "So, what do you expect me to do? Turn my head and ignore the fact that you had Harvey DuMont whacked in revenge for Johnny and Julie?"

"I do not expect you to *turn* your head," Vittorio replied. "I expect you to open your eyes and your mind and *use* your head. We are not responsible for the DuMont execution."

"With all due respect, Don Vittorio, I was there in 1975. As a detective sergeant, it was me who put the cuffs on you when we brought you in for questioning in the Hoffa disappearance. If memory serves me, you said you weren't responsible for that, either."

Vittorio chuckled. "I had wondered if you would remember. That was our first of many encounters, Captain

McAvoy. But, in this instance, an old man's memory is perhaps better than your own. I did not say I *was not responsible*. I said that *you would never make it stick*. There is a difference. Am I not right?" He winked, but continued before McAvoy could reply. "I am telling you now that we were not responsible for Harvey DuMont. And Salvatore, here, is my witness that everything I have said to you tonight and am about to say to you now was never said. Yes, we *were* planning to hit him." McAvoy's eyes widened. "Oh, yes, we were planning it. But someone else got to him first."

"Then what in the hell were Sal and Tony doing tonight? It damn well looks to me like they were trying to find out if anyone could finger them."

Vittorio deliberately and calmly said, "They were doing your job for you, Captain McAvoy. They were investigating the death of Harvey DuMont."

"Yeah. Right." McAvoy said with a trace of contempt.

Sal Merlino finally entered the conversation. "Let me put it to you this way, Chief McAvoy. Suppose," he held up a hand to stifle any protestations. "Just suppose for a moment that it *wasn't* us who ordered the hit." McAvoy switched his gaze back and forth between the two men and Sal continued. "Who would your suspects be?"

"We have no other suspects," McAvoy said and quickly followed up with, "We hardly need any other suspects."

"Play along with me," Sal cajoled him. "Without us for bogeymen, where would you usually start in an investigation of this type?"

McAvoy maintained his silence as he weighed the possibilities.

"In this matter," Vittorio interjected, "we are on the same side, *mio amico*. We, also, would like to see *Signor* DuMont's killer identified."

"And why this sudden public-spiritedness?"

Sal finished a last morsel of *Cenci alla Fiorentina*, wiped the powdered sugar from his fingertips onto the yellow napkin and stared down at his plate. Then, very quietly, he said, "Do you really think that a man like Harvey DuMont could have killed Julio, Giovanni, and Rosa Grimaldi by himself?" He looked up into McAvoy's eyes. "As believers in true justice, we would be as interested as would the police in knowing the name of Harvey DuMont's accomplice, for it is he who we think killed Mr. DuMont."

A chill slowly crawled up McAvoy's spine as two pairs of dark cold eyes bore into him.

Finally Vittorio smiled, again the ever-gracious host. "Can I have anything else brought to you? More cappuccino? More brandy, perhaps?"

"No thank you, Don Vittorio. You've given me more than enough to digest for one night." He stood and signaled to Larry, who had cleaned every plate in front of him and had just finished his second *Zabaione*.

The young officer gulped one last swallow of milk, wiped his mouth and met McAvoy and Sal Merlino at the head of the staircase.

The maitre d' hurried over and handed Larry a Styrofoam container. "A little something to take home with you, Officer Parker." He winked and Larry responded with a smile.

With that, Sal Merlino escorted the two men down the steps of the winding stone staircase to their waiting Jeep Cherokee.

McAvoy entered The Plough & Whistle and received a warm hug from Stevie Henderson. Bill Brinkmire had filled her in on the events at St. Mary's and told her where the chief had gone.

"Thought maybe we'd have to drag the Hudson for your overweight carcass," she said, poking him in the stomach and trying, unsuccessfully, to hide with a joke the anxiety that she really felt.

He returned the hug, secretly grateful that she had been concerned for him. "Take more than a chateau full of bad guys to do me in," McAvoy replied, doing his best John Wayne impression.

He bent down and kissed her lightly on the tip of her upturned nose as he unclipped the holster from his left hip. She blushed and self-consciously looked around the pub to see if anyone had been watching. From McAvoy's customary table by the dart board, both Bill Brinkmire and John Desmond raised their beer mugs in a salute.

"Tell me all about it later," she said, giving him a squeeze and pulling away. She tucked the holster in her apron pocket, then retreated behind the bar to deposit it under the counter and pick up a drink order that her brother had just poured.

McAvoy waved a greeting to Porky and, as he walked over to the table, he debated with himself on how much he should divulge to Bill Brinkmire regarding his conversation with Vittorio Gianelli. *He's either trying very hard to sidetrack me from the correct trail or trying very hard to steer me onto it. And if Vittorio is right and Harvey DuMont was killed by an accomplice, that accomplice doesn't believe anyone knows about him. For now, I think I'd better keep it that way.*

"What more do you have for me, Chief," Bill asked, turning over a fresh sheet in his note pad. "You still think it was a mob hit?"

"I'm more certain now than ever," McAvoy said, taking the empty third mug from the tray on the table and filling it from the quarter-full pitcher of Hudson Lager. "How else can you explain Tony and Sal's presence at St. Mary's? But I still don't have one shred of hard evidence to back it up. The only thing we know for certain is what Cynthia told us, that Harvey killed the Gianelli brothers and stole the diamonds from them. Right now as far as the law is concerned, it's only conjecture that the Gianellis whacked Harvey. Hell, officially, the Gianellis are still denying that Johnny and Julie boosted the diamonds. And why not? Again, it's only conjecture. There's no solid evidence to support it even though everyone involved knows they did it."

Look deeper, Ed, John Desmond silently implored his friend, while maintaining an impassive expression on his face. *Look much deeper.*

"Well, I'll tread lightly on that angle, then," Bill said. "I've got what Cynthia said at the arraignment, my interviews with Doc Krider and Fr. Desmond, plus more of the facts regarding the Detroit thing from you. I'll just lay it all out and let the readers draw their own conclusions. By the way," he added, "I also talked with Harvey DuMont himself just after the necklace was found and I printed that first article. I can use *that*, too."

McAvoy's interest was piqued but he didn't want to let Bill see how much. He tried to sound just mildly curious. "Oh, yeah? What did you talk about?"

"Well, I didn't really get to do any of the talking. He called and cussed me up one side and down the other for identifying the location of the find. I thought he was just some old codger who was overprotective of his privacy but, now, I can understand why he was so upset. He was afraid the Gianellis would find him.... Looks like he was right."

"Looks like," McAvoy said, then thought, *Looks like his accomplice might have felt the same way.*

Bill pushed his chair back and stood. "Thanks for the info, guys. I appreciate your time. And remember," he shook his finger at McAvoy, "when the whole story can be told, it's mine first." The chief nodded his assent and Bill crossed over to the bar to settle his rather substantial tab with Stevie.

"If you hadn't come in when you did back there, what do you think would have happened?" John asked, running a finger around the rim of his mug while he watched the bubbles rise in the beer. "Tony Gianelli wouldn't really have shot me would he?"

"If I hadn't have come in, Sal Merlino would have rescued you," McAvoy assured him.

"You told Bill that you were more convinced than ever that the Gianellis were responsible for the DuMont murder," John said, trying to sound nonchalant and realizing that he was venturing out on some pretty thin theological ice by even broaching the subject. "What did you mean?"

"Actually, I lied to Bill," McAvoy said. He then told John of Vittorio Gianelli's and Sal Merlino's assertion that they were innocent of the crime and that they thought it had been committed by Harvey's Detroit accomplice.

"I'm going to talk to Cynthia again tomorrow to see if Harvey saw or spoke to any old friends shortly before his death. If those guys are right, though, and not just trying to sidetrack me, when Danny's dog uncovered that necklace, Harvey's partner-in-crime knew that the mob would get wind of it. He whacked Harvey in order to save himself from possible exposure."

What John Desmond said in response was, "Well, let me know what you find out, will you? I've got sort of a vested interest in this case."

"I know you can't tell me anything that Harvey said in his confession, John, so I won't even ask. But did he say anything before or after the confession? Anything at all?"

"Not a thing, Ed," John answered. "Not a single syllable. I got to him, pulled him up on the bank and the first words out of his mouth were, 'Bless me, Father, for I have sinned.' He made his confession and then died as I gave him absolution."

The two men sat in silence for a few moments, sipping their beers, then John asked, "You're not going to solve this one, are you?"

"Not if the Gianellis did it I'm not," McAvoy answered, then he brightened up a bit and added, "But if it *was* someone else?" He smiled, nodded his head, and clapped the priest on the shoulder. "I'll find him, John. Don't you worry about that. I'll find him."

He downed the last of his lager, heaved himself out of his chair and walked toward the door. As he stopped to retrieve his revolver, the chief patted Stevie on the rear and told her to give him a call at the station when she was through with work.

Chapter 9

A despondent John Desmond watched McAvoy leave The Plough & Whistle, then sighed, left his mug of beer unfinished and waved to Stevie and Porky as he left for his short drive back to St. Mary's.

Parking his car in front of the rectory, John went directly into the church to resume his prayers at the point at which they had been interrupted by Tony Gianelli. But although he tried, he couldn't concentrate and caught his mind persistently wandering. He finally gave up, turned out the sanctuary light, and headed back up the south transept.

As he crossed through the office into the rectory, John was almost magnetically drawn toward the telephone, but then his gaze came to rest on *The Oxford Dictionary of the Christian Church*, lying on the desk, still open to the page on the *Seal of Confession*.

John switched off the office light and decided to turn in for the night. He needn't have bothered for the little time as he actually ended up spending in his bed. Sleep wouldn't come. He couldn't switch off his brain or shift it to any other topic aside from the one that consumed him.

He paced from bedroom to office to kitchen to office to bedroom and back again, trailing a cloud of smoke from St.

Mark behind him. At one point, he actually had his hand on the telephone receiver.

Dressed in pajamas and a robe, John abandoned the pipe and padded into the church in his bare feet to try the prayer route again. He flipped through *The Book of Common Prayer* and read various seldom-used services in an attempt to distract himself from his thoughts. He had just finished *The Decalogue*—the litany of the Ten Commandments—when he suddenly smiled and looked at the white space at the bottom of the page.

In his mind, he saw printed there what he had always considered to be the eleventh commandment. *Thou shalt not horseshit thineself.* John nodded his head, smiled more broadly, and made the same response as he had after meditating on all the other commandments. *Lord, have mercy upon me, and incline my heart to keep this law.*

The gold Piaget on his wrist, another Christmas gift from Kate Winthrop, read six-thirty. Wednesday morning had snuck up on him. He closed the prayer book, went back into the rectory, showered, shaved, and packed a suitcase.

As he hung up the telephone, John's heart felt immeasurably lighter. The arrangements had been made. Neither the call to the Suffragan Bishop's office in New York City nor the one to upstate New York had resulted in any difficulties. Neither party had asked for an explanation.

He jotted a short note to Marsha Daniels, asking her to make sure that the guest bedroom and bath were presentable, and then wrote a much lengthier and more detailed note regarding church services and parish business. Marsha's note he placed in the empty wicker letter basket by the office doorway. The second note he folded, placed in an envelope, scrawled the name *Tess* on the outside, and placed it on the telephone.

After locking the front door to the rectory, John Desmond carried his suitcase out to the car and glanced skyward. The sun shone brightly. Only a few wispy clouds floated overhead—a beautiful day for a drive.

Thank you for this day, Dear Lord, and all that it may bring.

He tossed the suitcase into the back seat of the Cougar and headed over to The Poplars for his Wednesday staff meeting and visitation with the sick.

❦ ❦ ❦

Fortunately, all the guests at The Poplars were recovering nicely from their ailments and the visits went rather quickly. As John reached the reception area on his way out, accompanied by Kate Winthrop, the large clock on the wall read nine-fifty-three. At the main entrance, Kate and John said their good-byes.

Letting go of his arm and steadying herself with her scrimshawed-handled cane, Kate reached up with a gnarled hand and patted the priest's cheek. "I'll be praying for you, John, that you'll be able to come home soon."

"Thanks, Kate." He smiled, affectionately kissed the old woman on the forehead and walked out to the parking lot.

Kate watched as the Cougar increased speed down the winding private road and disappeared from sight. "And, although you couldn't tell me why you're going, I think I had better pray for Edward as well," she muttered as she turned from the door and hobbled back to her suite.

❦ ❦ ❦

An elderly man, dressed in a Cistercian habit, opened the door to Sacré Coeur Monastery in response to the clanging of a time-weathered iron bel that hung amid the vines on the outside wall. His age-creased face carried an exceptionally warm and expansive smile.

"Fr. John?" he asked, and without waiting for a reply he introduced himself. "I'm Fr. Paul. Come in, please come in."

John Desmond, suitcase in hand, entered the mammoth foyer and looked around self-consciously, admiring the paintings of religious scenes that hung there. "I'm sorry to impose upon you with such short notice," he began but was interrupted by the old priest.

"No, no, Father. There is no need to apologize nor to explain. We are here to serve. Come, your room is ready."

He chuckled and put his hand on John's shoulder, partly to guide him in the right direction and partly to assuage the younger man's apprehension. Just before passing out of the foyer through one of the three stone lancet arches, Fr. Paul stopped and picked up a sheet of paper from a marble-topped table.

"This is a map of the compound," he said, showing John the piece of paper on which all four levels of the main buildings were sketched as well as the grounds and the outbuildings. "You will want to keep this with you at all times. We've had guests who didn't turn up at meals for weeks." He winked in response to the anxious expression on John's face. "A joke, Father. A joke. You're surprised at that, hmm? You thought all we did was solemnly pray and make wine and jelly?" He chuckled again. "We joyously pray and make wine and jelly…and think up jokes."

The elderly monk pointed a finger at one of the outbuildings on the map that was joined to the refectory by a covered walkway. "This is the hospice. Your room is on the second floor—room 214." Turning the paper over, he continued. "And here are the times for chapel and meals."

The seven canonical hours were listed by name along with the times assigned for their start. Meal times were also listed as well as some general guidelines to be followed by the guests. Fr. Paul had briefly reviewed these rules with John during their early morning telephone conversation and since NO SMOKING headed the list, the meerschaum evangelists had remained behind in the rectory office.

"Pay special attention to meal times, Father," the monk cautioned with a twinkle in his eye. "The refectory is not a Burger King annex. You don't get it your way. You miss a meal and you go without." He gave a conspiratorial wink. "But the map does show the location of the kitchen, does it not?"

John snickered. Fr. Paul's relaxed manner had put him at ease.

Pointing to the archway, the monk became slightly more serious. "Now, Father, once we pass through that portal, there is no radio or television, no newspapers, no telephone calls, except for the one which we discussed earlier. Also, since we refrain from speaking, if you have any questions, you'd better ask them now."

"No, Fr. Paul," John replied. "I'm all set. Lead the way."

After being up with Stevie until three in the morning, McAvoy hadn't gotten into the office until about nine on Wednesday. He checked the night logs and then telephoned Cynthia DuMont, arranging to drive out to Big Indian Mountain in the early afternoon. Also, he asked her to think back to the time between the finding of the Isabela Pendant and Harvey's death to see if she could remember any telephone calls that her husband received from old friends or associates, in fact, from anyone at all. Cynthia promised that she would.

A ten o'clock meeting with his sister Colleen, the mayor, to keep her apprised of his progress with the case, had taken the better part of the next two hours. Colleen and the Village Council did not relish the thought that the term "mob hit" might be associated in print with their fair village of Peekamoose Heights. It played hell with tourism, they reasoned.

McAvoy reckoned that the city mothers—the majority of the councilpersons were women—certainly were not going to be overjoyed with Bill Brinkmire's article in this afternoon's edition of the *Ashokan Register*. Not saying anything about it, though, kept him out of the thankless and pointless position of either having to call Bill or argue with the mayor.

Asking the newspaper man, on behalf of the village, to kill the story would only result in Bill telling him to go perform an unnatural act with himself. Trying to convince the mayor of the importance of Harvey's accomplice, if one really existed, believing that a mob hit remained the focal point of the investigation would have taken up another two hours of his time.

McAvoy emerged from the Village Hall, just on the east side of the police station, and stepped off the curb to cross Irving Boulevard for lunch at The Plough & Whistle. As he did so, he observed a woman on the west side of the station, peering through the glass in the door of John Desmond's CPA office. From his vantage point a quarter block away, McAvoy pegged her to be in her late thirties.

She had short black hair, wore a gray pinstripe suit with a mandarin-collared white blouse, and high heels. The pleated skirt fell just at knee-level and McAvoy, being a trained investigator, noticed that she had great-looking legs. In fact as she bent over slightly at the waist, facing away from him and looking through the glass, those legs were not her only attribute that the chief admired. From her clothing, he assumed the woman to be one of John's CPA colleagues so he was quite unprepared for what he discovered when he walked over and spoke to her.

"May I help you, Miss?" he asked.

The woman turned toward him and he saw that she had an extremely pretty face to go along with the cute figure. He also discovered that what he had thought to be a mandarin collar was, in fact, a clerical collar.

McAvoy hurriedly tried to erase the previous impure thoughts from his mind. *Sorry, God,* he prayed silently.

"I'm not sure," she answered, showing him a full set of perfectly aligned white teeth. "I was supposed to pick up a key to the rectory from Fr. Desmond's secretary..." She looked at a piece of paper in her hand. "A Cindy Blake. But apparently she's already left for lunch."

McAvoy looked at his watch. "Yeah, she's got two dogs at home. She usually leaves at eleven-thirty to let them out. She's generally back by one, but, listen, ma'am, I've got a key to the rectory. I can let you in." He quickly answered the woman's unspoken look of cautiousness by introducing himself and pointing to the police station. "I'm Ed McAvoy, the Chief of Police."

"I'm Theresa Hitchcock," she replied, crossing over to him and extending her hand.

McAvoy made note of her firm grasp and that she maintained eye contact during the handshake. She had gray eyes like his own. Hers, however, seemed to penetrate his mind.

No delicate little flower, this one, he thought. What he said was, "I was just going to grab a bite to eat, myself. Why don't you join me and then I'll lead the way over to the rectory." He looked over at The Plough & Whistle, then back at Theresa Hitchcock and stammered, "It's a...it's a pub, but they serve...they serve real good food."

Theresa smiled again and patted him on the shoulder. "I'm an Episcopal Priest, Chief McAvoy, not a cloistered nun. Believe me, I *am* familiar with the inside of a bar. It'll be just fine."

As they walked across Irving Boulevard, McAvoy asked, "What is it you're going to be doing here, Ms. Hitchcock?"

"I'll just be filling in for the next few weeks while Fr. Desmond is away."

The chief stopped in the median of the boulevard. "Away? Away where...when?"

"I'm not sure where, but he left sometime this morning. I didn't have a chance to talk to him myself. I'm on the Suffragan Bishop's staff. She called early this morning and asked me to come up here and pinch hit for a few weeks."

"I just saw him last night," McAvoy said, trying to understand why his friend hadn't mentioned anything to him about leaving. "But we did have a few distractions to deal with. Probably just slipped his mind." It bothered McAvoy, though, that John would go off this way.

Inside The Plough & Whistle, the chief introduced Theresa to Stevie, Porky, and Danny, checked his revolver at the bar and led the lady priest to his customary table. "Lady priest" seemed to be a more correct terminology to McAvoy than "priestess." "Priestess" conjured up images of witchcraft and pagan sacrifices.

When Stevie came over to take their order, he asked, "Did John say anything to you last night about leaving for a couple of weeks?"

Stevie thought for a moment, remembering the priest waving to her as he exited the bar. "No. But he *did* look a bit preoccupied when he headed for home last night. I figured the events of the evening had taken their toll on him."

Theresa ordered a chef's salad and a glass of white wine. Stevie didn't even bother asking what McAvoy wanted. He was a creature of habit—ham and American cheese on whole wheat with lettuce, mayonnaise and mustard, and a large glass of milk.

After the barmaid left the table, McAvoy, not being able to shake "lady priest" and "priestess" from his mind, thought that he might as well get a clarification. "If you don't mind my asking, what are we supposed to call a lady priest? Certainly not 'Father.'"

Theresa laughed and when she did so, her nose crinkled up and her eyes sparkled. "What did you call John Desmond?" she asked in return.

"He was my friend," McAvoy replied. "I called him John, although sometimes, in a more formal setting, I called him Fr. Desmond."

"Well, how about if I be your friend, too. You can call me Theresa or Tess, and if you feel uncomfortable with either of those in a more formal setting, you can call me Ms. Hitchcock."

Theresa moved her head slightly closer to McAvoy's and lowered her voice somewhat. "When I filled in at Holy Cross in Kingston for four weeks earlier this year, I understand that they got to calling me Fr. Mother." She shook her finger at him in a mock warning. "Never to my face, though." She laughed again. "*Never* to my face."

Stevie brought their orders and since business was a little slow, she sat with them while they ate and she and McAvoy filled Theresa in on both the village and the parish.

When they arrived at St. Mary's, a light-green metallic Nissan Altima sat in the parking lot and all the windows in the rectory were wide open. The chief pulled his Jeep Cherokee in next to the Altima and Theresa parked her burgundy Mustang next to the Jeep. Instead of using his key, McAvoy rang the bell.

Marsha Daniels opened the door. "Come in, come in," she gushed.

After McAvoy made the introductions, Marsha directed Theresa toward the guest quarters. "You'll find your bedroom and bath down there, ma'am. I'll try to stay out of your way, but I got me a good half-hour left of cleaning up after Fr. Piglet."

As Theresa carried her suitcase down the hallway, the housekeeper vented on McAvoy. "You'd think he could give me a little notice, you know, instead of me turning up here to find a note." She reached into an apron pocket and pulled out a piece of paper which she waved in front of the chief's nose. "He's just lucky my regular Wednesday people are on vacation for two weeks. I won't need to do their place until next week just before they come back."

"You didn't know he was going away?"

"Lord, no. I usually come by in the late afternoon to tidy up, but like I said, my regular Wednesday people are away so I came by about eleven. I've been at it ever since. And the smell. He must have been smoking that infernal pipe of his all throughout the house, not just in the office like he's supposed to. I'll close the windows just before I leave. Maybe the air-freshener will have taken effect by then."

Theresa rejoined McAvoy in the foyer and Marsha started for the kitchen, shouting back over her shoulder. "And, ma'am, if you go by the name of Tess, there's a letter for you on the telephone in the office." With that, she disappeared around a corner.

McAvoy pointed Theresa toward the office door and the two of them went in. He noticed as he entered that Marsha Daniels had already wiped Tony Gianelli's blood off the doorjamb and wondered why the woman hadn't said anything about it. Marsha, though, had a reputation for not gossiping about her clients' business.

Theresa sat behind the desk and opened the envelope.

After a few moments, McAvoy asked, "Does he say where he's gone?"

She shook her head. "No. And, not only that, he isn't sure how long he'll be away."

She held out the letter to him. It contained information on the services to be conducted on which days and his hospital and prison visitation schedule. McAvoy noted that John had made his visit to The Poplars that morning before leaving. A list of the names and telephone numbers of vestry members and club and guild chairpersons was attached. The note indicated that John had not had a chance to notify any of them of his hastily-arranged trip.

"Well," Theresa said, "it looks like there's nothing more on the docket for today, so I might as well start making some phone calls and introduce myself."

"I'll leave you this," McAvoy said, removing a key from his key chain. "I'll get the spare from Cindy. Also, if you need any typing done or photocopying or anything like that while you're here, you can give that to Cindy, too."

As he set the key on the desk pad, McAvoy focused in on two things which triggered an alarm in his mind. First, he noticed that all four of John's meerschaum evangelists sat in their proper places next to the humidor in the pipe rack. *Must have been in a hurry. John didn't smoke much but he sure did enjoy that late evening pipe.*

In the back of his mind, he wondered if Tony Gianelli's visit the night before had had a greater effect on the priest than he had imagined. *Is he afraid? Is that why he left without telling anyone where he was going? So that Tony couldn't find him?*

The second item lay on the desk. *The Oxford Dictionary of the Christian Church* that John had forgotten to put back on the bookshelf was still open to the page containing the write-up on the *Seal of Confession*. As McAvoy scanned the page, a bad feeling crept over him. *He knows who did it. Harvey saw his assailant and told John as part of his confession. I was right after all. That greaseball came here last night to find out if Harvey had fingered him. But John can't say anything because of the Seal.*

"Earth to Ed, Earth to Ed." As Theresa waved a hand in front of his face, McAvoy realized that the woman had been speaking to him.

"I'm sorry, Tess. My mind is off on a case we're working. What were you saying?"

"The schedule says that on Thursdays John visits the Eastern New York Correctional Facility and the Ellenville

Community Hospital. Could you point me in the right direction?"

"I'll do better than that. Why don't you join me for dinner tonight at the pub? I'll have an area map for you and point out the various places you're apt to go. Also, you'll get a chance to meet some of your parishioners."

"Sounds good. What time?"

"Why don't you meet me there about seven?" She nodded her acceptance and he added, "And don't just order a salad. Porky is a world-class chef. If you don't try one of his specials, you'll hurt his feelings."

"You're on," she said with a laugh. "See you at seven."

McAvoy left Theresa to her phone calls. As he turned out of the rectory parking lot and drove the one block north to Irving Boulevard, thoughts of John Desmond consumed his mind. He paid no attention at all to a red Mazda Miata MX-5 that had been parked in the lot beside the Mountain Gap Repertory Theatre, a block further south.

No sooner had the chief turned right onto Irving, the MX-5 shot out of the theater parking lot, past St. Mary's and down to Irving where it, too, turned right. The driver of the Miata slowly drove the one block from Church Street to Vanderdonk Street, keeping an eye on McAvoy's Jeep Cherokee two blocks away. When McAvoy pulled the Jeep into the small parking lot in front of the police station, the driver of the Mazda eased his vehicle into the IGA parking lot. Finding a parking place between two pickup trucks that faced down Irving Boulevard toward the police station, he shut off the engine and waited.

❦ ❦ ❦

McAvoy picked up Lucille and drove over to Big Indian Mountain to keep his appointment with Cynthia DuMont. On the way, he told his sister-in-law about John Desmond's hasty vacation and about Theresa Hitchcock, but somehow

Lucille already knew everything. He also mentioned the four pipes in the rack and the *Dictionary* and his interpretation of their meaning.

"You may be right about him leaving because he's scared," Lucille croaked. "But I think you're wrong about the confession on two counts." McAvoy raised a solicitous eyebrow and she elaborated. "First of all, if DuMont were going to identify his killer, wouldn't he have done it first thing? He wouldn't have started his confession then said, 'Oh, by the way, Father, that greaseball Antonio Gianelli shot me.' Secondly, even if he had, that would have been a kind of aside and not really part of the confession itself. There's no way DuMont would have intended or assumed that that information would be kept secret under the Seal. He would have told John because he *wanted* his killer identified and brought to justice."

"You're right," McAvoy said. "And John would have told me. What do you suppose it means, then?"

"Maybe he had it out to show the Gianelli kid why he couldn't answer any questions about DuMont's confession."

McAvoy shrugged his shoulders, acknowledging the possibility.

❧ ❧ ❧

The initial enthusiasm Cynthia exhibited as she opened the door to McAvoy's knock diminished slightly upon seeing Lucille standing there next to the chief. Although the woman disguised her feelings well, Lucille imagined that she heard a catlike hiss emanate from Cynthia's aura. As they smiled and shook hands, Lucille couldn't help but check Cynthia's paw to see if her claws were extended.

Not immune from a trace of cattiness herself, Lucille gave the other woman the once-over as Cynthia led them into the living room. On her previous visit to the house, she had only seen Cynthia's long legs as the woman had performed her panther-pose for McAvoy in the black funeral dress. This time, the dress was absent, replaced by a black shorts-and-halter ensemble.

Nice mourning clothes, she thought.

Over coffee and the freshly baked brownies that seemed to be ever-present at the DuMont house, McAvoy asked Cynthia about the possibility that Harvey had had an accomplice in the Detroit robbery.

"He never said and I never asked," Cynthia replied. "I guess maybe I didn't *want* to know too much about it, Ed. Thought that the less I knew the less guilt I shared."

Lucille looked up from her note pad. "Who were his buddies back in Michigan?" Cynthia looked perplexed and Lucille continued. "Who did he fish with? Who did he hang out with?"

"Different guys," Cynthia answered, giving Lucille the names of a half dozen men that Harvey had fished with over the years. "And there was the poker game," she added. "They played once a month. Some of the same people that he fished with and"—she hesitated, trying to remember—"two other guys who didn't fish."

Lucille recorded those names as well.

"Were you able to remember if there were any phone calls?" McAvoy asked.

"Yes. There were two on that Thursday you took everyone fishing near town."

"Who from?"

"Well, actually there was only one. The first one wasn't really what you'd term a phone call. When Lenny drove me home after bringing you guys your lunch, the phone rang. I answered it and whoever it was hung up without saying anything. I thought it was just a wrong number."

McAvoy and Lucille traded looks with eyebrows slightly raised and a common thought. *If a woman answers, hang up?*

"What about the other call?" McAvoy asked.

"Later that evening while the four of us were eating dinner, the phone rang again. This time Harvey answered it. Matt and Lenny and I were talking so I didn't pay any attention to what Harvey said. He wasn't on very long and said it was someone trying to sell an alarm system. Those are the only calls I remember."

McAvoy finished his fourth brownie, washed it down with the remainder of his coffee and rose. "Well, thanks for the info. Make sure you let me know, though, if you think of anything else."

Cynthia accompanied him and Lucille to the door and as they stepped out on the porch, Lenny Damien and Matt Christiansen drove up in their white Ford Explorer.

Matt had reverted to his cover of *Field & Stream* look. Lenny was dressed in jeans and a madras shirt. The tails of the shirt were not tucked in and McAvoy noticed the bulge in back from his ever-present paperback book. Both men smiled and waved.

"Thought I'd spend a few hours down by the stream, if that's all right with you, Cyn," Matt said as they approached the house.

"You know you're always welcome, Matt," Cynthia assured him and they kissed each other affectionately on the cheek.

McAvoy introduced Lucille to the two men. As soon as Lucille opened her mouth, they both remembered her voice— Matt, from the call that he had made to McAvoy on the previous Thursday and Lenny, from his phone call after the funeral.

In response to Matt's query on how the investigation was progressing, the chief told him about exploring the angle of Harvey having an accomplice as well as continuing to pursue the mob-hit scenario. "Either of you aware of any old friends of Harvey's that turned up between the time Danny found the necklace and the day Harvey was killed?"

Lucille stood off to one side, continuing to take down in shorthand exactly what everyone said. Matt and Lenny looked at each other for a moment. Lenny rubbed his hand over his chin while Matt removed his tweed hat and ran his fingers through his white thinning hair, then both men shook their heads.

"Danny found the necklace on a Tuesday," Matt said. "On Wednesday, we fished here like always, just the two of us— and Lenny and Cynthia, of course. Thursday we were with you and Danny. Friday, Lenny drove me into Kingston to the orthopedist. Harv didn't see anyone else during the time *we* were with him." He looked at Lenny for verification.

"Nobody, Chief," Lenny confirmed.

"Did he mention anyone he had seen recently or did he say anything that, thinking back on it now, might seem out of the ordinary?"

"Nothing at all," Matt replied.

Lenny glanced over at him. "That's not altogether true, Uncle Matt."

All eyes focused in on the young man.

"What are you talking about?" Matt asked.

"Well, it may not mean much of anything, but remember just before we left here Thursday night when you asked Harvey about fishing in the afternoon on Friday? Because of your appointment in the morning?"

Matt nodded. "He said he'd rather fish in the morning and that by the time I'd finished up in Kingston, he'd have caught his limit and gone home. So?"

"I just don't recall Harvey ever fishing alone before, that's all," Lenny said. "On other days when you've had doctor appointments, he's waited for you to get back and when you were in the hospital for tests during those three days back in May? The only day he fished was the day Danny came over. Remember, he told us that?"

"That's right," Cynthia said. "He puttered around in the garden those two days and complained like an old grumble bug."

"Any indication that he was meeting anyone else?" McAvoy asked.

Cynthia, Lenny and Matt shook their heads in unison.

"It may mean nothing at all, Chief," Lenny said. "But I thought I'd toss it out for what it's worth."

"No, you did right, Lenny," McAvoy said. "No matter how insignificant something might seem, tell me. I'll be the judge of whether it's worth anything or not."

Lenny nodded and walked back to the Explorer to unload the camp stools and his uncle's fishing gear.

Remembering the phone calls that Cynthia had told him about, McAvoy said, "Matt, Cynthia mentioned a telephone call that Harvey took during dinner last Thursday night. By any chance did you overhear anything that was said?"

Matt thought for a moment. "I remember the call, but Cyn and Lenny and I were talking so I didn't pay any attention to what Harvey said. He wasn't on very long and said it was someone trying to sell an alarm system."

As McAvoy turned to go, Matt stopped him. "Because we were tied up this past Tuesday," he said, referring to Cynthia's arraignment, "Danny and I didn't get to dedicate that catch to Harv's memory like you and I talked about at the cemetery. Convince him to come out tomorrow, Mac. It'll be good for both of us."

McAvoy promised that he would try and he and Lucille said their good-byes and headed down the driveway toward the Cherokee. As they reached the car, Lenny had just finished closing up the back of the Explorer. McAvoy asked him about the phone call as well.

"Yeah, I remember that," he answered. "But Uncle Matt and Cynthia and I were talking so I didn't pay any attention to what Harvey said. He wasn't on very long and said it was someone trying to sell an alarm system." He shrugged his shoulders and told McAvoy that he wished he could be more help.

The chief thanked Lenny for his time and he and Lucille headed back toward Peekamoose Heights. As he made the turn from Maben Hollow Road out onto County Road #47, McAvoy said, "Nobody saw anything, nobody heard anything, and nobody knows anything. You got any thoughts?"

Lucille gave a derisive snort through her nose. "The widow DuMont would have preferred that you had shown up alone. Watch yourself with that one, Ed." She gave him a sidelong glance.

"She's a bit of a flirt, but that's all it is."

"I know what it's like to have a husband die," she reminded him. "It's a lonely feeling and people deal with those feelings in different ways. Black shorts and a black halter are not the usual mourning clothes to be greeting gentlemen guests in. Just be careful."

He reached over, took Lucille's hand and gave it a squeeze.

So engrossed in their own conversation were Ed and Lucille McAvoy, neither noticed a red Mazda Miata MX-5 that had followed them out of Maben Hollow Road and now trailed the Jeep Cherokee at a comfortable distance of about a quarter mile.

By the time McAvoy and Lucille returned to the police station, it was close to five o'clock. Jim Culpepper and Larry Parker had already started their watch and a grateful Mickey Campbell had gone home. Don Ralston, the other officer assigned to the day watch had been off sick and, since Lucille had been at the DuMont home with McAvoy, Mickey had had to ride the desk most of the afternoon.

Now that the afternoon watch was underway, Jim patrolled the village in one of the police vehicles while Larry sat at the desk, taking care of paperwork and manning the switchboard. The young officer looked up with relief as McAvoy and Lucille entered, quickly rose and picked up his trooper's hat. He, as indeed all the officers, liked being out on patrol much better than sitting in the office.

"Sergeant Bassett wants you to call him," he told McAvoy. "Other than that, nothing much is happening. I told Mrs. Bigelow that as soon as you got back, I'd take a run out to her place."

Lucille snickered and McAvoy gave him a "Now what?" look.

Larry shrugged his shoulders and explained. "She claims there's a dwarf or a troll prowling around in the woods beside her house."

"What do you plan on doing about it?" McAvoy asked as he crossed into his office.

"Go over there, wander around the woods and fire a few shots into the ground, tell her I scared it away and that it won't be back, eat my cookies, drink my milk, and then come back here."

"Don't make a career out of it," McAvoy said and sat down at his desk to call the sheriff's office.

Larry touched the brim of his trooper's hat with a little two-fingered salute and left for his mission of mercy.

Actually, it was more a mission of pity. Ginny Bigelow had been a widow almost as long as anyone could remember. While still bodily strong, her mind tended to stray a bit from time to time—not enough to cause her to be a menace to herself or anyone else, but just enough to label her as an eccentric. She periodically imagined that prowlers or dwarfs or trolls or even, on one occasion, a goblin roamed the woods behind her house on the slope of Slide Mountain.

The police responded to these calls as promptly as they could and always treated the lonely old woman with respect, checking out the area as if a legitimate threat actually existed.

They usually managed to convince her that they had dealt with the problem, although sometimes it took two or three visits. In addition to giving the officers her heartfelt gratitude, Mrs. Bigelow invariably rewarded them with freshly-baked chocolate chip cookies and a glass of milk.

Martin Bassett had called to let McAvoy know about two items. First, the sheriff wanted to have a DuMont-case progress meeting with everyone concerned on Thursday morning. Secondly, and the reason for the meeting, Assistant District Attorney Ledbetter had called to report a bit of a snag with Cynthia DuMont's extradition—not so much a snag, actually, as an unusual development.

The Wayne County Michigan DA wasn't so sure that he wanted to bother with the expense of an extradition and trial. The only evidence they had that Harvey DuMont murdered the Gianellis was Cynthia's testimony that Harvey had done it for the diamonds. No concrete proof existed. The Gianellis, of course, would continue to deny that Julio and Giovanni were responsible for the jewel heist or that they *had* any diamonds. Indeed, no hard evidence had ever been uncovered to prove otherwise. Harvey was dead and Cynthia was the only witness against herself. Her attorney, no doubt, would plea-bargain the charge down from aiding-and-abetting to obstruction-of-justice and Cynthia would, at the very most, receive a suspended sentence.

In short, Wayne County had enough on it's plate and too little money as it was to waste its time with the likes of a Cynthia DuMont. The Wayne County DA had summed it up succinctly. "If Mrs. DuMont agrees to return the Isabela Pendant and what loose diamonds remain, and as long as she hasn't broken any laws for which Ulster County wants to prosecute, cut her loose. If the diamond wholesaler wants to go after her in a civil suit for retribution, that's up to him."

McAvoy said that he would pass the word and agreed to be at the meeting at eleven the next morning, then he hung up and made two other calls. Cynthia DuMont was happy and relieved and, yes, she would gladly turn over the jewels. Jerry Gardner, still at work in Detroit even though it was now well past five o'clock, was neither happy nor relieved but, yes, he would follow up on the accomplice theory. McAvoy had Lucille read Jerry the names of Harvey's old cronies that Cynthia had given them earlier.

"This may well turn out to be a waste of time," McAvoy said, "but see if any of them are living beyond their visible means or if they took a recent trip out this way."

"I'll see if I can flush anything out, Mac, but the smart money on this one says the answer is up there at Garibaldi House. Talk to you later."

McAvoy recradled the phone and walked out of his cubicle to where Lucille sat deciphering her notes. "I'm going home to clean up a bit. Care to join me for dinner at The Plough? Theresa Hitchcock will be there and you can talk with her directly instead of having to wait for any more gossip to filter through."

Lucille gave him a middle-finger salute without looking up from her notes. Her penchant for gossip was no secret in Peekamoose Heights. Somehow, she knew every single detail, no matter how trivial, about everyone's business dealings and personal life.

During their drive out to Cynthia's that afternoon, McAvoy had thought to blind-side Lucille with the news about John Desmond's sudden departure and Theresa Hitchcock's arrival. He had been surprised to find out that she already knew about it. In the short time that it had taken for him to drive over to St. Mary's with Theresa and return to the office for his sister-in-law, Lucille's mysterious sources had provided her with all the available gossip about the lady priest.

"I'm having dinner at Bev's tonight," she croaked. "I'll wait here until Larry or Jim return before I leave. But I plan on coming back later to transcribe these notes so you'll have them for your meeting tomorrow. Maybe I'll drop over for a drink, if you're still there."

"Do that," McAvoy said and exited the station.

The Bev whom Lucille mentioned was Beverly White, an English teacher at Onteora Junior and Senior High School in Boiceville and the managing director of Mountain Gap Repertory Theatre. The friendship between Lucille and Bev went back to kindergarten and had been maintained throughout the decades. Lucille's husband Dave, Ed's brother, had died of a heart attack a few years ago while Bev's husband Mitch had been given his walking papers within months of the honeymoon many, many years ago. With both women being alone, their friendship now grew even stronger.

The Plough & Whistle had begun to wind down from one of the busiest nights in everyone's recent memory. Had Porky Jarvis known that the presence of Theresa Hitchcock would have brought in so many customers, he would have laid in some extra help. As it was, he, Stevie, and Danny had been kept hopping all evening.

Theresa had been the belle of the ball, having abandoned her high heels, Arthur Andersen suit, and clerical collar in favor of tassel loafers, Dress Stewart-plaid slacks, and a white jewel-neck blouse. She captivated everyone she met—men and women alike. Women liked her because she seemed so genuine and did not talk down to them. Men appreciated her easygoing manner and the fact that if she were a closet man-hater, as most had suspected before they met her, she kept those feelings well disguised and didn't come across like a recruiter for NOW.

The welcoming reception that the St. Mary's vestry had planned for Sunday afternoon would be redundant. Almost everyone who might attend that sort of shindig had already made an appearance at the pub during the course of the evening. Even villagers who were not parishioners of St. Mary's stopped by her table to say hello and introduce themselves. Bill and Diane Donovan, who McAvoy knew attended Calvary Baptist on State Road #28A in West Shokan, came over to let Theresa know that if she needed her car serviced while in town, Donovan's Shell Station would be happy to take care of it.

The dinner crowd gradually thinned out and was replaced by the smaller drinking-and-sitting-around crowd. Just about the time the Mets-Dodgers game started out in Los Angeles and everyone's attention shifted to the big screen TV, Theresa thanked McAvoy, Porky, Stevie, and the rest of the villagers for their hospitality. Endearing herself to the TV crowd, she sent pitchers of St. James Pale Ale to every table on her way out.

McAvoy was sure that the attendance for Sunday services at St. Mary's would not decline due to John Desmond's absence.

🐟 🐟 🐟

McAvoy sat alone at his table by the dart board, two manila folders on top of the blue-and-white checkered tablecloth, a yellow legal pad in front of him, and his reading glasses resting on the bridge of his nose. He had walked over to the office for the material after Theresa had left and now reread all the notes on the Harvey DuMont case, all except the ones Lucille had not yet transcribed. His sister-in-law had not made an appearance at the pub and, when he had gone over to the office, Larry said she hadn't been back there, either.

Must be some juicier gossip over at Bev's, McAvoy thought.

He had just started to draw a box diagram on the pad. A single box at the top of the paper he labeled MURDERER. A branch coming down from that box split and fed two more boxes. These were labeled ACCOMPLICE and THE GIANELLIS, respectively. A line coming down from THE GIANELLIS box split into three other boxes—TONY, SAL, and HIT-MAN. McAvoy exed-out the SAL box. Somehow he could not picture Sal Merlino killing anyone himself.

Porky stopped by and looked over the chief's shoulder? "Care for a box of crayons?"

"Maybe that would help," McAvoy answered with a laugh. "I'm just trying to do as you suggested and find the right ingredients for my recipe."

"Appears as if you need some additional ingredients, considering the sparsity of information on that sheet of paper." He patted McAvoy on the shoulder and walked away.

More ingredients, McAvoy thought. *Yeah, Porky, that's all I need. I don't even know what to do with the ones I've got now.*

Then Sal Merlino's voice from the night before echoed in his mind. *Play along with me. Without us for bogeymen, where would you usually start in an investigation of this type?*

He took a critical look at his sketch, then added five more boxes to the same level as ACCOMPLICE and HIT-MAN. These he labeled ENEMY, WIFE, LOVER, LOVER'S HUSBAND, and WIFE'S LOVER.

Danny stopped by the table and asked, "Ed, would you please empty that pitcher for me?"

Being underage, the boy could clear away plates and glasses and deliver food but he could not handle alcoholic beverages. Friend or no friend, he was not about to violate the law in front of the chief of police. His Uncle Roz would pitch a fit. McAvoy absently poured the remainder of the Hudson Lager from the pitcher into his mug as he continued to study his diagram.

"Thanks," Danny said and picked up the pitcher.

Suddenly, McAvoy remembered his conversation with Matt Christiansen. "Sit down for a minute," he said, pulling out the chair next to him and taking off his glasses.

Danny looked around the room and judged everything to be taken care of for the time being. "What's up?" he asked as he hopped onto the chair.

McAvoy told Danny about Matt's request that the two of them have a little private wake and catch the creel limit in memory of Harvey. At first the youngster remained silent, running his finger around his tray in little circles. Finally he looked up, smiled and said softly, "Yeah....Mr. DuMont would like that. He'd like that a lot. Besides," he said, giving a small laugh, "some of the customers have been asking Uncle Roz about trout." Then looking down at the sketch on the table, he asked, "What's that?"

"Just a list of possibilities. You know on TV where the cops write all their clues on the blackboard?" The boy nodded. "Well, this is sort of like my blackboard."

Danny pointed to the box labeled WIFE and a look of panic entered his blue eyes. "You don't think Mrs. DuMont had anything to do with it?"

Stevie had joined them and she raised a questioning eyebrow at McAvoy.

"Probably not," he said. "But a good cop has to cover every angle. Suppose you tell me about Mrs. DuMont."

Stevie had taken the chair next to Danny but she didn't say anything.

"Okay," Danny agreed. "What do you want to know?"

"First of all, do you know what it means to flirt?"

"Jeez, Ed, I'm fourteen," Danny answered, a bit put out that the chief seemed to think of him as a little kid. "Of course I know what flirting is. It's what Mom does with the customers."

"I beg your pardon, young man!" Stevie came about three inches off her chair.

"Well, you *do*, Mom," he insisted, surprised that she had taken offense at something he considered to be common knowledge.

"I most certainly do *not!*"

Danny gave her a patronizing look then turned to McAvoy. "Doesn't she flirt?"

McAvoy shrugged his shoulders at Stevie and nodded in the affirmative.

"See, I was right," Danny said to his mother. "You *do.*"

Before Stevie could turn his quest for information into an argument, McAvoy jumped in. "What about Mrs. DuMont?" he asked. "Does she flirt?"

Danny thought for only about a half a second. "Yeah," he answered with a snort that said "You bet she does." "Big time."

"You spent a lot of time out there, Danny, so you probably know those people better than anyone else. Is there any difference between the way Cynthia DuMont flirts and the way your mother does it?"

This time he took a few seconds longer to consider the question. "Mom's all show and no go," Danny said finally. "It's just a game with her and all the customers know it."

Stevie patted him on the hand and he continued. "I'm not so sure about it being 'no go' with Mrs. DuMont, if you know what I mean."

"Anything that you actually *saw?*"

"Naw, just what I felt. You know? It's definitely different from the way Mom does it. But," he added, "she would never do anything to hurt Mr. DuMont. I'm positive of that."

"I'm sure you're right, Danny," McAvoy said and the boy's anxiety level dropped, but only for a second.

Porky came storming in through the back door after having taken out a load of trash. There were deep furrows in his bald head as he approached Danny. "Who took the trash out last?" he bellowed, standing there rocking on his heels with his hands folded behind his back. "Hmm?"

It was a rhetorical question and Danny knew why it was being asked. Sandy had gotten into the trash can *again* and had strewn garbage all over the back yard. He shot out of his chair as if fired from a cannon and raced for the back door.

Porky looked down at Stevie and verbally took the remainder of his wrath out on her. "How many times do I have to tell him to make sure the lids are on tightly? Hmm? How many times? I don't blame the dog, Stephanie." He always called her "Stephanie" when he was angry. "If I've said it once I've said it a hundred times. If the animal can smell it, she'll dig into it. That's what bloody animals do, for God's sake." He threw his arms into the air in frustration and waddled back behind the bar.

As soon as Porky moved out of earshot, Stevie let out a snicker that she had been suppressing and winked at McAvoy. "He's so cute when he gets mad." Then she picked up Danny's tray and the empty pitcher and went back to work.

McAvoy put on his glasses and concentrated again on his sketch. He erased and rearranged the second tier of boxes so that ACCOMPLICE and GIANELLIS were together on the left-hand side of the paper and the other five were together on the right. With the diagram redrawn in this manner, the importance, or lack of importance, of the Isabela Pendant became obvious. If Harvey DuMont had been killed by an enemy, his wife, his lover, his wife's lover, or his lover's husband, the Isabela Pendant didn't enter into the equation at all.

The door to the pub opened and Lucille poked her head in. Seeing McAvoy, she crossed to his table, signaling Stevie for a fresh pitcher of beer. In her hand she carried a manila folder.

McAvoy looked up from his notes. "You missed her," he said, referring to Theresa Hitchcock.

"Dress Stewart-plaid slacks, white blouse, loafers, charmed the socks off of everyone, and even bought a round of drinks."

"How do you *do* that?" he asked.

She shrugged her shoulders, pulled out the chair next to the chief, sat down and tossed the manila folder in front of him. "If she carried an umbrella and could sing 'Chim Chim Cher-ee,' I'd swear Mary Poppins had come to town." McAvoy laughed and directed his attention to the folder. "The notes from today?"

She reached over and took his mug of beer. "Do you believe that when I take notes for you that I accurately recount what people say?" She took a swig of the lager.

"It's verbatim. You're as *good* as a tape recorder," he answered, then a puzzled expression came over his face. "Why?"

"Take a look at Cynthia DuMont's answer to your question about the telephone call that her husband took the night before he was killed. Page five. It's highlighted."

McAvoy opened the folder. Lucille had neatly typed the notes from his interview with Cynthia DuMont. On page five, she had highlighted one of his questions in pink. The answer had been highlighted in yellow. It read:

McAVOY: What about the other call?

CYNTHIA: Later that evening while the four of us ate dinner, the phone rang again. This time Harvey answered it. Matt and Lenny and I were talking so I didn't pay any attention to what Harvey said. He wasn't on very long and said it was someone trying to sell an alarm system. Those are the only calls I remember.

"Okay," McAvoy said. "That's how I remember it."

Stevie had brought a fresh pitcher and Lucille abandoned McAvoy's mug with the lukewarm beer, pouring two new mugs from the pitcher. "Page eight," she said. "Same question to Matt Christiansen."

McAvoy turned three pages while Lucille sipped her beer. Another section was highlighted.

McAVOY: Matt, Cynthia mentioned a telephone call that Harvey took during dinner last Thursday night. By any chance did you overhear anything that was said?

MATT: I remember the call, but Cyn and Lenny and I were talking so I didn't pay any attention to what Harvey said. He wasn't on very long and said it was someone trying to sell an alarm system.

The hair on the back of McAvoy's neck prickled. He flipped back to page five, reread the first answer, turned again to Matt's answer then looked over the top of his glasses at Lucille.

"Page nine," she said and took another sip.

He turned the pages and read the third highlighted section.

McAVOY: Do you remember a phone call that Harvey took during dinner the night before he was killed?

LENNY: Yeah, I remember that. But Uncle Matt and Cynthia and I were talking so I didn't pay any attention to what Harvey said. He wasn't on very long and said it was someone trying to sell an alarm system.

The chief closed the folder, removed his glasses and rubbed his eyes with his knuckles.

"You should be so lucky with the next play you direct at Mountain Gap Rep," Lucille rasped, sliding the second mug of beer across the table to him, "to have three people who can memorize lines so well."

McAvoy set his glasses on the tablecloth and picked up the mug. After a long drink of the lager he sighed, set the mug down and said, "Well, now."

"Indeed," Lucille replied with a nod. "Have we uncovered DuMont's accomplice?"

"I doubt it. After all, it was Matt who told Danny to report the finding of the pendant to me. Also, it was Matt who had

Lenny call me after the funeral to tell me that Cynthia was confessing that Harvey murdered the Gianellis. We may, though, have uncovered something else." He slid the pad across the table to Lucille and pointed at the box labeled WIFE'S LOVER.

"Matt?!" she croaked. "He couldn't have killed DuMont. He wouldn't have been able to walk that far."

"But Lenny could have. They only have each other for alibis."

"Then how does the dog finding that pendant figure into it?"

Just then Danny entered from the back door and crossed to the bar. "Sorry, Uncle Roz," he said.

Porky reached over, tousled the boy's hair and smiled. "All cleaned up?"

"Yes, sir."

As he watched the two of them, McAvoy remembered Porky's tirade of a few minutes prior to Lucille's arrival. *If the animal can smell it, she'll dig into it. That's what bloody animals do, for God's sake.* "Maybe the dog was *supposed* to find the pendant," he said. "To throw the blame for Harvey's death onto the Gianellis."

"Then why not just sit back and wait for the Gianellis to do the job *for* them? You said yourself that Don Vittorio admitted that that's what they intended to do."

And suddenly it began to come together for him. "Because even as rash as Tony Gianelli is, he would have first forced Harvey to give him the name of the accomplice. And he would have discovered in no time at all that Harvey had no accomplice because Harvey didn't commit the Detroit murders and steal those diamonds."

"Then Cynthia lied."

"Yes. Cynthia lied." He tapped the legal pad where the box WIFE'S LOVER was drawn. "To protect her lover"—he moved his hand so that his finger pointed to the ACCOMPLICE box—"a lover, who along with his nephew murdered the Gianellis and stole the diamonds."

"Can we prove it?"

"Not yet, but now that we suspect the truth, we can go about *finding* the proof."

They raised their mugs and toasted each other.

Chapter 10

The same cast of characters was present at the Thursday morning meeting as had attended the previous Saturday afternoon—the Ulster County Sheriff, Deputy Sergeant Martin Bassett, Deputy Sergeant Stanley Jurocik from the forensics department, and Ed McAvoy. After listening intently to McAvoy's suppositions for about twenty minutes, the sheriff stopped the meeting and called the DA's office. A half hour later, McAvoy went through his entire analysis again, this time with Assistant District Attorney Frank Ledbetter present.

ADA Francis Xavier Ledbetter was a rising star in the Ulster County DA's office. Young, tall, handsome, articulate, bright, and very ambitious, Frank had higher political aspirations and, for that reason, as sharp a prosecutor as he was, he also tended to be very cautious. Rarely did he take a case to trial when the odds of obtaining a conviction were not at least a few percentage points in his favor. Conviction rates meant a great deal to the future DA/Mayor/Congressman/Who-knows-what-else.

When McAvoy finished, Frank Ledbetter stood, crossed over to the window and looked out at the parking lot. "Great story, Mac. You had me captivated. Is this one for the brothers Grimm or do you have any evidence to go along with it?"

"No hard evidence, Frank, but surely there's enough circumstantial evidence to—"

"To get me laughed out of court," Frank interrupted. "Give me one piece...just one piece of factual evidence that points to Mrs. DuMont, Christiansen, or Damien and we'll talk further. Right now all you have is a cop's hunch." He waved off the protests from the four policemen in the room. "Yes, I know, I know, people, sometimes those hunches pay off, but if I went to court on every cop's hunch that's been brought to me, I'd have the worst conviction record in the state."

"But I know I'm right about this one," McAvoy protested.

"I'm sure you *are* right, Mac. And as soon as you bring me some evidence to back it up, I'll ask for an indictment." He headed toward the door.

"Can we get a search warrant or a phone tap?" the sheriff asked.

"Not with what you've got now," Frank replied.

Stanley Jurocik asked a question. Up until this time, he had been merely a spectator, invited to the meeting simply because he had done the crime scene analysis on both the woods where the diamond was found and the creek bed where Harvey DuMont was killed. No one expected anything from him until any actual evidence was uncovered.

"What if I can come up with proof in the lab that the pouch was treated with something that the kid's dog would smell so that it would dig up the diamond?"

Frank Ledbetter pulled on his nose with the thumb and forefinger of his left hand as he thought. "Stosh, you prove that the pouch was doctored with something that would not normally be associated with that type of pouch and I'll get you the search warrant *and* the phone tap." He opened the door and strode out of the conference room.

The sheriff motioned to Jurocik. "Pick up the pouch from Dunlavy's and let me know when you've got something. Until then, gentlemen, let's all keep thinking about this."

As the three men left, the sheriff returned to his office, reached into the desk drawer for a plastic bottle of Maalox and popped four of the lemon-creme antacid tablets into his mouth.

McAvoy hardly needed the sheriff to tell him to keep thinking about the case. Unlike the Ulster County Sheriff's Department with a backlog of cases, Peekamoose Heights had only one active case at the moment, aside from Mrs. Bigelow's troll. And case number PMH-247-38, the Harvey DuMont murder, consumed him. He could think of nothing else.

On the drive back from Kingston, the chief mentally sifted though his notes again—notes that were now committed to memory. So great was his concentration that he took no notice at all of the red Mazda Miata MX-5 that followed along about a quarter mile behind.

It had been extremely difficult for McAvoy not to tell Danny Henderson to forget about the fishing date with Matt Christiansen. After promising to arrange it, though, he couldn't risk that Danny's absence would alert Matt that something was amiss. He did, however, in an offhand way, he hoped, prevent the youngster from saying anything that might tip his hand.

The night before, as Danny came by the table on his way to the kitchen with a load of dirty dishes, McAvoy had motioned to the diagrams on the legal pad. "I'd appreciate it if you wouldn't mention this to Cynthia, Matt, or Lenny tomorrow. Even though you and I know it's just police procedure that I consider all the angles, they might be a little offended."

"Mention what, Ed?" the boy replied with a wink. "I don't see anything." He then looked at Lucille. "Do you see anything, Lucille?"

"Nope," she croaked in response. "Not a thing."

Danny went about his chores and McAvoy and Lucille finished their beers in silence.

🐟 🐟 🐟

While waiting to hear from the forensics department, McAvoy placed a few phone calls. The first one was to Martin Bassett back in Kingston to ask him to have someone check with Matt Christiansen's orthopedic surgeon to see if Matt and Lenny indeed were there at the time of Harvey DuMont's death. The second call was to Jerry Gardner in Detroit.

"I haven't gotten around to it yet," the detective lieutenant said upon hearing McAvoy's voice, not giving the chief a chance to say what he had called for. "You think I got nothing to do but run down information for you. Jeez, Mac, you just gave me the fucking names yesterday, for Christ's sake."

"Take it easy, Jerry, or they'll be pensioning you off for hypertension. I called to do you a favor."

"Oh, yeah?" Lieutenant Gardner sounded skeptical.

"Yeah. Forget those eight names that Lucille gave you yesterday. Run these two, instead." He gave Jerry the names of Matt Christiansen and Lenny Damien. "Matt was an investment broker of some sort and I don't know what Lenny did."

Even though he grumbled, the lieutenant acknowledged an eight-for-two swap to be a good deal and promised that he'd try to come up with something soon.

🐟 🐟 🐟

McAvoy had just returned from lunch at The Plough & Whistle and sat at his desk resifting the information for the umpteenth time. He had been relieved to see Danny Henderson at the pub. The boy had gotten back from fishing with a full creel of trout and Porky had already entered Baked Stuffed Trout Almondine on the blackboard as the CATCH OF THE DAY.

In response to his question about Matt Christiansen, Danny had told him that both Matt and Lenny had gone home as he was leaving Cynthia's.

Lucille's buzz-saw of a voice filled the station. As usual, she hadn't bothered with the intercom. "Martin on line one."

McAvoy picked up the receiver. "Yeah, Martin. What's up?"

"Jurocik called a while ago. He ran some sort of gas chromatography test on that pouch and said it's loaded with fatty acids."

"Fatty acids?"

"Yeah. Bacon or sausage grease, he thinks. Something on that order."

"Isn't that nice?" McAvoy couldn't help but smirk a little. "Do we have the search warrant and phone tap?"

"Only for Cynthia DuMont's house and the DuMonts' two cars. Not for Christiansen or Damien."

"What?"

"Frank tried, Chief. Judge Elliott said that since Cynthia has already admitted that Harvey had the pendant and since it had been dug up on the DuMont property, he could go along with the warrants for her but not for Christiansen and Damien. He said that we have no evidence tying them to anything."

"Shit!"

"Yeah. That's what the boss and I said when Frank told us."

"But it's Matt and Lenny's house and car I want to search."

"We know, Chief. We'll just have to come up with something else. How do you want to handle the Cynthia DuMont search?"

McAvoy thought for a moment. "You got any mug shots of known mob hit-men over there?"

"No. But you can bet your ass Greene County has. Why?"

"Suppose you come out here and drive Cynthia, Matt, and Lenny over to Catskill to look at those photos. Play up the mob-hit angle as if that's all we're considering and ask them to see if they recognize seeing any of the hit-men around. Meanwhile, your people can tap the phone and I'll have a look around the house and in Cynthia's cars. Okay?"

"Okay. When do you want it done?"

"As soon as possible and, Martin, you call them instead of me. Make it sound real official and important. And, whatever you have to do, make sure you pick them up at their separate homes and drop them off again. I don't want them to be alone with each other even for a minute. We have to force them into using the telephone."

"I'll call you back as soon as it's arranged."

McAvoy recradled the receiver and sat there at his desk, thinking about what his next move should be.

Lucille poked her head into his office and her voice abraded his thoughts. "What's the word?"

He filled her in on the plan. "As soon as Martin picks up Cynthia, I'll go over there and poke around. Legally, I need to have one other person with me while I search. Care to come along?"

"Yeah," she croaked. "I'd love to get a look at that wardrobe of hers."

❧ ❧ ❧

When McAvoy and Lucille made the turn off of County Road #47 onto Maben Hollow Road, they spotted a Bell Atlantic van parked next to a green switching box that serviced all the homes in the immediate area. One phone company serviceman had his head and arms poked inside the box while another stood and watched.

Must be union, McAvoy thought, but as they neared the van, he recognized the idle workman as Bill Layman, an Ulster

County Sheriff's deputy from the Phoenicia post. He pulled the Jeep up behind the van and the deputy came over.

"How long?" McAvoy asked.

"About ten more minutes," Bill replied. "We'll be monitoring it from a vacant store over in Oliverea." He handed the chief a slip of paper with a phone number scrawled on it. "Here's a number that you can reach us at if you need to."

McAvoy thanked him and continued on to Cynthia DuMont's home.

The search of the DuMont house and the two vehicles turned up nothing at all—no sawed-off shotgun, smoking or otherwise. But, then, McAvoy hadn't really expected it to.

Lucille seemed intrigued with Cynthia's wardrobe. "Do you realize that this woman has eight different shorts-and-halter ensembles?" she croaked as they searched the master bedroom. "And damn near everything else she owns is low cut? She sure is proud of those boobs, isn't she?"

McAvoy laughed in response.

As they left the bedroom and Lucille finished her detailed description of the room, she said, "Well, nothing hidden in with her undies, which, by the way, come from the *Victoria's Secret* catalogue, nor in the shoe boxes, eighteen in all, nor in among her husband's stuff either."

They had saved the desk for last and had just finished with it, making sure they returned everything to its proper place. Unfortunately, nothing incriminating, like love letters from Matt Christiansen, had been found lying around. Among the papers, bills mostly, was the log sheet from Wagner Brothers Mortuary, showing who sent flowers to Harvey's funeral, and a box of lemon-yellow note cards embossed with a large script letter *C*. Each card had a plain lemon-yellow envelope. Lucille sat on the desk chair and completed her list.

"Let's hope she trades information with Matt on the phone tonight and something slips out," McAvoy said, glancing over the living room for a third time.

"What if he just comes over here after Martin drops him off and doesn't use the phone?"

"Got it covered. I'll be waiting to take her to dinner at The Plough. Sort of a thank-you gesture for her being so helpful. By the time I drive her back here, believe me, it'll be very late. He'll *have* to call her. Either that or she'll call to fill *him* in."

Everything had gone as planned. Matt, Lenny, and Cynthia had been more than happy to go over to Greene County with Martin and look through the mug books. They would do whatever it took, so they said, to bring Harv's killer to justice—anything, of course, short of turning themselves in.

Periodic surveillance of the road up to Deep Notch had yielded the Greene County Sheriff's Department a volume of blurry through-the-car-window-photographs of visitors to Garibaldi House. At the end of the session, though, no identifications had been made and Martin had driven the trio home, stopping first at Big Indian Mountain as planned to drop Cynthia off to a waiting McAvoy.

The chief offered to treat Matt and Lenny to dinner as well, but they declined, thanking him profusely for his generous offer.

McAvoy had to admire their style. *They're bound and determined to keep up the charade that they're no more than casual friends with Cynthia, brought together simply by Matt and Harvey's mutual love of fly fishing.*

McAvoy had dressed up for the occasion. He had on a solid burgundy knit tie with a burgundy-and-gray tattersall shirt, gray slacks and a burgundy sportcoat. Cynthia insisted on changing her clothes prior to going and asked him in to wait for her.

As she walked through her house, the chief watched her carefully, trying to tell whether she would notice anything out of place from the search. He knew that he and Lucille had meticulously replaced everything that they had moved, but sometimes even a half-inch difference, unnoticeable to a stranger, can appear as a half-foot variation to someone intimate with the surroundings.

With an, "I'll just be a moment," Cynthia flashed a smile to McAvoy and flounced into the bedroom, neglecting, on purpose, to close the door behind her.

No wonder she doesn't notice anything, he thought. *She thinks she's being courted.* He crossed into the kitchen and waited there, as far from the open bedroom door as he could get without leaving the house.

In less than ten minutes, the yellow sun dress had been replaced by a black-and-white jump suit. An elasticized white sleeveless and strapless top barely contained Cynthia's ample bosoms. The black silk georgette pants fit quite snugly over the hips and seat before billowing out in genie-style legs to be gathered in again at the ankles.

McAvoy sensed rather than actually heard her come up behind him. He turned and, as she stood there leaning against the kitchen doorway with that sort of panther look in her eyes, he knew how prey in the jungle felt.

With his gaze drawn to her cleavage—cleavage that could hide a small dog—he silently answered Lucille's boob question, asked earlier that day. *Mighty proud, and rightly so.*

❧ ❧ ❧

Stevie could hardly keep a smile from her lips as McAvoy and his "date" entered The Plough & Whistle. She took possession of his revolver and showed them to the table by the dart board.

Porky didn't even attempt subtlety. He screwed up his face and rubbed his eyes with his fists as if a thousand watts of light had blinded him.

After Stevie took their drink order and returned to the bar, Danny crept up behind her and whispered, "Pay attention, Mom. Now you'll see how world-class flirting is done." A stern look from his mother sent him scampering back into the kitchen.

McAvoy excused himself and went over to explain the situation to Stevie. Lucille had already filled her in that the chief would be bringing Cynthia for dinner and assured her that it was strictly business. Nevertheless, Stevie unmercifully let McAvoy squirm through his own explanation.

"I hardly know what to think, Ed," she told him when he finished his stammering. "Last night a lady priest, tonight a bimbo. What do you have planned for tomorrow? Is there something I should know?"

"Honey, I told you it's—"

"If you ask me to wear a Little-Bo-Peep outfit, I'm going to start to worry about you," she said, then smiled and whispered in his ear, "I didn't say I wouldn't wear it, mind you. I just said I'd start to worry." Then she turned serious and as she straightened his tie she said, "I hope I'm right in assuming that there are limits to the actions you consider to be in the line of duty."

"Don't worry," he said with a sigh. "Nothing's going to happen."

As McAvoy returned to his seat, Martin Bassett entered the pub, removed his Glock Model 17 semiautomatic pistol from it's holster, slid it across the bar to Porky, placed a drink order, and came over to the chief's table.

"Lucille needs to see you for about five minutes," he said. "I'll keep the lady company while you're gone."

McAvoy could tell from the tone of Martin's voice that Lucille's information had a direct bearing on the case and could not be broached in front of Cynthia. He made his apologies to the woman and left the pub for his office.

When he opened the door to the police station, he found Lucille, Larry Parker, and Jim Culpepper crowded around Lucille's desk. "What's up?" he asked.

"Plenty," Lucille croaked and, as McAvoy came through the gate in the counter and sat on the edge of the duty desk, she filled him in. "Martin said that Matt Christiansen *did* keep his doctor's appointment on the day of the DuMont murder and, in fact, was in the examining room at the exact time of the killing. However, because they were extremely busy that day, no one remembers whether Lenny remained in the waiting room during his uncle's stay or whether he was there when Matt finished up with the doctor."

"Okay, we're no better or worse off then we were before but at least now we know that Lenny doesn't have an alibi and *could* have done it."

"Oh, we know much more than that." She cackled like the Wicked Witch of the West and turned the page of her notebook. "Your old friend Lieutenant Gardner called. There is no record that either a Matt Christiansen or a Lenny Damien ever existed in the Detroit Metropolitan area." McAvoy raised an eyebrow and Lucille continued. "But because you told him that Matt had been involved with investments, the lieutenant checked with the people in bunko. Their computer turned up another uncle and nephew team by the name of Matthew Christiani and Leonardo Damilano. He faxed their mug shots."

Jim Culpepper handed two photographs to McAvoy. The faces of Matt Christiansen and Lenny Damien looked up at him from each hand.

"Well, well, well," McAvoy said, nodding his head and smirking.

Lucille continued. "They were involved with a land development scheme. Supposed to build an enormous self-contained retirement community on Lake St. Clair. They spent thirty grand for an option on the land, another fifteen for full-color brochures, architectural plans, and advertising. After collecting about a half a million in down payments from elderly people, they were never seen nor heard from again."

"Real sweethearts," McAvoy said, eyeing the faxed photos.

"Guess when they dropped out of sight?" Lucille asked, then, in response to the eyebrow again, answered her own question. "Sometime in the week following the murder of the Gianelli brothers. Left their apartment, their clothes, their cars, a boat and"—she hesitated for effect as she tossed the notebook on the desk—"fly fishing gear."

McAvoy selected one of the two photos and held it up for Lucille, Larry, and Jim. "Think perhaps a girl like Rosa Grimaldi would have been attracted to someone like this?" A handsome Leonardo Damilano looked out at the trio.

"The sarge wants to know how you want to handle it," Jim spoke up. "He said it would be okay with the sheriff if we invited them over here for some reason or another and made the collar ourselves within our jurisdiction."

Both Jim and Larry liked that idea. They exuded excitement. An arrest of fugitives from justice sure beat wandering through the woods looking for nonexistent goblins.

McAvoy turned to Lucille. "Get Deputy Dawg on the phone, would you?"

She made the call, asked Porky to have Martin come to the telephone but cautioned him not to let anyone else know who was calling. After thirty years in the Air Force, Porky recognized an order when he heard one and followed this one to the letter. Lucille put the call on the speaker so they all could hear.

"You don't have to say much," McAvoy told the deputy. "Just listen. If we make the arrest now, all we'll get them for is the bunko rap. Anything else at this point is still too circumstantial. They'll go back to Detroit, make restitution to the old people in return for a slap on their wrists. Maybe they'll draw a couple or three years of soft time but be out in eighteen months for good behavior with their millions of dollars in diamonds. I want them for murder. Let's stick with our plan."

"Why not take what we've got?" Martin whispered. "Even if we only get them for fraud, they ain't coming out in eighteen months, Chief. They ain't coming out ever. Once we draw the tie-in to the Gianelli brothers, whether or not we get the murder conviction, they won't live beyond their first week in prison. Don Vittorio will see to that."

"But we don't get Cynthia and she's as guilty of Harvey's murder as Matt and Lenny. Let's play out our hand. We can always pull them in on the open fraud warrant whenever we like."

"Okay, Chief. It's your show."

McAvoy hung up and walked back across the street to the pub, thinking that it would take some of his theatre skills to act as if nothing had happened. He opened the door, though, to find that he wouldn't have to entertain Cynthia by himself with only Martin for backup.

Ben Krider had joined the twosome and so had Theresa Hitchcock, fresh from her first official duties at St. Mary's— Thursday evening vespers. Dressed in tan slacks and a brown blouse that tied with a bow at the neck, she looked quite the contrast to Cynthia DuMont.

Originally, Theresa had wandered in and sat herself down at a small table for two against the back wall. She felt pretty good about her first service at St. Mary's. John's note had said to expect only the regular quintet so she had been surprised to see thirty-eight parishioners in the pews when she intoned the opening greeting.

Must be the curiosity factor at work, she thought. But even so, it pleased her.

Seeing Theresa by herself, Ben Krider came over and collected her, informing the lady priest that part of her official duties as John Desmond's replacement included taking his spot in the Thursday-night dart tournament. She graciously accepted, thinking about how difficult it would be to leave this village when John returned. It differed so much from downtown Manhattan. The people here were so very friendly.

Had she known the doctor better, she would have realized that friendliness comprised only half of his motive for insisting that she join the group. Although Martin Bassett *usually* ended up losing the dart tournament, it was not an absolute certainty. Sometimes the blind-squirrel theory came into play. The ever-frugal Ben figured that the more people in the game, the less his own chances became of coming in last.

Theresa let Ben carry her drink over to the table as she excused herself and headed for the ladies' room. Once alone, though, she crossed over to Stevie by the bar. "Fill me in," she whispered.

"Thursday-night darts," Stevie said. "Ed, Ben, Martin, and John meet here every Thursday. After dinner, they nurse a few pitchers and play darts to see who picks up the tab. Don't worry, none of them are very good and they don't run up that big of a tab."

"Who's the...uh...?" Theresa glanced sideways at Cynthia DuMont.

"The woman with the healthy looking figure?" Stevie asked.

"Yeah," Theresa admitted with a grin. "Healthy. That's the word I was searching for."

"She's the widow of the guy who got murdered by the creek last week but, Ms. Hitchcock—"

"Tess," Theresa interrupted.

Stevie smiled. She liked this woman. If Theresa were going to stay on at St. Mary's, Stevie knew they'd become very good friends. "Tess, don't ask a whole lot of questions or talk about it. I'm not exactly sure what Ed and Martin are doing but there's police business going on that's not supposed to look like police business."

"Gotcha," Theresa said, then winked and walked over to the table.

With drinks, dinner, and after-dinner drinks, McAvoy managed to keep Cynthia DuMont busy and away from Matt Christiansen for almost two hours. After Danny had cleared away the dinner dishes and glasses, Stevie had brought the pitcher of Hudson Lager and mugs that customarily signaled the beginning of the dart tournament.

Martin, ever the male chauvinist, unilaterally decided that the girls shouldn't be required to throw darts, since it obviously wouldn't be a fair contest and that only the men should take the line and compete for the entire tab. Cynthia, who thoroughly enjoyed being pampered and treated like a princess, oohed and cooed over this noble gesture.

Theresa, silently fuming over the patronizing use of the word "girls," simply walked over to the wall and removed the clutch of missiles from the dart board. After setting all but three of them on the table, she moved behind the hockey line and flicked the first dart into the triple-eighteen. With no more than a second or two between throws to take aim, her next two darts scored a triple-twenty and a single twenty-five that was only a gnat's whisker out of the bull's-eye.

She turned to Martin, folded her hands just below her chin, batted her eyelashes and asked in a pitiful little voice, "Mr. big, strong deputy man, would you please add those up for me? You know how awful we *girls* are at mathematics."

Martin stood staring at the dart board with his mouth agape. He didn't just see three individual darts that totaled up to one-hundred-and-thirty-nine points. He saw his worst nightmare about to come true. It was bad enough getting beat almost every week by John, Ben, and McAvoy, but to get beat by a girl? So strong were his feelings of dread that he even imagined feeling a twinge in his groin as his testicles shrunk down in size by half.

Martin's premonition had come true. They had played five matches. McAvoy and Ben had each won two apiece and Theresa had won one. Worse than that, Martin had not even won one leg of any of the matches and now sat there holding the tab in his hand, going through the calculations in his head.

He couldn't believe the amount entered below the total line. Usually, the four regulars just had two pitchers of beer. *This* tab included dinner for five, drinks before and after, and four pitchers. He was going to have to schedule himself for a lot of road-patrol overtime to make this up.

"Add it up any way you like, Martin, but it still comes out that high," Stevie said, patiently standing beside his chair with her tray extended, waiting for the deputy to haul out his wallet.

Over behind the bar, Porky loudly cleared his throat. When Martin turned and looked at the barkeeper's round, innocent cherub face, Porky cracked his knuckles and asked, "Might tonight just be the night, do you suppose, hmm?"

Martin glanced again at the total of the tab, added Stevie's fifteen percent, then doubled that amount. He tried swallowing the lump in his throat but it wouldn't go down so he took a swig of beer and looked again at the dart board. He hadn't thrown badly tonight. Everyone else had just been on their game.

Maybe tonight is the night, he thought. "Usual rules?" he asked, warming to the challenge.

"Usual rules," Porky confirmed, removing a tungsten/ nickel tournament-quality dart from a black leather case and attaching a chromolux flight to it.

"You'll enjoy this," McAvoy whispered across the table to Theresa and Cynthia. Then he stood, crossed to the wall and turned the dart board around so that the concentric circles, numbered one through ten from the outside in, faced the room.

Whenever Porky found himself in a particularly playful mood, he would offer someone the opportunity to throw darts with him—the stakes being double or nothing on that person's tab. The rules of the game varied, depending on the quality of the opponent. For Martin Bassett, Porky would only throw one dart to Martin's two; however, if Porky's dart hit the bull's-eye, he would be declared the winner, regardless of Martin's total score. It was a sucker bet. After thirty years of pub-crawling in England and daily practice on the board in The Plough & Whistle, Porky could hit the bull's-eye nineteen out of twenty times.

After his first humiliating encounter with the double-or-nothing bet on a snowy December night, Martin had whined until Porky agreed to a further modification of the rules. The normal throwing line, or hockey line as it was called, was at a distance of seven feet, nine-and-a-half inches from the wall. In an extremely weak and generous moment, Porky had agreed that *he* would throw from a line twelve feet from the target. At that distance, Porky's accuracy slipped to a mere fourteen out of twenty.

As Martin and Porky finished shaking hands before taking up positions behind their respective throwing lines, Cynthia made a grand production of coming over and kissing each one of Martin's darts for luck. Then she planted a final kiss full on the deputy's lips.

"And, what about me?" Porky asked, as if his heart were broken. "Am I to be reduced to having only my little sister give me a good luck kiss?"

Theresa, stood and walked over to the portly bartender, made a small sign of the cross over his dart, looked at Cynthia then back at Porky, shrugged her shoulders and smiled. "We each do what we do best," she said, then returned to her seat.

Whether or not the power of the blessing overshadowed the power of the kiss would be discussed for months to come, but this night turned out to be one of the fourteen in twenty. Martin, who's pitiful score of fifteen would have won if Porky had not hit the bull's-eye, dug into his wallet and laid the required number of bills on Stevie's tray. Everyone thanked Martin for his hospitality, then they all, except Martin, walked out to the street together—Ben for his short drive to The Poplars, Theresa for her even-shorter drive back to the rectory, and McAvoy to take Cynthia over to her home on the slopes of Big Indian Mountain.

The liquid crystal digits on McAvoy's Seiko read twelve-thirty. It had been an hour since he had delivered Cynthia DuMont to her front door. He had returned to the pub a half hour ago and this was the seventh time he had looked at his watch in that thirty-minute time span. The telephone still had not rung.

Martin got up, walked to the corner of the bar, picked up the receiver and punched in the numbers for the phone that had been installed in the vacant store in Oliverea. He spoke to Dave Stratton, the Ulster County deputy on the other end of the wire, and after a few moments returned to the table.

"Nothing," Martin said. "Nothing at all." Looking again at his own watch, he sighed. "I'm going to call it a night, Chief. I'll check with you tomorrow morning but if anything develops in the meantime, you know where to reach me."

He stopped at the bar on his way out and retrieved his pistol.

McAvoy hung around for another fifteen minutes, then he, too, placed a call to the vacant store and told Deputy Stratton that he was leaving the pub for the police station. He hung up the phone, picked up his service revolver from Porky, and walked across Irving Boulevard.

Although the night was clear and warm, it did nothing for the chief's mental state. During the short walk from the pub to his office, depression began to set in. It was obvious that Cynthia and Matt were not going to contact each other. Matt, the consummate con man, had schooled Cynthia well. Adapting one's lifestyle as if the con were true was what made a good con job work.

Well, we can always pull Matt and Lenny in on the fraud warrant. What Martin said is true. They'll never walk out of prison alive. I guess I should take some consolation in that.

But he took no consolation at all. It really irked him that a murder had taken place within his jurisdiction and would officially remain unsolved. There just *had* to be something he could do about it.

Seeing Lucille's silver Chrysler Sebring convertible in the small parking lot in front of the police station made him smile. His sister-in-law was more anxious about this case than she would admit. She didn't like the thought of someone getting away with murder any more than he did.

Upon opening the door, he was greeted by a sight that made his depression dissipate. Lucille had knocked a pen off the side of her desk and, while still sitting on the chair, had stretched over to retrieve it. The view from the doorway of Lucille's hind quarters and a gorgeous leg stretched out for balance, skirt hiked to the top of her thigh, made McAvoy do a double-take.

Chapter 11

The early afternoon sun shone warmly and brightly on the stretch of the Esopus Creek that flowed between Maben Hollow and Eagle Mountain Roads on the slope of Big Indian Mountain. A chaise lounge sat on an outcropping of shale. A woman, dressed in a powder-blue shorts-and-halter ensemble, lay stretched out on the lounge, sunning her middle-aged but still firm and voluptuous body.

She had just completed the ritual of applying a second coat of tanning oil to her tapered, movie-star legs, her shoulders and arms, her bare midriff and chest, and the tops of her ample breasts that could not be contained within the confines of the halter. Now, as she set the bottle of oil down on the rock next to the chaise and lay back, she adjusted the large-brimmed straw hat downward to shade her face from the sun's rays.

A crackling of branches from behind her announced the approach of someone descending the slope of Big Indian Mountain, coming down the path from the DuMont house to the creek.

❦ ❦ ❦

Early on Friday morning, Mickey Campbell had shown up at Cynthia's. He had come to drive her to the county courthouse in Kingston so that she could take care of the paperwork regarding the release of the Isabela Pendant and the sixteen loose diamonds.

When she claimed not to have any knowledge of the court date, the young Peekamoose Heights police officer seemed bewildered and stammered an apology. "I'm sorry, ma'am. Didn't…uh…Chief McAvoy call you? He…uh…was supposed to call you this morning and tell you I would pick you up."

At barely five foot six, with bright red hair and a face full of freckles, Mickey Campbell was hardly a prototype for a policeman. He had a friendly, puppyish way about him that made everyone he met take an instant liking to the young officer.

Cynthia was no exception. "It's no problem, Officer," she said, smiling at his awkwardness. "Of course I'll come with you. Just let me get my purse."

At that moment, the telephone rang. On the other end of the line, McAvoy told her that ADA Ledbetter needed the releases signed and that an Officer Mickey Campbell would be out to drive her to Kingston and back. When informed that Officer Campbell stood on her doorstep at that very minute, McAvoy, too, apologized for the communications' foul-up. Again, Cynthia asserted that it was not a problem. Five minutes later, she climbed into the blue-and-white Jeep Cherokee and Mickey headed it in the direction of Kingston.

As he made the turn out onto County Road #47, Cynthia smiled, shifted her position slightly, and crossed her legs so that the hem of her yellow sun dress road up to mid thigh. She was going to enjoy making the awkward young officer feel even more so all the way to Kingston and back.

❧ ❧ ❧

Martin Bassett had shown up very early that morning on the western slope of Panther Mountain to take Matt and Lenny over to Greene County again to look at another set of mug books. He told the two men that the Greene County Sheriff's Office had neglected to show them the books on the previous day. The mug books, four volumes in all, actually belonged to the New York City Police Department. They had been relayed pony-express style during the nighttime hours, from sheriff's deputy to sheriff's deputy, through all the counties on the New York Tollway from King's County in Manhattan to Greene County in the Catskills.

Martin apologized profusely that Matt and Lenny had been caughtby surprise over the trip, explaining that it was his understanding that McAvoy had notified them. Matt assured the deputy that no harm had been done and that he and Lenny would be more than happy to go along.

When they reached County Road #47 and headed toward State Road #28, away from Oliverea, Matt showed a bit of concern. "Aren't we going to pick up Cynthia?" he asked.

"This will probably just turn into another wild goose chase," Martin replied. "The chances of her, or you, for that matter, having seen Mr. DuMont's killer are slim to none. The Sheriff didn't think we should trouble Mrs. DuMont anymore than we already have so it'll just be the two of you today."

Both Matt and Lenny expressed their agreement with that reasoning and Martin proceeded on to Catskill.

At the Greene County Sheriff's Office, the two men did a marvelous job of acting as if they were actually studying the mug shots. Martin wondered how many of their old friends they were able to spot as they leafed through the pages. After about two-and-a-half hours and a half-dozen cups of bad coffee, Matt and Lenny shrugged their shoulders and shook their heads. Martin thanked them for their time.

It was close to noon when he delivered them back to their home, apologizing once again that this, like the previous day's trek, had turned out to be a wasted effort. Both Matt and Lenny dismissed the deputy's apologies, expressing their willingness to do whatever was necessary to bring Harvey's killer to justice.

The two men waved to Martin as he turned the Caprice around and eased it down the winding driveway and out of sight, then they mounted the steps to their house. A lemon-yellow envelope protruded from the edge of the screen door and Lenny retrieved it as he opened the door. It was a small note card-sized envelope and had the name *Matt* scrawled across the front in a woman's handwriting. He gave the envelope to his uncle and entered the house.

Matt, needing the cane and, therefore, not able to walk and open the envelope at the same time, had stopped in the doorway to slit the envelope with his finger. He removed a lemon-yellow note card, embossed with a large script *C*, and the blood drained from his face.

"Jesus Christ!" he said with a gasp, almost in a state of apoplexy. "Is she out of her fucking mind, leaving this here in plain sight?!"

Lenny took the note from Matt and helped his uncle inside. As he glanced down at the note, he, too, paled. It read, "Never was much good at math, but good enough to realize my share isn't anywhere near large enough. I think it's time to renegotiate." It was signed with a simple initial—a *C*. A postscript beneath the initial read, "You should have been up-front with me about the girl in the boat."

Lenny hastily crossed over to the stove and turned a knob for one of the gas burners on the rangetop. When the propane ignited, he touched both the note and the envelope to the blue flames and deposited the burning papers into the sink. While the fire consumed the note card and envelope, he shut off the burner then, turning his attention once more to the sink, he twisted the faucet handle and rinsed the ashes down the drain.

"If you'll recall," he said as he shut off the water, still facing the sink and away from his uncle, "I warned you about something like this."

Matt just leaned on his cane, attempting to figure out why Cynthia had been so careless.

When he didn't respond, Lenny continued. "I said she was too flighty to maintain the con."

Still Matt did not reply, lost as he was in his own thoughts. Lenny went on. "I believe I used the term 'loose cannon?'"

Matt maintained his silence and Lenny turned to face him. "Rosa was also too flighty, Uncle Matt. She also would have been a loose cannon. We did what we had to do then and you know what we have to do now. Instead of guaranteeing our freedom, this middle-aged sex kitten is going to get us caught. And killed."

Matt sighed resignedly then looked directly at Lenny, raised a cautioning finger and softly said, "I'll talk to her." He waved off Lenny's protestation and raised his voice. "I said I'll *talk* to her!"

"Yes, Uncle Matt," Lenny answered, then took in a deep breath, shook his head and exhaled audibly through his nose.

❦ ❦ ❦

The freshly mopped pub floor had dried and Danny removed the last chair from on top of the last table and reset it in its proper place. He was on his way to the linen closet for fresh tablecloths and napkins when Porky hailed him from the kitchen.

"I know your mum and you had an agreement that you would confine your fishing to Tuesdays, Thursdays and Saturdays, lad, but there are circumstances that pop up sometimes to alter agreements."

"Like what?" Danny asked. A flicker of hope registered in his blue eyes.

"Oh, like the fact that you didn't get to go this past Saturday because of helping your mum and me prepare for the picnic and you didn't get to go Tuesday because of that spot of legal business that your friends had to take care of."

Danny smiled at his uncle. "Would the fact that you completely sold out the entire trout catch last night be one of those circumstances, too?"

"Could be, lad. Could bloody well be." Porky said, rocking back and forth on his heels and chuckling. "Now since your mum is at the bank, that sort of leaves you in my custody, say what?"

"Sort of," Danny agreed. A broad grin began to form on his face.

"Then I think it's within my purview to give you permission to go fishing if I so choose. Providing, of course, that you've left by the time your mum gets back."

"Color me gone," Danny shouted over his shoulder as he headed out the back door to collect his fishing equipment, his bike, and his furry buddy.

Porky waddled over to the blackboard, picked up the piece of chalk that dangled from a string fastened to the frame and scrawled *Baked Stuffed Trout* underneath the CATCH OF THE DAY heading.

❦ ❦ ❦

Matt emerged from the woods and hobbled halfway to the chaise lounge. Although dressed for fishing, he carried no fly rod, just his cane. "Leaving that note in the door like that was a very stupid move, Cyn," he said. "What if someone else had found it?"

The bare shoulders raised themselves from the chaise in a shrug of indifference.

Gingerly crossing the rest of the way to the woman, he tried to reason with her. "I thought we had an agreement. You get your freedom from a stale and loveless marriage, *and* a cool one million dollars plus whatever Harvey's insurance pays. We, in turn, not only get *our* freedom from constantly looking over our shoulders, but your silence as well."

Again, no reply came from the lounge.

"We kept our part of that bargain, Cynthia. Harvey's dead and you're free to do whatever you like with your life. I told you the court would believe the story and be lenient with you and I was right. Don't make us think we can't trust you."

He waited for a response but, receiving none, switched his tack from reason to a veiled threat. "You mentioned Rosa Grimaldi in your note, Cyn. I'd like you to think very seriously about her. You see, we couldn't trust Rosa. No amount of money would have bought her silence so we were forced to deal with her in a more permanent manner."

Matt put his hand on the aluminum frame of the lounge back to steady himself while he paused again, expecting a response. Still getting none, his voice hardened. "Stick to our agreement, Cyn. For your own good. Please, don't compel us to take a similar approach with you."

He had reached down during that last sentence and lightly traced his finger across the bare breast tops that protruded from the powder-blue halter. Suddenly the woman brought her hand up, taking Matt's wrist and twisting it so that the elderly man lost his balance and came crashing down at the side of the chaise lounge.

"Touch me like that and you'd damn well better have an engagement ring in your pocket, Pops," Lucille McAvoy's raspy voice croaked from beneath the straw hat.

Matt Christiani lay there speechless. Lucille shifted the hat off her bulldog face and winked at him. "Looks damn good from the neck down, doesn't it?" she rankled as she reached beneath the chaise and shut off the small tape recorder.

From his hiding spot in the woods, twenty yards downstream, McAvoy approached the shale outcropping, giving a wink and a nod to Lucille for a job well done.

"It's over, Matt," he said. "It's finished." The chief helped the old man to his feet and handed him his cane.

"You conned me, Ed," Matt said with just a speck of admiration mixed in with the surprised tone to his voice. "You out-conned a con." He stood there and shook his head in disbelief.

McAvoy removed a small dog-eared card from his shirt pocket and began to read. Having done this so often, he didn't need to use his reading glasses to make out those words that had been committed to memory many years ago. But still he used the card out of habit. "You have the right to remain silent. Should you give up that right—"

"It's okay, Ed," Matt interrupted with a wave of his hand. "I know the speech."

"Why, Matt?…Why?"

The elderly con man shrugged his shoulders. Defeat was beginning to settle in. "No matter how well we stayed hidden, as long as the Gianelli crowd continued to look, there would always be the possibility that they'd come up with something. Maybe they'd make the connection between our disappearance so close to the heist. Maybe someone would remember Lenny with Rosa. We thought that if we could give them a reason to stop looking, maybe…just maybe we'd be free. That's one reason why we came here in the first place. Figured they wouldn't look too awfully hard in their own backyard."

"Why Harvey DuMont?"

"Coincidence, Ed. Pure and simple coincidence. He just happened to be in the wrong place at the wrong time. Meeting up with someone from the Detroit area made us think about it, especially when we realized that Cynthia considered him a millstone around her neck. Twenty years of age difference may not have seemed that big a deal when he was in his late thirties and she in her late teens but it's a whole different ball game when it's sixties and forties. Once we knew we had Cyn on our side we really began to believe it would work."

McAvoy nodded. "Is Lenny up at the house?"

❧ ❧ ❧

Danny Henderson had bicycled over to the DuMont home from Peekamoose Heights, followed by his faithful canine companion, and had just propped his bike up next to the porch, happy to see Matt and Lenny's white Ford Explorer in the driveway. As he headed for the path that would take him through the woods and down to the creek, Lenny emerged from the opposite direction. Danny waved but Lenny, for only the briefest of moments, stood there with a blank stare on his face, then smiled his usual expansive smile, tousled Danny's hair, and petted a tail-wagging Sandy.

"Tell you what," he said in a conspiratorial voice. "Cynthia and Matt are down by the stream. What say you and I sneak down there quietly and surprise them?"

"Okay," Danny replied. "But Sandy doesn't sneak so good."

"I'll open the windows of the car and we'll leave her here until after our surprise. Then you can come back up and get her."

Danny thought that was a good idea. While he coaxed the dog up into the back of the Explorer, Lenny went around to the passenger side, opened the front door and removed an item wrapped in an old towel from beneath the front seat. Also, unseen by the boy, he removed a Browning BDM from the glove compartment and stuffed it in his belt at the small of his back. The tails of his shirt, worn outside his jeans, hid the 9mm semiautomatic pistol from sight.

"Come on," Lenny said. "Let's have some fun." He ushered the youngster in front of him and, as they started down the path, he discarded the towel.

❦ ❦ ❦

The answer to McAvoy's question, as to whether Lenny was up at the house, came not from Matt Christiani, but from the direction of path. "No, Chief, Lenny's over here."

McAvoy, Matt, and Lucille turned toward the sound of the voice. Leonardo Damilano had Danny Henderson by the collar and held a sawed-off twelve-gauge pump shotgun to the side of the boy's head.

Danny tried to fight back the tears but failed. He had never been so frightened in his entire life.

"Unclip your gun and holster, Ed, and toss them into the creek," Lenny ordered as he guided Danny closer to the foursome. "Very slowly, Ed," he cautioned as McAvoy drew back his sportcoat lapel with his left hand and reached for the revolver with the right. "And, use your left hand."

McAvoy unclipped the holster from his belt and tossed it into the center of the stream. "The game's over, Lenny. Give it up before you hurt someone else."

Matt hobbled over to his nephew. "Take them to the house. We'll tie them up and leave them there. It'll give us at least a four-hour head start before anyone finds them."

"You go on up, Uncle Matt," Lenny said. "I'll take care of things down here." He looked at Lucille, who, by this time, had sat up on the chaise lounge. "On your feet. Over by the chief."

Lucille complied. She and McAvoy unconsciously reached out and held each other's hand.

Lenny gave Danny a little shove. "You, too, Danny."

The boy did as he was told and Lucille enveloped him in her arms.

"Bring them up to the house, Lenny," Matt said. "We disappeared before. We can do it again."

Lenny turned to his uncle. "We did it before because we left no witnesses. Go on up to the house."

"That was different," Matt insisted. "They were two mobsters and a slut. We're *not* killing *these* people. Now take them up to the house!"

Lenny gave no verbal response but, instead, raised his sawed-off shotgun to the firing position.

Matt put a hand on the stock and tried to muscle the gun away from where it was aimed—at the threesome by the stream. "I said *no!*"

Pushing his uncle away, Lenny deliberately pointed the shotgun at him and pulled the trigger. Matt Christiani, wide-eyed in disbelief, was lifted off his feet and blown three feet away. He came to rest in a heap by the back of the chaise lounge.

Lucille screamed and shuddered and turned Danny's head away from the sight, burying it in her bosom and wrapping her arms tightly around him. McAvoy started toward the man with the shotgun but the distance turned out to be too great for an out-of-shape, middle-aged man with a bad leg to cover in time. He was brought up short as Lenny trained the barrel on him and pumped another shell into the chamber.

A second shot rang out and Lucille screamed again, not opening her eyes for fear of seeing her brother-in-law splattered all over the stream bed.

But the shot had not come from the shotgun.

McAvoy in his frozen position watched as Lenny's head snapped backward and blood oozed from a hole in his forehead. The young man crumpled to the ground, firing off one last blast into the loose shale beside him as he toppled over onto his back.

Lucille and Danny opened their eyes and turned to look in McAvoy's direction but then quickly followed the chief's surprised gaze back across to the opposite side of the stream. Antonio Gianelli rose from a kneeling two-handed firing position behind the pudding-stone boulder and holstered his Beretta.

No one spoke. McAvoy went to Lucille and Danny and put his arms around both of them while Tony carefully picked his way across the creek, using the stepping-stone boulders to avoid getting his handwoven calfskin Farragamo loafers wet.

The young mobster slowly walked up to the body of Matt Christiani and spat in the dead man's face. He repeated the display of contempt with Lenny Damilano and hissed, "*Vendetta*. The living avenge the dead."

"What...what are you doing here?" McAvoy asked, still in a state of semi-shock.

As Tony Gianelli turned and spread his arms open wide, the look of hatred in his dark brown eyes quickly changed to amusement. "What? No 'Thanks, Tony?' No 'We appreciate you saving our lives, Tony?' Just, 'What are you doing here?'"

Lucille and Danny sat on the edge of the chaise lounge, still holding onto each other, avoiding looking in the direction of Matt and Lenny.

McAvoy approached their rescuer. "Okay. You're absolutely right. Thanks, Tony! We appreciate you saving our lives! We really do. But, what *are* you doing here?"

"I been following you for three days now. Papa swore you'd solve this case and he was right. He's got a lot of respect for you, you know? And he says that I gotta respect you, too."

Tony raised his hand to touch the bandage on his forehead and for an instant his smile vanished, then he shrugged his shoulders and the smile reappeared. "Okay, I do what my papa says. But let me tell you, this country life has ruined you. You ain't worth a shit anymore when it comes to spotting a tail. I been dogging your ass for three days now. Oh, by the way, the Beretta's registered, I got a permit to carry, and I assume that I'm gonna get some sort of commendation from the Peekamoosey people for coming to the aid of a cop in trouble. Ain't that a kick in the ass? I gotta go now."

With that, Antonio Gianelli turned and picked his way back across the boulders. Once on the opposite side of the creek, he waved and shouted, "*Ciao*," over his shoulder and disappeared into the woods to hike back to where he had parked his red Mazda Miata MX-5.

McAvoy walked over to Danny and Lucille. "Let's go," he said quietly.

Danny needed no other encouragement than that. He raced for the path up to the house to be with his best friend, tears still streaming from his eyes. McAvoy stretched out his hand to Lucille. She took it and when she rose to her feet, he put his arms around her and kissed her softly.

"I never thought it would go down like this," he said. "I'm sorry I put you and Danny in danger."

She looked up at him and put her arms around his neck. "You couldn't have predicted that Danny would be here. And if we had brought anymore backup, they might have been spotted. Then where would we be? And there's certainly no need to apologize to me, Ed. I'm a member of this department, too, remember? I knew what I was letting myself in for." She stood on her toes and kissed him back, full on the lips—a tender, loving kiss.

McAvoy had always wondered what his brother Dave had seen in Lucille, with her bulldog face and buzz-saw voice. Seeing her in the powder-blue shorts-and-halter ensemble, feeling her voluptuous body pressed against him and her soft full lips on his, he didn't wonder any longer.

"However, you *will* have to apologize to Heather," Lucille said, breaking the clinch and gesturing toward the tape recorder under the chaise. "There weren't any fresh cassettes in the cabinet and I think we may have taped over last night's class notes."

Chapter 12

Cynthia DuMont had been given the run-around all morning long at the Ulster County Courthouse, regarding the release forms that Mickey Campbell had taken her to sign. First, she was shuffled from office to office. Next, ADA Ledbetter had been unexpectedly called away. Then the forms had been lost and had to be prepared again from scratch.

Seeing Deputy Sergeant Martin Bassett's familiar face, Cynthia DuMont had initially been overjoyed. *Finally,* she thought, nearly at her wit's end. *Someone to shepherd me through this bureaucratic nightmare.*

The joy changed rapidly to shock as Martin read Cynthia her rights and placed her under arrest for complicity in her husband's murder. She was arraigned early that afternoon on a charge of conspiracy-to-murder and taken to the Ulster County Jail to await her trial.

Bill Brinkmire, tipped-off beforehand by a call from McAvoy, had been present at Cynthia's arrest and arraignment. He sat in his office with his elbows on the desk and his head in his hands, lamenting the fate of a weekly newspaperman. He would have McAvoy's interview exclusively, as promised, but by the time he published his *Ashokan Register* on the following Wednesday, the story would be five days old. Agnes Berman would have five days-worth of articles in the *Kingston Chronicle* before Bill's story could be told.

Actually, Aggie would have six articles. She managed to squeeze in the bare-bones facts of the case before the Friday afternoon edition went to press.

❧ ❧ ❧

Gail Simpson, one of the girls from Food Services, knocked softly on the door to suite #24 at The Poplars, then entered with the dinner trolley. As always, Kate Winthrop's trolley contained both the *New York Times* and the *Kingston Chronicle*.

Kate thanked the girl as Gail assisted her to the pink upholstered Queen Anne wing chair and placed a linen napkin across the elderly woman's lap. Then she poured part of the contents from a small bottle of Liebfermilch into Kate's wine glass, not filling it past the halfway mark.

As Kate sipped the wine with one palsied hand, she picked up her reading glasses with the other. A small article in the *Chronicle*, on the front page below the fold, caught her eye. She scanned the article first, then when she had reread it thoroughly, she set the wine glass and the paper down and glanced over the half-frames of her reading glasses at the Massachusetts tall-case clock. Thinking the time to be acceptable, she reached for the telephone receiver on top of the Queen Anne lowboy and punched in the numbers from a small piece of paper that had been tucked underneath the telephone.

"Sacré Coeur Monastery," the voice on the other end of the phone line informed her.

"My name is Katherine Winthrop," Kate said. "I'd like to leave a message for Fr. John Desmond, please."

"Yes, Mrs. Winthrop. I'm Fr. Paul. I'll be happy to give him the message myself."

"Just tell him, if you will, that the problem has resolved itself. He'll know what that means."

"Very well, Mrs. Winthrop, I'll be seeing him at vespers in a short while and—"

"Oh...uh...Fr. Paul?"

"Yes, Mrs. Winthrop?"

"Tell him there's no hurry. In fact...tell him to feel free to stay through the weekend."

"If you wish. But, may I ask why?"

"Well"—Kate hedged for a moment then confessed her true motive—"his temporary replacement here at St. Mary's is a woman and we don't often get the pleasure of hearing or seeing lady priests. They're really quite rare in these parts."

"Much more so in *these* parts, dear lady," Fr. Paul said with a chuckle. "*Much* more so."

⚜ ⚜ ⚜

A single bell tolled and John Desmond closed his bible and looked at his watch. It was time for vespers, the sixth of the canonical hours. From his perch on a black wrought iron bench amid the juniper, laurel, and rhododendron of the small rock garden, he watched as the monks began their evening migration across the garth toward the chapel.

He strolled across the quadrangle and waited at the sidewalk as a trio of young robed men coming out of the kitchen crossed his path. All three of them smiled warmly and nodded a greeting. John returned both the smile and the nod and fell in behind them, feeling very much at peace with himself and his decision.

As he entered the chapel and made his way to a pew in the rear, John Desmond heard in his mind, for perhaps the hundredth time, Harvey DuMont's dying confession. The man had confessed to several one-night stands with partygirls at various out-of-town dry-cleaning conventions which he had attended without his wife. He had taken the Lord's name in vain numerous times a day. He had cheated on his taxes. He hadn't been to Mass in over seven years, although John wasn't sure whether the latter failing was still a sin in the Roman Catholic Church or not.

However, what the priest had *not* heard from a man who had wanted to confess with the urgency that Harvey DuMont had exhibited—a man who knew that he was dying and wanted to be forgiven for his transgressions—was that he had stolen over four million dollars in diamonds and murdered three people in the process. And from that omission, coupled with Agnes Berman's coverage of the Cynthia DuMont arraignment, the frightening facts of the case had become obvious to Fr. John. Harvey DuMont didn't confess to the robbery and murders because he hadn't committed any robbery or murders for which to confess.

And if, in fact, Harvey DuMont had *not* committed those crimes, then the only reason John could think of for Cynthia DuMont to lie about them in court was that *she* had conspired to have her husband murdered.

Never one to intentionally violate the eleventh commandment, John knew that he could not have remained in Peekamoose Heights. Sooner or later he would have rationalized a way around the Seal of Confession and found some obtuse way of pointing McAvoy in the right direction. This self-imposed retreat had built the necessary firewall between his priestly obligation and his own human weakness.

Yet, in taking an unexpected sidestep from his daily duties, John realized he'd been blessed with the strengthening of his vocation. Bowing his head as the service began, he couldn't help but hope that McAvoy was being a little slow in working things out. He would truly miss Sacré Coeur when it was time for him to leave.

❧ ❧ ❧

"Martin on line one," Lucille croaked from the outer office.

McAvoy looked at his watch. Early evening on a Saturday was a strange time to hear from the deputy. He picked up the receiver and punched the button that was lit.

"Just came in to clean up some things and happened to see a copy of a report from the Kingston PD," Martin said. "Someone broke into Dunlavy's jewelry store last night."

McAvoy sat bolt-upright in his chair, fully attentive as the deputy continued. "They snatched the Isabela Pendant. Nothing else in the whole shop was touched, just the necklace. From what it says here in the report, these guys knew their stuff. A real professional job. But strange, too. Blew the entire door off Dewey's safe but didn't touch another thing. No gold, no diamonds, no nothing. Just the pendant. And no clues. It's bound to turn up, though. There's no way they can fence something that well known without us finding out about it. Well, just thought you'd like to know."

McAvoy thanked Martin for the information, pushed the disconnect button and got another dial tone, then punched in a number from a card in his wallet.

"Garibaldi House," Mario, the chateau's *maggiordomo*, answered on a telephone in Greene County. "May I help you?"

"This is Ed McAvoy over in Peekamoose Heights. I'd like to speak with Vittorio Gianelli, please."

"I'm sorry, Captain McAvoy, but Don Vittorio is currently out of the country."

"As of when?"

"As of this morning, sir. I believe he boarded an early morning flight for Rome."

"Italy?"

"Yes, sir. Of course, Italy. From there, I believe, he had a connecting flight to Palermo. In fact,"—there was a slight pause and McAvoy guessed that the man was looking at his watch—"he should have landed in Palermo about an hour or so ago."

"Then let me talk to Sal Merlino or Tony Gianelli."

"I'm sorry, sir. Both Mr. Merlino and Antonio are with Don Vittorio. Can anyone else be of assistance?"

McAvoy thanked the *maggiordomo*. Then he recradled the receiver and sat there, staring off into space and remembering the story that Vittorio Gianelli had related to him over coffee and dessert a few nights before about a July Sicilian night in 1943.

❧ ❧ ❧

On the northern slope of Busambra Mountain, overlooking the town of Villafrati, hundreds of guests, most of them "friends-of-friends," had gathered for the marriage of Maria Franchese to Guido Ragucci. Maria was the only child of the late Tito Franchese and granddaughter of Leonardo Franchese. Guido was an up-and-coming Palermo attorney.

Scores of bouquets of pink-and-white flowers graced the formal gardens of Il Castello Rimini for the occasion. Yards and yards of bunting of the same color combination had been stretched around the perimeter of the garden and from the terrace of the villa on down the center aisle, between the two sections of white folding chairs. A gazebo had been set up in front of the reflecting pool. A smiling Monsignor Montano stood in front of the altar, which had been temporarily moved from the medieval fortress' small chapel to the gazebo, waiting to begin the Nuptial Mass.

The many guests craned their necks, trying to catch a glimpse of either the bride or of her cousins from America. Murmuring began as two strangers, a young man in a gray silk suit with a bandage on his forehead and a middle-aged, impeccably dressed, bald man, took their seats in the second row on the bride's side of the garden.

Back in the villa, final preparations were being made for the bride's appearance. Since both Maria's father and grandfather were deceased and she had no brothers, she considered the presence of her Uncle Vittorio, all the way from

America, to be a blessing indeed. She was thrilled that he had consented to give her away.

Vittorio was not really the girl's uncle, but the term "Uncle" had always been simpler than "First Cousin Twice Removed." Maria had always heard him referred to as her Uncle and had, thus, always called him that herself during his infrequent visits to Sicily or when she wrote to him in Detroit and, later, at Garibaldi House.

Vittorio Gianelli had been her late grandfather's cousin. After inheriting Il Castello Rimini upon the death of his sister, la Contessa Sophia Campi, and then deciding to leave Sicily for America, Vittorio had left the villa under Leonardo Franchese's stewardship. Now he was back to stay—some said, to finish out his life in retirement where it had begun. Others guessed that he was there to accept membership in the Cupola, the Sicilian Mafia hierarchy.

Betting money favored the latter supposition. The presence of Giuseppe Savarese, Antonio Mazzetti, Salvatore Gordiano, and Benedetto Cognitore could not be explained away as mere courtesy calls. Even the don of dons, Franco Pesavento, the man who most probably had ordered the assassinations of antimafia crusaders Judge Giovanni Falcone and Prosecutor Paolo Borsellino, was in attendance.

"Do you have something old?" Vittorio asked as the bride pushed his wheelchair toward the French doors that led out to the terrace.

He looked more robust than he had in years and had discontinued wearing his cashmere overcoat and black fedora since arriving in his native land. Also gone was the slouch. He sat erect in the chair, looking remarkably handsome, dressed in a fifteen-hundred-dollar black silk suit that had been fitted by Sal Merlino's tailor.

"Yes, Uncle Vittorio. Both my mother and grandmother were married in this dress."

"And beautiful they both were. I knew your grandmother well. But it never looked so gorgeous on either one of them."

Maria blushed. "Thank you, Uncle Vittorio. I didn't think you'd be able to come. I'm so happy you could share this day with me."

"So am I, little one. So am I. Fortunately some very important family business was able to be concluded satisfactorily and that enabled me to get away. Now, before we go out, there is something I wish you to have."

"But your wedding gift was delivered a week ago," the girl protested.

"This is not a wedding gift, little one," he replied, reaching into an inside pocket of his suitcoat and removing a small brown leather pouch. "This is a gift from one generation of our family to another."

There were tears in the old man's eyes as Maria took the pouch from him. She wondered what it contained and also wondered about the little nicks all over the leather surface. The indentations looked very suspiciously like teeth marks.